"Camilleri's Inspector Montalbano mysteries might
sell like hotcakes in Europe, but these world-weary
crime stories were unknown here until the oversight
was corrected (in Stephen Sartarelli's salty translation)
by the welcome publication of *The Shape of Water* . . .
This savagely funny police procedural . . . prove[s]
that sardonic laughter is a sound that translates ever so
smoothly into English."
                              —*The New York Times Book Review*

"Hailing from the land of Umberto Eco and La Cosa
Nostra, Montalbano can discuss a pointy-headed book
like *Western Attitudes Toward Death* as unflinchingly as
he can pore over crime-scene snuff photos. He throws
together an extemporaneous lunch of shrimp with
lemon wedges and oil as gracefully as he dodges ad-
vances from attractive women."   —*Los Angeles Times*

"[Camilleri's mysteries] offer quirky characters, crisp
dialogue, bright storytelling—and Salvo Montalbano,
one of the most engaging protagonists in detective
fiction."   —*USA Today*

"Like Mike Hammer or Sam Spade, Montalbano is
the kind of guy who can't stay out of trouble . . . Still,
deftly and lovingly translated by Stephen Sartarelli,

Camilleri makes it abundantly clear that under the gruff, sardonic exterior our inspector has a heart of gold, and that any outburst, fumbles, or threats are made only in the name of pursuing truth."

—*The Nation*

"Camilleri can do a character's whole backstory in half a paragraph." —*The New Yorker*

To access Penguin Readers Guides online, visit our website at www.penguinrandomhouse.com.

© Elvira Giorgianni

THE OTHER END OF THE LINE

Andrea Camilleri, a bestselling author in Italy and Germany, is the author of the popular Inspector Montalbano mystery series as well as historical novels that take place in nineteenth-century Sicily. His books have been made into Italian TV shows and translated into thirty-two languages. His thirteenth Montalbano novel, *The Potter's Field*, won the Crime Writers' Association International Dagger Award and was longlisted for the IMPAC Dublin Literary Award.

Stephen Sartarelli is an award-winning translator and the author of three books of poetry.

Also by Andrea Camilleri

Hunting Season

The Brewer of Brewston

Montalbano's First Case and Other Stories

THE INSPECTOR MONTALBANO SERIES

THE OTHER END OF THE LINE

ANDREA CAMILLERI

Translated by Stephen Sartarelli

M

PENGUIN BOOKS

PENGUIN BOOKS

An imprint of Penguin Random House LLC

penguinrandomhouse.com

Copyright © 2016 by Sellerio Editore
Translation copyright © 2019 by Stephen Sartarelli
Penguin supports copyright. Copyright fuels creativity, encourages diverse
voices, promotes free speech, and creates a vibrant culture. Thank you for
buying an authorized edition of this book and for complying with copyright
laws by not reproducing, scanning, or distributing any part of it in any form
without permission. You are supporting writers and allowing Penguin
to continue to publish books for every reader.

Originally published in Italian as *L'altro capo del filo* by Sellerio Editore, Palermo.

ISBN 9780143133773 (paperback)
ISBN 9780525505617 (ebook)

Printed in the United States of America
1 3 5 7 9 10 8 6 4 2

Set in Bembo Std
Designed by Jaye Zimet

THE OTHER END OF THE LINE

1

They were sitting out on Livia's little balcony in Boccadasse in silence, enjoying the cool evening air.

Livia had been in a bad mood all day, as was always the case when Montalbano was about to return home to Vigàta.

Out of the blue Livia, who was barefoot, said:

"Would you do me a favor and get my slippers? My feet are cold. I guess I'm just getting old."

The inspector gawked at her.

"Why are you looking at me like that?"

"You're starting to age from the feet up?"

"Why, is there a law against that?"

"No, but I thought it was some other body parts that started aging first."

"Cut the shit with your foul mouth," said Livia.

Montalbano balked.

"Why are you talking like that?"

"I'll talk however I feel like talking! Is that okay with you?"

"Anyway, I said nothing foul. The body parts I was referring to are, I dunno, the eyes, the ears . . ."

"Are you going to get me those slippers or not?"

"Where are they?"

"Where do you think they are? Right beside the bed. The ones that look like cats."

Montalbano got up and headed for the bedroom.

Those slippers no doubt kept her feet nice and warm, but he hated them, because they looked like two long-haired white cats with black tails. Naturally, they were nowhere to be seen.

Surely they must be under the bed.

The inspector crouched down, thinking:

The back! That's another body part that gives you the first warning signs of aging!

He reached out and started feeling around with one hand.

It came up against a furry slipper and was about to grab it when a sharp pain took him by surprise.

Jerking his hand back, he noticed he had a deep scratch on the back of it that was even bleeding a little.

Could there possibly be a real cat under there?

But Livia didn't own any cats.

So he turned on the lamp on the bedside table, grabbed it, and shone its light under the bed, to see what it was that had scratched him.

He couldn't believe his eyes.

One of the two slippers had remained a slipper, but the other one had turned into a cat, a cat cat, and was now glaring at him threateningly, ears pressed against its head and hackles raised.

How could this be?

He suddenly felt furious.

And he got up, set down the lamp, went into the bathroom, opened the medicine chest, and disinfected his scratch with a bit of rubbing alcohol.

Moments later he was back out on the balcony and sat down without a word.

"So where are my slippers?" asked Livia.

"You can go and get them yourself, if you have the courage."

Glancing at him scornfully, Livia shook her head as if in commiseration, got up, and went into the apartment.

Montalbano contemplated the gash on his hand. The blood had clotted, but the scratch was deep.

Livia returned, sat down, and crossed her legs. On her feet were the slippers.

"Wasn't there a cat under the bed?" asked Montalbano.

"What are you saying?" said Livia. "I've never had a cat in this apartment."

"Then how did I get this scratch?" the inspector asked, showing her his wound.

The only problem was that, to his great surprise, there was nothing on the back of his hand. The skin was perfectly intact.

"What scratch? I don't see anything."

Montalbano suddenly leaned down and took off one of her slippers.

"My scratch, which your fake slipper gave me," he said angrily, throwing it off the balcony.

At this point, Livia yelled so loud that . . .

. . . Montalbano woke up.

They weren't in Boccadasse but in Vigàta, and Livia was

sleeping like a baby beside him, the morning's faint first light filtering in through the window.

Montalbano realized it was going to be a day of libeccio, the southwest wind.

The sea was making a lot of noise.

He got up and went into the bathroom.

An hour and a half later Livia joined him in the kitchen, where the inspector had made breakfast for her and prepared a mug of espresso for himself.

"So, what's the plan?" asked Livia. "I'll be taking the three o'clock bus for Palermo airport."

"I'm sorry I can't drive you there, but I can't be away from the station for even an hour. You've seen for yourself the kind of situation we're in. Let's do this: When you're ready, give me a ring, and I'll come and give you a ride to the bus station."

"Okay," said Livia. "But will you keep your promise to come to my place this time? I won't accept any excuses."

"I said I would come, and I'll come."

"With your new suit?" asked Livia.

"All right, with my new suit," Montalbano replied through clenched teeth.

They'd argued about this for at least two hours a day during Livia's short stay in Vigàta.

When she first got there, Livia, the moment she was off

the plane, before even embracing Montalbano, had wanted to give him some good news.

"Did you know that Giovanna is getting remarried in a few days?"

Montalbano opened his eyes wide.

"Giovanna? Which Giovanna? Your friend? Who's she marrying? What about the kids?"

Livia started laughing and gestured to him to go and get the car.

"I'll tell you the whole story on the drive home."

As soon as he'd put the car in gear, Montalbano asked his first question.

"What about Stefano? How did Stefano take the news?"

"How do you expect? He was delighted. They've been married for over twenty years."

Montalbano sank into complete incomprehension.

"But how can a man who's been married for over twenty years and has two kids be delighted that his wife is marrying another man?"

Livia broke into a laughing fit so extreme that, through her tears, she'd had to undo her safety belt to hold her stomach.

"What on earth are you imagining? Where do you get these ideas? Giovanna's getting remarried to Stefano."

"Why, did they get divorced? You never said anything to me about it."

"No, they did not get divorced."

"So why are they getting married all over again?"

"They're not 'getting married all over again.' Quite the contrary. They want to reconfirm their marriage."

"Reconfirm . . . ?"

Montalbano was so confused by this point that he was afraid to keep on driving, so he pulled over and stopped.

"Listen," he snapped, "I haven't understood a fucking thing in all this!"

"Don't start spouting obscenities or I won't explain anything to you!"

They'd resumed driving, and Livia began to fill him in on the story of Giovanna and Stefano.

Happily married for twenty-five years, the couple was about to celebrate the renewal of their vows.

At the sound of the word "renewal," Montalbano couldn't restrain himself.

"Renewal?" he said. "You mean like renewing a lease on a car? Or renewing your membership in a club?"

Bewailing Salvo's lack of romantic sentiment, Livia proceeded to explain the whole ceremony of matrimonial renewal.

"When a couple has been married for twenty-five years, they celebrate their silver anniversary, which in fact means renewing their vows. They go to a church, with their relatives, and their children if there are any, and whoever else they want to invite, and they reenact the service. They reconfirm their vows: *Do you take, as your lawfully wedded husband . . .* and so on. It's all very romantic. The wedding rings are blessed again, and I'm told the couple take two candles and light a third, which symbolizes their union. Then there's a proper wedding feast afterwards, with all the usual celebrations as well as silver confetti. And you have to come, because I promised Giovanna and Stefano you would be there. You can come first to Boccadasse to get me, and then we'll go to Udine together."

This had been the first blow.

The second came that same evening, as they were eating, and it was enough to extinguish Montalbano's appetite in an instant.

"I had a look in your closet," Livia said, all serious.

"And did you find any skeletons?"

"Worse. I found the corpses of your old suits. You haven't got a single decent one. For this occasion I want you to have one tailor-made."

Montalbano broke out in a cold sweat. In all his life he had never been to a tailor. He felt so discouraged he didn't even have the strength to open his mouth.

Only after recovering from the shock had he managed to speak, and he tried to change the subject.

"Livia, I want you to come to the police station with me tomorrow. I've already informed Beba."

"What for?"

"You know, it's possible that living in Boccadasse you don't have a clear sense of just how dramatic things are down here. Lately the migrant landings on our shores are more punctual than the bus from Montelusa. They come by the hundreds every single night. No matter the weather. Men, women, children, old folks. Freezing, starving, thirsty, and frightened. And in need of everything. Every single one of us at the station is busy twenty-four hours a day trying to manage these arrivals. And in town people have formed committees of volunteers who collect living necessities, cook warm meals, provide clothing, shoes, and blankets. Beba directs one of these committees. Do you feel up to lending her a hand?"

"Of course," said Livia.

The inspector was hoping, and feeling like less than a worm in so doing, that Livia, in helping those poor wretches, might forget about the "marriage renewal" and the concomitant need for a new suit.

The following day, Montalbano had taken Livia to Beba's place and didn't see her or hear back from her for the rest of the day.

They'd met back up that evening at his place in Marinella, and before telling him what she'd been doing, Livia saw fit to deal the third and decisive blow, once again at dinnertime, as if she'd decided to impose a crash diet on him.

"In spite of everything else I had to do today, I managed to drop in at the tailor's. Unfortunately, they're really busy tomorrow and can't see you. But they were very nice and promised me that they'll manage to make you a suit in time for the celebration. They'll be expecting you day after tomorrow—in other words, the day I leave—at three in the afternoon. I'm sorry I won't be able to come with you, but will you promise me you'll go?"

Montalbano bristled.

"That's all I've been doing for the past two days, is making promises. I promise I'll go. Just give me this tailor's address."

"Via Roma, 32. It's right next door to the stationery shop, but there's no sign outside. They're right on the ground floor. You'll see, I think you'll find Elena quite charming."

"Elena?!"

"Yes, Elena. Why do you ask?"

"Sorry, but I'm not going," the inspector said decisively.

"What do you mean, you're not going? You just promised me you would."

"I said I would go and see a tailor, not a seamstress."

"Oh, come on, she's a woman tailor who makes men's clothes, too. What's the difference?"

"Oh, there's a difference all right."

"And what is it?"

"I'm not going to get undressed in front of a woman. And I don't want a woman measuring my crotch and circling around me with her measuring tape telling me how broad my shoulders and waist are. I would rather be embraced by a woman for other reasons . . ."

"I don't know whether to call you a disgusting sexist or a cheap whoremonger!"

At that point, Livia had slammed the kitchen door behind her and locked herself in the bedroom.

Just to make a point, Montalbano had gone into the dining room, turned on the television, and spent a good hour watching a detective drama of which he managed to understand not a thing. After turning it off, he made up the sofa bed and, to avoid going into the bedroom to get some covers, he kept his clothes on and lay down, covering himself only with his bathrobe.

He tossed and turned for a good while, unable to fall asleep. Then he heard the bedroom door open and Livia's voice calling to him.

"Stop acting like an idiot and come to bed."

Without answering, he got up and, hollow eyed, went into the bedroom and lay down, right at the edge of the bed, like someone just passing through.

A short while later, he felt Livia's warm hand caressing his hip. Followed by his total surrender, when he promised he would go and see the woman tailor.

On the evening of the third day, when Livia came home she luckily made no mention of the new suit, and so Montalbano was able to make up for the lost meals of the two previous evenings.

Livia, on the other hand, had been unable to bring so much as a spoonful of fish soup to her lips, so keen was she to find out from the inspector about a person she'd met while working with Beba who'd impressed her quite a bit.

"I met a gentleman of about sixty, tall, slender, and very elegant, with glasses. Apparently he's friends with everyone here in Vigàta. He spoke perfect Italian and Arabic—also perfectly, I assume—with all the immigrants he encountered. They all call him 'Doctor'—Dr. Osman. Do you know him?"

Montalbano laughed.

"Of course I know him; he's my dentist. He's a very

special person, aside from being an excellent doctor. You know those old-time doctors with a clinical eye who could take one look at you and make an accurate diagnosis?"

"Sure," replied Livia. "But where's he from?"

"He's Tunisian. Just imagine, aside from being a dentist, he's also quite the art expert. He works as a consultant for the Museo del Bardo. And that's not all. For the past few summers—and not only the summers, unfortunately—Dr. Osman gets up in the middle of the night and goes to the port to help with the immigrant arrivals, both as an interpreter and as a doctor."

"I'd like to get to know him a little better."

"The next time you're here we can invite him to dinner."

"And where did he do his studies?"

"He got his degree in London."

"So how did he end up in Vigàta?"

"Dr. Osman is very discreet, and he's never told me his life story, but apparently he got engaged to a woman from Vigàta when he was a student. The engagement eventually went by the boards, but he'd fallen in love with Sicily, and especially with the sea here, which is the same sea that washes his own country's shores."

"I've been to Tunisia. And in fact, aside from the language, it's not that different from here."

"I agree, Livia, but I don't think there are that many people who feel that way. And there isn't even any difference in the fact that in order to survive, they're forced, even now, in 2016, to leave their homes, their land, and their families, in order to find a job, just like our own young people."

"You know, Salvo," Livia continued in a melancholy tone, "I'm really sorry I have to leave tomorrow. I wish I could stay just to be with you, but also to keep helping Beba."

They embraced. And their embrace, over the course of the evening, grew longer and more passionate.

They finished breakfast. Montalbano got up, went over to Livia, bent down, and kissed her. But Livia held on to his hand.

"I don't feel like leaving you just now. Couldn't you stay a little longer with me, just a little bit longer?"

Montalbano didn't feel up to saying no. He moved his chair and sat down beside Livia, who held her hand out to him. He took it, and they sat there for a few minutes, just like that, in silence, each looking the other in the eyes the way they used to do, sometimes for an entire morning, just feeling the warmth of each other's hands and diving deep into each other's gaze.

The telephone rang.

Neither of the two had the courage to unclasp their hands, but the temperature suddenly dropped just the same. Then Livia, resigned, said:

"Go and answer."

Montalbano was expecting to hear Catarella's voice, but it was Fazio calling instead.

"Sorry to bother you, Chief, but could you come to the office as soon as possible?"

"Why, what's happened?"

"What's happened is that early this morning a patrol

boat came in packed with a hundred and thirty migrants, including three pregnant women and four corpses, two of which were small children."

"And so?" said Montalbano.

"Well, the fact is that the registration center counted only one hundred and twenty-nine. One is missing."

"Were you able to find out whether the missing person is male or female, old or—"

"Yeah, Chief, apparently it was a fifteen-year-old kid traveling by himself."

At that moment, out of the corner of his eye Montalbano saw Livia opening the French door onto the veranda. The wan light of before had become the shadowy light of a gray day. The sea boomed more loudly.

"But now," Fazio continued, "the problem is that the commissioner is having conniptions and demanding that this person be found at once. So we've all been busy looking for him for the last three hours, and there's nobody at the station."

"I'll be right there," said Montalbano, thinking that by this hour the lad had no doubt already reached, only God knew how, the German border.

No sooner had he hung up than the phone rang again.

"Montalbano!"

He immediately recognized the imperious voice of Commissioner Bonetti-Alderighi.

He felt like hanging up. Then he thought better of it, realizing that he would have to answer sooner or later anyway. Sighing deeply, he said:

"I'm sorry, who am I speaking to?"

"It's me, for the love of God!"

"Me who?"

The commissioner's voice exploded in rage:

"The commissioner! Wake up, Montalbano!"

"Sorry, sir. Good morning."

Bonetti-Alderighi returned the greeting.

"Good morning my ass! There you are, lolling about your house instead of going to the station and taking control of this very delicate situation."

"What delicate situation?"

"Do you not consider the escape of a terrorist a deli—"

"Sorry to interrupt, Mr. Commissioner, but we're only talking about a poor migr—"

Bonetti-Alderighi, furious, interrupted him in turn.

"Poor migrant, my ass. I've received a confidential memo from the antiterrorism bureau. Apparently an extremely dangerous ISIS militant was hiding among that boatload of refugees."

"Apparently, or do they know for certain?"

"Montalbano, don't start cavilling with me, for the love of God. It is quite simply our duty, and responsibility, to track him down and take him to the proper processing center, where he will be detained."

"I beg to differ, Mr. Commissioner. In this instance, it is absolutely essential to cavil with you, as you put it. These boatloads are full of poor migrants, most of whom are Muslim, and if we don't distinguish between regular Muslims and ISIS militants, we're only adding to the general ignorance and creating more panic and hostility by playing right into the terrorists' hands."

Bonetti-Alderighi fell silent. But for only a few seconds.

"Find me that terrorist, goddammit!" said the commissioner, hanging up without saying good-bye.

Two "asses," two "for the love of Gods," and one "goddammit" in four minutes. Bonetti-Alderighi must really be in a state.

Montalbano got up slowly.

He went over to Livia, who was looking out at the rough sea. Putting his arm around her shoulders, he pulled her towards him.

"I'm sorry, Livia, but I really have to go."

Livia didn't move.

Montalbano went into the bedroom to get his jacket and the car keys.

Then he returned to Livia's side.

"All right, then, I'll wait for your phone call."

Only then did Livia turn to look at him, and with her forefinger pointing out at the sea, she asked:

"What's that bundle out there?"

"What bundle?"

"That black thing floating there off to the left, near the far end of the port."

Montalbano took two steps forward on the veranda and started carefully looking where Livia was pointing.

They stayed that way for a few moments in silence. Then the inspector went down onto the beach.

"You stay here," he said.

The inspector got as close as he could, given that the libeccio had eaten up a good part of the beach, and then he leaned

against an overturned boat that the usual early-morning fisherman had pulled ashore to safety.

He stood there briefly looking out at the sea, then made
his way very slowly back to the veranda.

His eyes were spooked.

"That's no bundle," he said.

2

Livia's face turned white as a sheet.

"Is it a dead body?" she asked.

"Yes," said the inspector, starting to take his jacket off and unbuckling his trousers.

"What are you doing?" Livia asked.

"I should go and get him before the current carries him back out to the open sea. Go and get me my sandals and bathing suit."

Livia rushed into the house, and when she returned she found Montalbano completely naked with the telephone receiver in his hand.

"Hello, Fazio? Listen, I'm about to recover a dead body from the sea right in front of my house. Inform the circus and try to get here as soon as possible yourself."

He hung up, put on his bathing suit and sandals, and, the moment he reached the veranda, found himself face-to-face with the early-morning fisherman.

"Good morning, Inspector. Have you seen that there's a dead—"

"Yeah, I know. I was about to go and get it."

"We can go in my boat."

The two men turned the boat right side up and pushed

it towards the wet sand, and then the first wave grabbed hold of it and pulled it into the water.

Montalbano and the fisherman hopped in. The man laid on oars and started rowing forcefully. Minutes later they were beside the floating corpse. The fisherman let go of the oars and went over beside the inspector, and together they got a good grip on the body and hoisted it onto the boat.

The inspector studied it.

The sea hadn't yet had time to inflict any damage. The naked body was still intact. It was clear it hadn't been in the water for very long. It belonged to a boy who looked barely fifteen years old. Death had rendered his facial features more childish.

Montalbano became suddenly aware that he was now in control of the "very delicate situation" that Bonetti-Alderighi had alluded to.

The fisherman, while steering the boat shoreward, said:

"You know, Inspector, lately there's been no point in going out to fish. You haul in more dead bodies than fish."

They touched the shore. Montalbano hoisted the corpse onto his shoulders and brought it onto dry land.

———

Livia meanwhile had come running up with a bathrobe, which she handed to the inspector.

"Dry yourself off. It's cold out," she said, never once looking at the corpse.

Montalbano took the robe and, instead of drying himself off, covered the boy's dead body with it.

From afar they began to hear the sirens of the approaching police cruisers.

Once he was dressed, to satisfy a whim, Montalbano phoned Hizzoner the C'mishner:

"I just wanted to let you know the case of the dangerous terrorist has been solved. I found him dead in the water."

"How can you be so sure that it's the same person?"

"Dr. Pasquano has just reported to me that the victim died no more than five hours ago, at the very moment the patrol boat was outside the harbor. The boy must have fallen accidentally and nobody noticed. So I'd like authorization to suspend the search."

Bonetti-Alderighi had a moment of hesitation.

"And you will take responsibility for this upon yourself?"

"Full responsibility," Montalbano replied, hanging up without saying good-bye.

"It's almost noon," said Livia. "What are you going to do? Go to the office?"

"No," said the inspector. "Let's stay another half hour together, and then I'll take you to the bus."

He took Livia by the hand and led her into the kitchen.

"We need something hot to drink."

He prepared another mug of coffee for himself and some tea for Livia.

They drank in silence, then Livia finally went into the bedroom and grabbed her suitcase while Montalbano put on his jacket and closed the French door to the veranda.

They went out of the house.

After saying good-bye to Livia, who didn't forget to remind him of the promise he'd made, the inspector went to his favorite trattoria to eat.

"So, what have you got for me today?" he asked Enzo.

"I've got something new for you today I want you to try, Inspector."

"And what's that?"

"I call it 'migrants' soup.' Since Signora Beba's committee asked us to help feed those poor folks, I invented a kind of fish soup that's also full of pasta and a variety of vegetables. So it's also very nutritious. Wanna try it?"

"Sure, why not?" said the inspector.

Montalbano liked the new dish so much that he asked for another helping. It revived his spirits and filled his belly so nicely that he felt no need to order a second course.

Since it was still early, and the weather was too nasty for a walk along the jetty, he headed in the direction of the Caffè Castiglione, where he ran into Mimì Augello, who was coming out on his way back to the office.

Montalbano had an idea.

"Excuse me, Mimì, do you by any chance know a woman tailor by the name of Elena?"

Mimì smiled and gestured with his head as if to say, *Man, do I ever know her.*

"Why do you ask?"

"Because Livia has forced me to agree to get myself a tailor-made suit, and she made an appointment with this Elena. But for me it's a pain in the ass."

"The pain'll go away the minute you see her," said Mimì.

"Why do you say that?"

"Because she's a very beautiful woman. Exceptionally so. She's just over forty, but, believe me, Salvo, her most impressive gift is her ability to win people's sympathy almost immediately. I'm sure it'll be the same with you."

"So you also had her make a suit for you?"

"I certainly wasn't going to pass up the opportunity, but as soon as Beba found out about it, she threatened not to let me back in the house if I was wearing a suit made by that woman."

As he drank his coffee Montalbano realized that he didn't find Mimì's words at all reassuring, since for his second-in-command, every woman who came within reach seemed extremely beautiful and not to be missed.

The rolling metal shutter outside number 32 was raised. Montalbano stopped and had to make a huge effort not to turn his back and head on to the police station.

Then he made up his mind, tried turning the knob on the glass door, but it was locked. He rang the doorbell. It had a pleasant sound. Opening the door was a slender, brown-skinned woman of about thirty with her hair gathered under a white headscarf, two deep, dark eyes, and a friendly smile.

"*Buongiorno*, I'm Meriam. Please come in."

She spoke perfect Italian, but with a slight foreign inflection.

Montalbano followed the young woman down a long

corridor. The walls were a dark, welcoming Pompeiian red. On the left was a row of furnishings—armoires, small tables, bookcases, glass cupboards, a hutch—that had originally been made for a kitchen but were now stuffed with fabric, sweaters, shirts, ties, and the like, all so colorful that it would have put the rainbow itself to shame.

Along the right-hand wall was instead a long tree branch, all white, probably found in the sea, bleached and eroded by salt water. Appended to this branch were a great many coat hangers displaying men's suits, overcoats, and raincoats.

At the end of the corridor they twice turned right, whereupon the inspector found himself in a very large room.

"Hello," a pair of male voices said in unison.

"Hello," Montalbano replied.

"Please sit down," said Meriam, indicating a blue sofa. "The signora will be with you momentarily."

And she went and sat down in front of a sewing machine.

Montalbano settled in and started looking around.

It was an open, luminous room. Next to the sofa were two armchairs and a coffee table. The two voices that had just greeted him belonged to two workers, one older, the other quite young, seated behind a large tailor's table.

They had an old-fashioned manner of going about their work. They would lay the fabric out on the wooden surface, measure it with an outdated measuring tape, then circle around it as if performing a strange sort of ballet step. Apparently sensing they were being watched, they turned around, met his eyes, and smiled instinctively.

The wall behind them was entirely covered with a set of shelves full to bursting with colorful fabrics.

The inspector felt lost.

He could no longer tell whether he was in Jemaa el-Fna Square in Marrakesh, the Cairo spice bazaar, or a shop in Beirut, but at any rate he felt at home.

Then Signora Elena came in through the door, hand extended towards Montalbano and a big smile on her face.

"Inspector Montalbano! What a pleasure to see you here!"

In a flash the inspector realized that, this time, Mimì was absolutely correct.

Montalbano stood up and shook her hand. Still holding his, Elena sat down beside him and then let go.

"Would you like a cup of tea?"

Normally tea made Montalbano want to throw up, but to his immense surprise he heard his lips form the words:

"Sure, why not? Thanks."

Meriam got up and left the room.

Elena began speaking:

"Your companion—who I must say is a beautiful, elegant woman—told me you need a dress suit. I was thinking of something relatively light, given the season, in summer wool, but not too dark, say, London-fog gray, a more autumnal sort of color . . . Or how about rust? I have some new fabric, very soft, almost like flannel, which I would like you to feel. You could even use the items separately, as sports jacket and trousers. A classic shirt for the wedding ceremony, of course, though the trousers would also go with an unstructured sports jacket . . ."

As the woman was talking, Montalbano couldn't take his eyes off her legs.

When Meriam set the mint tea down on the coffee table

along with a sugar bowl, the inspector's eyes had come up to Elena's bony knees. The tailor herself then bent down to the table, picked up the cup, and handed it to the inspector, who was thus forced, reluctantly, to take his eyes off her legs and look at her face.

Which was no less appealing. Elena was blond, with an open, serene, smiling countenance as welcoming as a soft, comfortable pillow when one is dead tired.

Montalbano did notice with some surprise, however, that the woman's eyebrows were black. And so he wondered whether it was the blond hair or the black eyebrows that were fake. Then he concluded that, in a woman like that, it was all natural, genuine, real. As natural as her slender, sumptuously curvaceous body.

Montalbano decided not to sip his tea. He would never manage. So he took a long draft instead, half emptying the cup.

The taste it left behind in his mouth was not, however, unpleasant.

Elena, meanwhile, had got up and gone over to the shelves.

Montalbano watched her. She moved with unaffected elegance. Moments later she returned with two long bolts of fabric. Sitting back down beside Montalbano, she took his hand and had him touch the first bolt. The cloth was indeed soft and warm. And seemed comfortable to him. Then Elena had him feel the second bolt, which was even softer and more pleasing than the first.

"That's the one," said Montalbano.

The cloth was rust colored.

"Oh, I'm so happy! You've chosen the one I thought would be best for you."

The woman then blushed, as if she felt she'd been too familiar with him.

"I'm sure you know what's best," said Montalbano, to put her at her ease.

She smiled and, taking his hand, made him stand up. They went over to the worktable.

"Please take off your jacket."

As he was taking it off and setting it down, Montalbano realized, with some embarrassment, that the critical moment for measuring the crotch had come.

Elena, however, touched the shoulder of the older of the two male workers and said:

"Nicola, please show the gentleman into the dressing room."

Nicola looped a measuring tape around his neck, put on his glasses, grabbed a pencil and a piece of paper, and said:

"Please follow me."

They went out of the big room towards the corridor and turned left this time, just once, then stopped. Nicola moved a velvet curtain that looked as if it had come from a theater, then gestured to the inspector to come forward. The dressing room was rather spacious and illuminated with warm spotlights. There was a three-paned mirror, two chairs, a metal clothes-stand, and a small table.

Nicola started quickly taking his measurements, and as soon as he was done they heard Elena's voice outside the curtain.

"May I come in?" she asked.

"Yes, go ahead," said Nicola.

"All done?"

"Yes, ma'am," said the helper, pulling the curtain aside and going out.

Elena went and stood with her back to the central mirror and said:

"Could you take two steps backwards, please?"

Montalbano, at a loss, obeyed.

Elena started looking him over slowly. Her eyes went from his shoulders to his chest, then from his belly to his legs.

"Now turn around."

Montalbano felt like he was in a doctor's office getting X-rays taken.

He felt Elena's eyes taking the same route over his body as before.

"Thank you," she then said. "We can go back out now."

Once in the big room, Montalbano went over to get his jacket and put it on.

"Your lady friend told me you'll be needing the suit in just a few days. I've got a lot of work on my hands, but I'll try to put your job in the fast lane. Is it all right with you if we have the first fitting three days from now, at the same hour?"

"That's perfectly fine with me," said the inspector, "as long as nothing unexpected comes up for me at work."

"All right, then, we'll leave it at that," replied Elena. "Here are the phone numbers for the shop and my cell phone, so you can call me if there's any change of plan. Come, I'll see you out."

Montalbano said good-bye, and the others replied in chorus.

He went back up the long corridor, with Elena beside him this time. She opened the glass door for him, handed him a business card, kissed him on the cheeks, and said:

"It was a pleasure to meet you. You're a very nice man."

"The pleasure's all mine," Montalbano replied in all sincerity.

The moment the glass door closed behind him, the inspector heaved a big sigh. For a short while he'd felt as if he was briefly in heaven. And he knew that what awaited him now at the station would be hell.

Upon entering, he immediately noticed that Catarella's eyes were all red and swollen and he was holding a handkerchief in his hand, which he used to wipe his nose.

"Catch a cold, Cat?"

"Nah, Chief," said Catarella, as if to cut the conversation short.

Montalbano persisted.

"Tell me what happened."

"No, sir, Chief."

"That's an order. Speak."

The corners of Catarella's mouth began to quiver, as if he was about to cry.

"Wha' happen izzat lass night when the 'vacuees all came offa the boat—"

"They're not evacuees, Cat," Montalbano said, interrupting him, "they're migrants. Evacuees were the people who would flee one town for another in the last war to escape the constant bombing."

"'Scuse me, Chief, but ain't these people also runnin' away from bombs?"

Montalbano didn't know what to say. Catarella's logic was flawless.

"Go on."

"Anyways, 'tween all 'ese 'vacuees a girl lookin' nine-month prennant and big as a jug so that she cou'n't e'en walk, fell inna my arms. An', holdin' 'er up wit' one arm roun' 'er waist, I started walkin' 'er right tord a amblance, wit' 'er wailin' alla whiles. An' so I ast 'er what 'er name was an' she said 'er name was Fatima. Finally, when we got to the amblance—"

"Sorry, Cat," the inspector interrupted him again, "but weren't there any nurses there on the scene?"

"Yeah, Chief, but they 'adda take care of a guy witta serious inchery. Anyways, I 'elped 'er get into this ambulance, an' when I was about to leave, she says to me in perfect Italian: 'Don't leave me.' So I ast if I cou' stay wit' 'er an' 'ey said no. An' so I got in my car an' went to the hospital in Montelusa. When I foun' Fatima there, still lyin' onna same goiny inna hallway, I took 'er 'and an' 'eld it rilly tight till they took 'er into the 'livery room, an' 'en I came back 'ere."

"Have you got any news of her?"

"Yeah, Chief. I got a call 'bout half a hour ago. It was a boy. Bu' she died."

Catarella couldn't contain himself any longer, and the tears began gushing out of his eyes.

"Be strong, Cat," said the inspector, who was about to go back to his office when Catarella stopped him.

"Chief, can I make a riquess?"

"Go ahead."

"C'n I be azempted from port duty? Please, Chief, if I have to go troo anyting like 'at agin, I'm not so sure my 'eart c'n take it. I migh' jess get a 'eart attack."

"All right," said Montalbano, "I'll see what I can do."

He'd just sat down when Mimì Augello walked in.

"How'd it go with the lady tailor?"

"Quite well," said Montalbano, "but let's talk about more serious matters."

"Why, don't you think that woman is a serious matter?" Augello retorted.

"There's something I have to ask you," said Montalbano. "Why did you summon Catarella for port duty last night?"

"I had to replace someone who called in sick."

"Try not to do it again."

"Why?"

"The rest of us are used to that sort of thing. We've been forced to grow thicker skin. But Catarella's like a little kid, and he can't really fathom what's happening. And maybe he's right."

"Okay," said Augello.

At that exact moment, Fazio came in. His face looked weary and dark. He sat down in front of the desk.

"I've just heard a rumor," he said, "which I hope isn't true. Supposedly almost four hundred more desperate souls are arriving tonight."

Mimì reacted.

"Right, like the other night when a thousand were sup-posedly arriving and in fact it was barely a hundred and thirty. I really don't understand why people always like to bullshit."

The telephone rang.

"Chief, 'Specter Sileci wants a talk t'yiz poissonally in poisson."

"Put him on."

"I can't, Chief, insomuch as 'e ain't onna line, but 'ere onna premisses."

"Then show him in."

Sileci was a colleague of Montalbano's, around fifty years old, a bit portly, and sporting a big mustache, whom the commissioner had put in charge of the squad dealing with the emergency situation created by all the migrant landings.

Upon entering, he greeted everyone roundly and sat down in the chair Fazio had vacated for him.

"We're in deep shit," he declared.

They all looked at him questioningly.

"I've just received an official communiqué," Sileci went on, "stating that two ships are on the way here. The first has picked up two hundred shipwreck victims, the second, two hundred and twelve. They're about seven hours' sailing from here." He glanced at his watch and continued: "In other words, all hell should be breaking loose again around midnight."

"Then that means that this time," said Montalbano, "we risk drowning in shit."

"That's exactly right. Therefore we need to come up with a plan. Any ideas?"

A heavy silence descended.

Each was looking at the others in the hopes that someone might have a solution, any solution.

Moments later, Montalbano was the first to speak.

"Well, I think I have an inkling of a plan. But first there are two things I need to know. Fazio, do me a favor and ring Dr. Osman right now and find out if he's available to lend us a hand. If so, tell him to come here to the station tonight around eleven-thirty."

Fazio got up and dashed out of the room.

"The second thing," the inspector continued, turning to Sileci, "is this: Do you think you can call the harbormaster and arrange for the second boat to dock about half an hour late?"

Sileci stood up, pulled his cell phone out of his pocket, and went over to the window. He spoke briefly and then returned.

"Yeah, they can manage that. I wanted to add that before coming here, I got a call from the commissioner, who gave me a warning. He said that this time—and these are his words—we mustn't let so much as a needle slip through our net."

"What's this about?" asked Montalbano. "The usual business of the terrorist who's weaseled his way into the mass of migrants?"

"Exactly. Ever since Cusumano was named chief of Antiterrorism, he practically checks under his bed every night before going to sleep, to make sure there isn't a terrorist hiding there. So you think it's not true?"

"I suppose it's possible some nutcase could be hiding among the refugees. But why would he face the risk of an extremely dangerous passage across the sea, not to mention the security checks he'd be subjected to upon arriving? If you ask me, any terrorist, if and when he comes here, will waltz blithely off a plane with a regular passport in hand and get his explosives later, from some accomplice already here."

Fazio returned.

"Osman says he's completely available."

"All right, then, tell us your plan."

3

"I think I know what the most critical point of the landing process is," said the inspector, "the point where our surveillance becomes very difficult and the meshes in the net become so large that anyone who wants to can escape."

"And when would that be?" asked Sileci.

"It would be the moment the boat's gangway touches the dock. At that moment there's total chaos on board, despite the efforts of the sailors to maintain some semblance of order. The migrants become overwhelmed with the irresistible need to set foot on dry land, immediately. They can't stand being at sea any longer. And that's not all. These poor folks have staked everything, every hope they've ever had, on this one sea crossing, all the spare change they've saved up or borrowed from their families over the course of an entire existence. They're well aware that the journey is very dangerous and might even cost them their lives, and so all their chances of living are concentrated in taking that first step on dry land. So, what happens, then? They all rush headlong to be the first to disembark, pushing every which way, falling into the water, climbing over one another. When they reach the bottom of the gangway, we find ourselves having to sustain the violent impact of twenty or thirty people unable to control themselves. They scream, wail, cry, and laugh, but mostly they're trying to run somewhere—where, even they don't know. It's just instinct, and they race blindly. And there are never enough of us to contain the thrust of this great mass. Clear?"

"Perfectly," said Sileci. "So what do you suggest?"

"I'll tell you in a second," Montalbano replied.

Then he told him. After which, he asked:

"Are you in agreement?"

"Yes. Let's just hope it works," replied Sileci, rising to his feet.

The first thing the inspector did when he got home was, as usual, to look in the refrigerator.

He found it empty.

And so he raced over to the oven. But there was no need to open it. The wondrous aroma of Adelina's *pasta 'ncasciata* was already penetrating his nostrils.

He lit the oven to heat up the casserole. Although the wind had dropped, the evening air remained chilly, and so he set the table in the kitchen.

While waiting he went and watched a little TV. There was a news feature on the arrival, at Lampedusa, of a ship that had saved sixty people. Seven, however, had died. Rather than ruin his appetite, he turned off the set.

And at that moment the phone rang. It was Livia. Her first question was:

"How did it go with Elena?"

"Elena who?" said Montalbano.

"Don't tell me you didn't go . . ." said Livia, assuming the worst.

Only then did the inspector remember that that was the tailor's name.

"Of course I went. I keep my promises."

"And so? What was it like?"

"What was it supposed to be like? It was fine."

"I knew it would be."

"But tell me something, Livia. When I got to the tailor's shop, I saw that Elena had two male helpers and a seamstress who was working at a sewing machine. One of the helpers took my measurements. She then had me choose a fabric to my liking, and limited herself to looking at me from the front and back."

"So?"

"So she seemed more like the owner of a fancy café than a tailor."

Livia started laughing.

"I'm sure one look at you was enough."

"Enough for what?"

"Enough to understand the shape of your body so she could tailor the suit."

For whatever reason, Livia's words triggered in Montalbano the same embarrassment he'd felt when under Elena's penetrating gaze.

Moments later, Livia said:

"All right, then, good night."

Montalbano returned her good-night wishes, though he knew that it was going to be anything but a good night.

By this point the pasta was certainly as hot as it needed to be. He removed it from the oven, served it into a wide bowl, and began to enjoy its bounty.

When he'd finished eating, he realized that it was past ten. And so he went into the bedroom to look for a heavy sweater.

▬

He got to the station right on time, at half past eleven.

"Ah, Chief! Dacter Cosma be waitin' f'yiz in the waitin' room."

"And where's Damiano?" asked Montalbano.

Catarella balked.

"Ya waitin' for 'im, too? 'E ain't 'ere yet, but I'll let ya know soon as 'e gets 'ere."

"Okay. And don't forget, Cat, Cosma and Damiano always appear together," said the inspector.

But in fact, Catarella hadn't mangled the name too badly. And deep down, there was something saintly about Dr. Osman.

Montalbano went into the small sitting room; Dr. Osman rose and they shook hands and smiled.

"You don't know how much I appreciate your agreeing to come," said the inspector.

"Allah is forgiving and merciful," replied the doctor. "And I, a mere drop in the sea, try to follow His example."

They went into Montalbano's office and sat down.

"How can I be of use to you?" the doctor asked.

"An exceptionally large landing is expected for tonight. More than four hundred people, on two different ships."

Dr. Osman literally thrust his hands in his hair.

Montalbano continued.

"And so it's possible there'll be some incidents, even serious ones. We must try to avoid this at all costs. And that's why I need your help."

"Tell me what you want me to do."

"It occurred to me that it would be better for us to board the ships before they dock. That way you can make a speech to these people and persuade them that a calm, orderly disembarkation will facilitate and accelerate their transfer to the processing center."

"Then tell me what you think I should say."

"You must explain to them that the rules have changed and that anyone who does not follow the police's orders will be immediately arrested, declared undesirable and illegal, and will therefore be sent back to his country of origin."

"Really?! Is that true?" Osman asked in shock.

"No, Doctor, it's not. But it's a necessary lie."

"All right, then. I trust your judgment."

The inspector told him a few other things he should say, after which they got into the car and headed for the port.

When they arrived, there were some ten or so buses and three ambulances parked a good distance away from the berthing point.

The buses were all clean and shiny, as though waiting for a delegation of Arab sheiks come to visit the Valley of the Temples. The drivers were gathered in a circle, smoking and making small talk, all dressed in rather elegant uniforms.

Montalbano thought that a lot of people must be lining their pockets with this bus contract.

The twenty policemen, plus Sileci, Mimì, and Fazio, were already on the edge of the quay. Sileci came over to Montalbano and Osman, greeted them, then said to the inspector:

"We've received a wire directly from one of the boats that there are two men and a woman that need to be taken immediately to the hospital."

"Are there any dead aboard?" asked Montalbano.

"Luckily, apparently not."

"How about on the other ship?"

"No injured, sick, or dead."

"So much the better," said the inspector.

At that moment a coast guard lieutenant came over, holding a cell phone to his ear.

"The first boat is at the mouth of the port. What should I tell them?"

"Tell them to stop there and wait for us. We'll be there in ten minutes." Then, turning to Fazio, Montalbano asked: "Is the pilot boat ready?"

"Absolutely. Come with me."

"I also need two of our men to come with me."

"Okay," Fazio said promptly, then called in a loud voice: "Macaluso and Gianni Trapani, over here!"

Two policemen quickly peeled away from the group and came up to Fazio.

"You two go with Inspector Montalbano."

They boarded the pilot boat, which then put out immediately.

Montalbano turned to the two uniformed cops and said:

"As soon as you board the ship, go to the stern at once and post yourselves beside the gangway."

As they approached the ship Montalbano noticed a problematic little rope ladder hanging from its side. He wondered whether he would manage to climb it. He was afraid to look like a fool in front of everyone.

He summoned his courage.

"I'll go up first," he said.

That way, he thought, if his foot slipped and he fell into the water, there would definitely be someone to pull him out.

Meanwhile the ship had turned on all its lights, and one was pointed straight at the rope ladder, to make it easier to climb.

Montalbano raised one foot, set it down on the first rung of rope, closed his eyes because the light was blinding him, and then, just to be safe, commended himself to both God and Allah.

He was advancing nicely when he suddenly felt himself being held back by something pulling on his trouser pocket. It must have got caught on a hook. He was too afraid to let go of the ladder with one hand, and so he merely hoisted himself vigorously upwards to keep on climbing, and at that moment he heard the hiss of his trousers ripping.

Once he came even with the deck, he felt himself embraced by the powerful arms of an officer and pulled aboard.

"Commander De Luca's the name," said the man, lowering his paper face mask.

Despite an initial cleaning of the ship, the smell of shit, piss, and menstrual blood still filled the air.

"Pleased to meet you. I'm Montalbano."

They waited for the others to join them. The inspector and Dr. Osman were taken to the bridge while the two uniformed cops headed towards the stern.

When they looked out from the bridge, they saw a formless mass, since the refugees were all bundled up under the thermal blankets they'd been given on board. All that could be seen were their eyes, glistening wide in the dark, as keen as those of a dog awaiting a bone.

Unable to bear the sight of those desperate, rapid-fire glances, the inspector looked away.

Dr. Osman brought to his mouth the megaphone that De Luca had handed to him, and started speaking in Arabic.

Montalbano was certain that the doctor was repeating word for word what he had asked him to say. Though he didn't know any Arabic, he had the impression he understood a few words. As he was listening he remembered that once upon a time all the fishermen in the Mediterranean spoke a common language, known as "Sabir." It was anyone's guess how it had come into being, and it was anyone's guess how it had died. Nowadays it would have been extremely useful to everyone.

Then the doctor must have finished his speech with a question, because the inspector heard two hundred voices replying in unison.

"They've agreed to cooperate," said Osman. "We can go now."

De Luca gave the order for the boat to continue its approach to port.

When Montalbano and the doctor came down from the

bridge, they immediately found themselves facing the crowd, which then slowly opened for them as they passed. The inspector felt a few hands stroking him gently, and a few voices saying:

"*Shukran.*"

Astern, Montalbano noticed three people lying on the deck in front of the still raised gangway, and two sailors giving them aid. Taking out his cell phone, he called Sileci and told him to send the three ambulances to the quay.

When the ship came to a halt and lowered the gangway, nobody moved.

They'd kept their word.

The stretcher-bearers were now able to board quickly, grab the injured, and carry them away. Dr. Osman then said something in Arabic, and at once the crowd lined up two by two, and the migrants began descending onto the quay in perfect order, without making any noise. All one heard was a kind of litany of laments and a few whispered words.

When the first forty people were on dry land, Osman ordered the others to remain on the ship. The police escorted those who had disembarked towards the bus. Then it was the turn of another forty to come ashore.

Once the last migrant had landed, the commanding coast guard officer told Montalbano and Dr. Osman that the second ship was waiting for them at the mouth of the port.

And so they boarded the pilot boat once again.

The second landing likewise unfolded without incident. Apparently Montalbano's lie that he would arrest and immediately repatriate anyone who made any trouble had worked to perfection.

Since the migrants were disembarking in groups of forty, the last group to touch ground fell short, consisting of only twelve people. Montalbano, Osman, and the two policemen came up behind them.

Once the inspector was on the wharf, Fazio and Augello approached him.

"Chief," said Fazio, "your trousers are all torn. We can see your underpants."

"What's wrong with that? Does it shock you?" Montalbano replied rudely.

"No, Chief. I just thought I'd let you know," Fazio said resentfully.

At this point Sileci came over to greet his colleagues. But the handshakes were interrupted by two angry shouts that came from the last group of people to disembark, who were now near the bus. The men turned around to look.

One policeman was saying to a migrant:

"Take that blanket off. Take it off now!"

"No! No! No!" the man replied desperately, wrapping himself more tightly in it.

The cop tried to grab the blanket and tear it away from him.

Then something strange happened. The migrant let go of the blanket and started running wildly away. He was dressed like a Westerner, in a pair of corduroy trousers, a kind of sports jacket, and shoes so fancy they looked out of place.

"Stop him! He's armed!" the policeman yelled.

Upon hearing these words, Fazio dashed off like a rabbit,

followed by Mimì Augello. In the twinkling of an eye, they seized the man and threw him to the ground, and when Montalbano and Osman caught up to them, they saw Mimì trying to open the man's hands, which were clutching his chest with all his might while he kicked out wildly and shouted:

"No! No! No!"

Finally Augello succeeded in making him let go. He stuck one hand under the man's jacket and pulled out a long, black object.

"It's a flute!" he said in utter astonishment, showing it to the others. Upon seeing the instrument, they were all speechless.

A flute, in that situation, seemed so extraneous an object that it might as well have fallen out of the sky.

Stripped of his flute, the man lay on the ground with his arms spread and his head tilted to one side.

He looked like Christ on the Cross.

He was quietly weeping.

"Help him up," Montalbano said to Fazio and Augello.

When the man, with the help of the other two, was back on his feet, Osman took a step forward and looked him over carefully. Then he said something in Arabic.

But the man interrupted him at once.

"I speak good Italian."

"I'm sorry, but aren't you Abdul Alkarim?"

"Yes," the man said in a faint voice.

"I heard you play a couple of years ago at the Maggio Fiorentino. I think it was *L'après-midi d'un faune*, by Debussy."

"Yes," the man repeated in an increasingly weak voice. "That was my last concert in Italy. Could I have a cigarette?"

Montalbano pulled out his pack, the man took a cigarette, and the inspector lit it for him.

"You can keep the pack," he said, giving him the lighter as well.

"Thank you," said the man, taking a deep drag.

"But how did you end up in this situation?" Montalbano asked.

"Shortly after that concert," the man replied, "I learned that my brother had been arrested by Assad's men and that his wife and eleven-year-old daughter had been left without means and fearing for their lives. I felt I had to go back to my country, but secretly, because I, too, had expressed my feelings against the regime. But then, six months ago, I managed to deliver my sister-in-law and niece to safety, and so I took ship myself."

Mimì Augello handed the flute back to him. The man took it and brought it to his chest, stroking it lightly.

"You may still need it," said Osman.

"I doubt it," said the man. "If I'm lucky enough to be granted political asylum, I hope to get a job picking olives."

Sileci, who had approached the group and witnessed the scene, said:

"I think it's time to go."

"Thank you," the Arab man said to all of them.

And they watched him walk towards the group of refugees. The policeman gave him back his blanket, which the man draped over his shoulders before climbing into the bus. Montalbano told Fazio to send their men home.

Sileci got in his car and drove to the head of the column,

and they all headed off. Bringing up the rear of the queue was a large, covered flatbed truck with Sileci's men inside.

The dock seemed suddenly deserted.

Montalbano glanced at his watch. Half past three a.m.

Too early for the morning fishermen, too early for the fishing trawlers that had spent the night at sea to return to port.

"Where'd you leave your car?" he asked Osman.

"In the police station parking lot."

"I'll take you back there."

They said good-bye to Fazio and Augello, and the rest split up and went their separate ways.

In the car Montalbano and Osman didn't say a word.

When they pulled up in the parking lot, the inspector and the doctor got out.

They shook hands.

"Thank you for your tremendous generosity."

Osman made a gesture as if waving away a fly.

"I'll always be here when you need me, *inshallah*. Try to get some rest."

And he got into his car.

Though tired, Montalbano didn't feel like going straight to bed. He opened the French door, equipped himself with whisky and glass, went looking for the reserve cigarette pack and lighter he always kept in the drawer of his nightstand, and sat down outside.

He knew it was a cold night, but he didn't feel it much, because the adrenaline in his body was still having an effect.

He thought again of the flautist.

The man's dignity and composure had impressed him.

Then he had a thought: How many people were there, among all those wretched souls, with the ability to enrich the world with their art? How many of the corpses now buried in the invisible cemetery of the sea might have been able to write poetry capable of consoling, cheering, filling the hearts of those who read them?

But, aside from that, how many chances for altruism, for generosity towards one's fellow man, were being lost in the tragedy that was enacted every single night?

The flautist had given up a comfortable life, free of danger, refused the joy of applause, renounced his art in order to rush to his family's rescue, at the risk of ending up in jail like his brother.

What was drowning in the sea was not only all those poor victims, but the better part of mankind.

He got up, went into the kitchen, took his trousers off, threw them away, and went into the bathroom, intending to stay in the shower for at least half an hour.

━━━━━

He slept in the blackest darkness for three hours straight, and woke up in the same position he was in when he'd fallen asleep, like some sort of deadweight that had been tossed onto the mattress.

All the same, he now felt completely rested and lucid.

It was past nine o'clock.

Today he made himself two mugfuls of espresso.

When he got to the station he found Catarella sleeping in his chair, head thrown back.

He reached out and slammed his hand down on the table.

Catarella jumped straight into the air, eyes popping out in terror.

"Wha'ss goin' on? Wha'ss goin' on?"

Then he recognized the inspector and immediately shot to his feet and snapped to attention.

"Beggin' yer partin an' all, Chief, bu' I kinda dozed al-luva sudden."

"Tell me something, Cat. Did you get any sleep last night?"

"Nah, Chief. I's waitin' f'yiz to come."

"Then find yourself a replacement at once, and if in five minutes I find you still here at your post, I'm gonna kick you out."

"Yessir, Chief!"

The inspector went into Mimì's office to see if his second-in-command had shown up yet. But the room was empty. Returning to his own office, he sat down at the desk, noticing that the papers to be signed had grown into two small stacks.

For once, however, he did not look at them with hatred. Maybe sitting there for two hours signing papers would help lighten the weight of the night before.

Five minutes later, however, there was a knock at the door.

"Come in!"

It was Fazio, eyelids drooping. Indeed, as soon as he sat

down in the chair opposite the desk, he was unable to stifle a yawn.

"Chief," he said, "maybe we need to assign shifts for these landings at the port. 'Cause if something happens when we're all at the port, the only person here in the station will be Catarella."

"All right," said the inspector. "As soon as Augello gets here we can set up these shifts."

4

Mimì Augello didn't show up at the station until after eleven. If Fazio was dead tired, Mimì looked like he was sleepwalking.

He was literally in a state of catalepsy.

Montalbano asked him if he was of sound mind and body.

Augello didn't answer him in words, but merely waved his left hand as if to say *so-so*.

"Fazio suggested we work in shifts at the port. Are you all right with that?"

Augello nodded yes.

"Well, then," the inspector went on, "if there are any arrivals tonight, Fazio'll be there. The following day it'll be me, and on the third night you'll take over."

Augello repeated the same gesture he'd made a moment before. Then he raised a finger and said:

"But isn't there any hope of a night going by without any landings?"

"Of course there's always hope! Why don't you go to Syria yourself and talk to the caliphate?" Then he asked: "Have you got any news of new arrivals?"

"Not yet," Fazio answered. "We always get the bad news in the afternoon."

"If we've got nothing else to discuss," said Mimì, "I'm gonna go into my office."

"The meeting is adjourned," said Montalbano. "Barring any unexpected developments, we'll meet back up here at four."

Strangely enough, he felt like signing more papers. He had the impression that diving into the great sea of bureaucracy might have a therapeutic effect on him. But the illusion didn't last very long, because once again he was interrupted by the ringing of the telephone.

"Ahh, Chief! 'Ere's 'at Dacter Cosma onna line."

"Put him through."

"Good morning, Inspector. I wanted to let you know that unfortunately I won't be available if needed tonight."

Montalbano felt his heart sink.

"Why not?"

"Because I have a high fever. I already had a little yesterday evening, but apparently the cold last night . . ."

"But what am I going to do?" the inspector blurted out.

"I've already made provisions," the doctor reassured him. "I talked to a friend of mine. Her name is Meriam. She'll be an excellent replacement for me, you'll see. I've already told her how she should proceed with the migrants."

The sound of that name was not unfamiliar to Montalbano.

"I'm sorry, but does this Meriam by any chance work at a tailor's shop?"

"Yes, she does. That's the one."

"I've met her. Do you think she can manage?"

"I assure you she can. She speaks four languages perfectly."

"Could you give me her cell phone number?"

After he'd written this down, the inspector ended the conversation and summoned Fazio. When he told him the news, Fazio twisted up his face.

"That's not okay with you?"

"No, no, Chief, it's perfectly fine with me. But will it be okay with the migrants? Let's not forget, Chief, she's a woman . . ."

"I trust Dr. Osman. But if you still have doubts, here's a suggestion. Let's switch shifts: I'll go tonight in your place."

Fazio bristled.

"Chief, I was just mentioning a potential complication. But if you trust Dr. Osman, then you should trust me, too."

The trattoria was deserted, but all the tables had been arranged in a sort of horseshoe pattern.

One table, however, had been set a bit apart from the rest.

"What's going on? Some kind of banquet?" the inspector asked, alarmed.

"No, Inspector. It's a party for the ninetieth birthday of *cavaliere* Sciaino," said Enzo.

"So why didn't you set a table for me in the little room in back?"

"My apologies, Inspector. I'm having the walls repainted."

Montalbano had no choice but to make the best of a bad situation. He sat down.

He was secretly hoping to finish eating before the merrymakers arrived.

"What've you got for me?"

"Spaghetti with clam sauce?"

"Hell, yes! Bring me some, and quick."

Enzo vanished into the kitchen, and at that moment a few people who looked like they were coming to a wake started filing in through the door. Folks in their fifties and sixties of both sexes, all wearing sorrowful faces fit for the Day of the Dead.

They took their seats while other people, equally gloomy and sad looking, came in behind them.

Outside they heard a powerful, cheerful voice say:

"Here I am, kids!"

And in came an elegant, smiling, ruddy-faced old man with two young men, perhaps grandsons, holding his arms, though it looked more like it was the *cavaliere*, with his firm, swift gait, supporting the other two.

At last, with the ninety-year-old gentleman in his place, the table began to come to life.

During the entire meal, Montalbano heard nothing but the old man's voice telling joke after joke, each one dirtier than the last, all the while eating and drinking without cease and toasting to the health of his table companions.

The inspector left the trattoria with the firm conviction that the ninety-year-old would bury them all before going himself into that good night.

He went out onto the jetty for his customary walk and noticed that the two ships of the night before were no longer in the port. They'd surely gone back out to look for more migrants on the open sea.

As Fazio had predicted, the bad news came in around four-thirty, with Sileci as its messenger.

In Montalbano's office were also Augello and Fazio.

As soon as Catarella mentioned the caller's name, Montalbano turned on the speakerphone.

"Montalbano, I need to inform you that, as usual, around midnight tonight, a motor patrol boat will be coming into port. Luckily there are only thirty-five migrants aboard, all of whom were rescued from a barge that was sinking. So it shouldn't be too taxing tonight."

"Good. I won't be there. Fazio'll be taking my place."

"I'll be waiting for him at the dock at eleven-thirty. I think five of your men should be enough tonight."

"All right," said the inspector, looking Fazio in the eye to get his approval, which his assistant gave with a nod.

Montalbano said good-bye to Sileci.

Before leaving for home, he went into Fazio's office.

"It might be a good idea to get in touch with the girl who's replacing Osman."

"Already taken care of" was his reply.

Montalbano stifled the fit of pique that came over him every time he heard Fazio say those words, and simply asked:

"What was your impression?"

"She seemed like a determined young woman. With a clear head."

"So much the better," said the inspector, waving good-bye and going out.

Since he got home early, he felt like going for a walk, but the libeccio had littered the whole beach with plastic bottles, shopping bags, and even, go figure, an old, broken-down washing machine. The shoreline had become a literal dump.

At least there weren't any corpses this time, the inspector thought, remembering the dead boy he'd found the day before.

He spent a quiet evening, and even managed to read a few beautiful pages of a novel whose protagonist was a Roman assistant commissioner of police sent among the snows of Aosta. The mere thought of being in the same place as that fictional colleague of his sent cold chills down his spine.

Before going to bed he called up Livia. When he told her about the migrants' landing of the night before, Livia got angry at him for not having told her anything earlier. Then they made up and wished each other good night, according to the usual ritual. At least this time it would, for once, be a good night.

But here, too, he was wrong.

At one point he woke up with a start, positive that he'd heard the telephone ringing.

He pricked up his ears.

Nothing.

Dead silence. He turned on the lamp on the bedside table and looked at the clock. One o'clock on the dot. Turning the light off, he got back in his sleeping position, and the telephone rang.

He raced through the darkness. Surely if they were calling him at that hour something must have happened during the disembarkation.

It was Fazio.

"Sorry, Chief, but Sileci wants you here."

"What's happened?"

"It's a little complicated to explain right now, Chief, but we can't take any action till you get here."

He went into the bathroom, put his head under the tap, got dressed haphazardly, and dashed out of the house.

The full, Leopardian moon that accompanied him all the way to the dock reinvigorated him. When he got there the situation didn't seem so dramatic.

Fazio and Sileci were waiting for him on the steps of the bus, inside which the migrants were now all seated while the five cops from his station were chatting. Sileci's men were already in the flatbed. Everyone was ready to leave. No trace of Meriam, however.

"What's going on?" Montalbano asked Fazio and Sileci when they came up to greet him.

"The disembarkation all went quite smoothly," said Fazio, who then turned to Sileci as if to let him have the floor.

"The trouble began," Sileci said with irritation, "when I gave the order for everyone to leave. A young girl came running off the bus screaming and crying, though her parents tried to hold her back. So at that point that woman intervened . . . what's her name?"

"Meriam," said Fazio.

"So, this Meriam started talking to the girl. It took a while to calm her down. The two stepped off to the side to talk, and then Meriam came over to me and explained that something terrible had happened during the crossing, and that the girl didn't want to get back on the bus."

"So what happened?"

"Meriam didn't want to tell us," said Sileci. "But what do you expect happened, Salvo?"

"I don't know. You tell me," said the inspector, who was beginning to get a little irritated himself.

"Somebody probably grabbed her ass," said Sileci, "and we're wasting a great deal of time on chickenshit."

"But where are Meriam and the girl?" Montalbano asked Fazio.

"They're in my car, Chief."

Montalbano wasted no time, went over to Fazio's car, opened the front door, and sat down in the driver's seat.

In the semidarkness of the backseat, he recognized Meriam's smile. The girl, who looked barely fourteen years old and seemed to have fallen asleep, was lying across Meriam's legs as the woman lightly stroked her hair.

Meriam gestured to him to speak softly.

Montalbano questioned her with his eyes, without opening his mouth.

Then Meriam began to speak in a whisper.

"This child, whose name is Leena, told me she was raped by two men during the crossing. She didn't dare say anything, otherwise they would have thrown her and her family overboard."

"So I gather, from what you say," said Montalbano, "that the rapists are on the bus."

"That's right, and that's why Leena didn't want to get on. She's afraid it could happen again. I've even spoken with her parents, who had no idea of anything and didn't know what had happened. I reassured them and told them that Leena is exhausted from the journey and will stay with me for a little while. They were reluctant, but in the end they consented."

Montalbano made a snap decision.

"I'll be right back," he said, and he got out of the car, ever so softly closing the car door without shutting it completely.

A few steps away stood Fazio, waiting for him.

"So?" he asked.

Without answering, Montalbano kept on walking towards Sileci.

"The girl confessed to Meriam that she was raped twice on the barge during the journey. And you call that chicken-shit! There's only one solution: have all the migrants come off the bus."

"What?!" said Sileci, getting more and more upset.

"Don't worry, I'll handle it myself. There's no need to bother your men about it. Just give me a few minutes."

"Okay," said Sileci.

Montalbano turned to Fazio.

"Tell our guys to have them all get out of the bus and form a line. For starters, we'll separate the men from the women."

Ten minutes later, the thirty-four migrants were all lined up in single file in front of the inspector, who said to Fazio:

"Look at them one by one, and then have all the women get back on the bus."

That left only eleven men still outside. Six were old and decrepit, and Montalbano sent them back up on the bus.

Then he turned to Sileci.

"You can let them leave now. These five men and the girl will come to the station with us. I'll have a statement of detention drawn up and ready for you in the morning."

Sileci could hardly believe his ears. He shook the inspector's hand and was off in a flash.

On Fazio's orders, the cops from Montalbano's unit had the migrants get into the two squad cars, two in each. Accompanied by another of his men, Montalbano took with him a boy of about sixteen who didn't seem to know whether he was scared to death or just dead tired.

Fazio went back to his car and drove off with Meriam and Leena.

After Montalbano had been driving for a few minutes, Fazio rang him on his cell phone.

"Chief, Meriam says that at the moment the girl is in no condition to answer questions. She says it's better if she takes her home with her first, gives her something warm to eat, and lets her wash up and change clothes, especially since she's got a niece staying with her who's almost the same age. And then they'll come to the station."

"Maybe she's right," said Montalbano. "But how much time do they need?"

After a brief pause, Fazio answered:

"About an hour, max."

"Okay," said the inspector. "Then tell the two other cars that they should put the migrants in a holding cell. Our men can go home then, except for two, who must remain on duty."

When he was outside the station, he pulled up, let the officer and the sixteen-year-old boy out, then continued on to Marinella and home.

Having been woken up in the early stages of sleep had dulled his senses. He felt like he needed a major freshening up to clear his head.

He went into the house like one of those silent-movie characters whose movements are all sped up. He undressed, got into the shower, came out, dried himself off, prepared a pot of coffee, drank down a mug, grabbed two reserve packs of cigarettes, put them in his jacket pocket, and went out of the house. Just as he was locking the door, his cell phone rang again.

"What is it, Fazio?"

"There's a complication, Chief."

"Namely?"

"When Meriam was washing the girl, she noticed some traces of blood. So she rang her gynecologist, who said that the girl should be brought immediately to her office, which is right in her house. I drove them there myself, and so now I'm here outside in the car, waiting for news. I'll call you back as soon as I have any."

"All right," said Montalbano.

Reopening the front door, he went into the bedroom, took off his shoes, lay down in bed, and picked up the novel in which his unfortunate colleague was freezing amid the alpine snows.

Getting engrossed in his reading, he lost all sense of time. The phone rang, but this time it was the land line.

"I'm at Meriam's place, Chief. So here's what happened. The gynecologist examined the girl, gave her a pill that will prevent her from getting pregnant, and then wanted the kid to be taken to Montelusa Hospital, but Meriam managed to convince her to wait. The girl is now in bed, because she's not supposed to move. What should we do?"

"I'll come to you. Give me the address."

"Via Alloro, 14. The name on the buzzer is Choukri."

Good thing he knew where this street was located, otherwise he'd be wasting time driving around trying to find it.

He parked, rang the buzzer, pushed the door open, and climbed two flights of stairs instead of taking the elevator. The door was open. Meriam was waiting for him.

She showed him into a small living room. Fazio, who was sitting in an armchair with his head in his hands, sprang to his feet, then sat back down when the inspector settled into another armchair.

"The doctor said that luckily the lesions are only superficial," Meriam said at once. "Leena's in my bed. I woke up my niece, and she's keeping her company now."

"And where's your husband?" Montalbano asked.

"My husband comes home at seven. He's a night watchman."

"Listen," the inspector began, "I would like for the questioning to be as untroubling as possible for the child. So, could you tell me whether Leena told you anything about what happened on the barge, and relate it to me? That would spare her the pain of reliving the whole ordeal and reopening the wound."

"Yes, unfortunately, she did tell me," said Meriam. "She said that a few hours after the barge set sail, as she was sleeping at her mother's side, she felt someone put a hand over her mouth, and then she was lifted bodily by two men and dragged towards the rear. Everyone was exhausted from the long wait to board the ship, nobody had eaten or slept for days, nobody in her family noticed anything, and even Leena herself told me that she'd thought she was dreaming, trapped in a nightmare. The two men who carried her away, keeping her mouth covered the whole time, took turns raping her, forcing her to sit on top of them. Then they picked her back up like a bundle of rags and returned her to her mother's side, but not before threatening to throw her and her parents into the sea if she told anyone. It took some doing to get her to talk, but after a while she couldn't hold it in any longer and finally confided in me . . ."

"Thank you," said Montalbano. "Did she tell you anything else about these two men?"

"No."

"Do you think we can go and talk to her now?"

"Yes. Follow me. Just for your information, her name is Leena Marrash."

Leena was sitting up in the large double bed, three pillows behind her head. Along with Meriam's young niece, she was looking at a cell phone emitting the sound of some American pop music.

"Anna, could you please go into your room for a few minutes?" Meriam asked her.

The girl got up and left, taking her cell phone with her.

Montalbano and Fazio sat down in the two chairs that were in the room. Meriam, for her part, sat down on the bed beside Leena. The girl was wearing a veil over her head, and now that he could see her in the light, the inspector realized just how much pain and suffering were etched into that little face.

Fazio also looked at her, but then lowered his head to avoid her eyes.

"Here's what we'll do," said Montalbano. "I'll ask her the questions, and then you, Meriam, will translate them and tell me how she answers."

"Okay."

"Could you ask her if she was able to see the two men's faces?"

Meriam hadn't finished asking the question when Leena started sliding all the way under the bedsheet. Her head and shoulders completely disappeared.

Meriam said something to her. The only response was that Leena reached out from under the covers with two small hands and grabbed the edge, not to raise it but to hold it more tightly closed and keep herself better sealed in darkness.

"Maybe it's better if you go back out into the living room," said Meriam. "I'll try and talk to her myself."

Montalbano and Fazio went out of the room.

When they were back in the living room, Montalbano noticed that Fazio was as pale as a corpse.

"You tired?"

"Nah."

"Unwell?"

"Nah."

"So what's wrong? Tell me! That's an order."

"Chief, I have an awful, frightening desire to kick all five men repeatedly in the balls, the innocent as well as the guilty."

Montalbano gawked in surprise. He'd never heard anything so violent come out of Fazio's mouth before; but then his assistant, as he was speaking, seemed to gain some control over himself.

"I'm sorry," he said in a soft voice.

Montalbano felt the need to smoke a cigarette. He went over to the window, opened it, and lit the cigarette, making sure to blow all the smoke outside.

When he'd finished, he stubbed it out on the windowsill, put the butt in his jacket pocket, and said:

"Fazio, call the station and find out how things are going there."

Moments later Fazio reported to Montalbano that Catarella told him the five men in the holding cell were behaving themselves, and the two officers were awaiting further orders.

Meriam's sitting room was clean and orderly. Two pieces of furniture were covered with photos of children. Inside a large silver frame the inspector noticed a photo of a diploma in English and a dark-eyed young man, probably Meriam's son or relative. On the low table between the two armchairs was a hardbound Koran alongside two Italian fashion magazines.

A modest home like so many others, in other words.

As Montalbano was looking on, lost in thought, Meriam came in.

"Inspector, I don't think Leena is up to talking to you. I think I know what you wanted to know, and so I took the liberty of asking her a few questions."

"You did the right thing," said Montalbano. "What did she tell you?"

"She didn't get a good look at them. But I asked her whether the two of them had anything unusual that might help us to identify them."

"And?"

"Leena said she was able to bite the finger of the first man with all her might. The second man defended himself, but she remembers that when he was holding her he was wearing a soft down jacket. But that was all she could tell me."

5

They agreed that Meriam would take the girl to the hospital in the morning.

By the time Montalbano and Fazio made it back to the station, it was past four a.m.

Catarella was dead to the world, head resting on his table. Montalbano let him sleep and went into his office after telling Fazio to ring the processing center to inform Leena's parents that the girl was being taken to the hospital for tests but that in any case she wouldn't be held up for very long.

But while Fazio was making the call, a problem occurred to Montalbano: If none of the five men detained spoke a word of Italian, how was he going to interrogate them? Summoning Dr. Osman was out of the question. The only solution was to trouble poor Meriam again. By now she was probably in bed. He looked for the piece of paper with her number on it, found it, and dialed. She answered on the first ring.

"I'm sorry, Meriam, this is Montalbano again. I feel mortified to ask, but I need you again. Could you come to the station and act as interpreter?"

"Of course. The girls are both sleeping soundly in the double bed. Just give me time to make a pot of coffee and a bit of porridge for my husband, and I'll be on my way."

The mere thought of it gave Montalbano a nasty twist in the pit of his stomach. Porridge and coffee? At seven in the morning?

Fazio returned.

"All taken care of," he said, sitting down. "So, what do we do now?"

"We wait for Meriam to get here."

Fazio did a double take.

"What? Did you call her up?"

"Of course! I happen not to speak Arabic. Did you by any chance study it at school?"

"No way, Chief. I studied English, though it's starting to look like Arabic would have been more useful."

"I had an idea," said Montalbano. "You've seen the state these poor wretches are in when they arrive. Even if they're young, they're exhausted, at the end of their rope. They wait on the shore for days and days, without eating or sleeping, until it's their turn to leave. And so I asked myself: How could anyone feel like raping a young girl? . . . And, even if such a thought does cross your mind, where do you find the strength to do it, when you're barely strong enough to breathe? So, it's possible these two lowlifes are none other than the boatmen themselves. Remember when Sileci told us that the motorboat had picked them up from a barge that was sinking? Apparently the two boatmen hadn't managed in time to jump to safety and are now in the holding cell with the migrants."

"You're right!" said Fazio.

"Do something for me, would you? Go and peek through

the spy hole to see what's going on in there, and then tell me if one of them is wearing a down jacket."

Fazio returned a few minutes later.

"Chief, three of them are sleeping on the floor, and the two others are sitting on the straw mattress and chattering intensely. One of them is in fact wearing a red down jacket."

They sat there looking at each other, and then Fazio asked:

"Shall we make some coffee?"

"Excellent idea," said the inspector.

As they were going into a small room with the camping stove, he saw Pasanisi and Pagliarello, the two uniformed beat cops, sleeping deeply in the two armchairs in the waiting room.

The coffee lifted his spirits.

The moment they returned to Montalbano's office, the telephone rang.

Catarella's voice was ragged with sleep.

"Hello! Hello!" he yelled. "Hello!"

"Cat, what's got into you?"

"I was tryin' a see fer soitan 'at you was youse ann'at you was onna premisses! 'Cuz, seein' as how I din't see ya walk past—"

"Okay, okay. What is it?"

"'Ere's some lady calls 'erself Signura Marianna Ucrìa sayin' you called 'er."

How nice! thought the inspector. Catarella's becoming interested in literature!

"Show her into my office."

"Hello again. I got here as soon as I could," said Meriam, coming in.

"Thank you, and again, my apologies, but your presence here is absolutely indispensable."

"I understand," the woman said.

Fazio sat her down opposite the desk, leaving the other chair empty.

"I'm under the impression," Montalbano began, "that the sixteen-year-old boy I drove here was more frightened than he should have been about what was going on. I think he must have seen something he wasn't supposed to see, and he's not talking because the guys who raped Leena are the two boatmen."

"What do you mean, the two boatmen?" Meriam asked in surprise. "Usually the minute they spot the motor patrol boat, they throw the migrants into the sea and are the first to flee to safety."

"You're right, but this time they seem not to have had the time to do that, because the barge was sinking."

Montalbano then turned to Fazio.

"Wake up Pagliarello and tell him to go and get the youngest of the group, the sixteen-year-old who was in the car with me, and bring him here to me. And you come right back."

Fazio left and then returned.

"Are you armed?" the inspector asked.

"Yes," said Fazio, surprised by the question.

"Give me your weapon."

Fazio handed him his pistol, and the inspector set it down on the table, within reach.

At that moment Pagliarello came in, pushing the Arab boy from behind. The lad was visibly trembling in fear.

"Wait," said Montalbano.

The two stopped just inside the door.

The inspector then stood up slowly, pistol in hand, drew near to them, and gestured with the gun for the boy to go and sit down in the chair facing Meriam.

When the boy was seated, the inspector said to Pagliarello: "Handcuff him."

The boy hung his head and started crying silently.

Montalbano sat back down.

"Please tell him," Montalbano said to Meriam, "that he's been identified by a little girl who was raped during the journey as one of the culprits. And that's not all; the girl also told us he was one of the boatmen. He is therefore under arrest and tomorrow will be immediately repatriated and sent to prison."

"Inspector, I think you're going a little too far!" said Meriam, frightened by what she was seeing and hearing.

And so the inspector looked at her intently and spoke to her with his eyes, and the expression on Meriam's face reassured him completely that she realized they were playacting. And indeed, she started translating, in a soft but firm voice, what Montalbano had just said.

Once she finished speaking, the boy slid off his chair, went down on his knees, brought his cuffed hands in front of his face, and began striking himself in the forehead and shouting. The tears ran in rivers down his face.

"What is he saying?" asked the inspector.

"He says he's innocent, that he had nothing to do with it. He's desperate, Inspector," said Meriam.

"Then ask him if he witnessed the rape and who the rapists were."

The boy's answer was a literal torrent of words, and in the end he collapsed on the floor and curled up into a ball.

Montalbano looked at Meriam questioningly.

"He said they told him they would kill him if he talked," the woman said. "And that if he goes to the processing center with his companions they will definitely kill him. He swears up and down that he's innocent, but doesn't feel up to risking his life yet again."

"Fazio, go get him a little water and have him sit down," said Montalbano. Then, turning to Meriam: "Ask him if he feels up to answering simply with a nod or by shaking his head. Also tell him that I will ask the same questions of all the other five men we've detained, and therefore they'll never know who talked."

Meriam did as asked. Then the inspector followed up with:

"The first question is this: Did he see who committed the rape?"

The boy nodded yes.

"The second question is: Was one of the two wearing a red down jacket?"

The boy nodded again.

"The third and last question is: Are the rapists the boatmen themselves?"

With one last nod, the boy started weeping desperately.

And so the inspector asked Pagliarello to remove the boy's handcuffs, take him into Augello's office, and stand guard over him. Then he asked Fazio to go and wake up Pasanisi and, with his help, bring him the man who was talking to the one in the red down jacket.

━━━

While waiting he informed Meriam that he would be changing tactics entirely, and that she should still translate everything he said, exactly as he said it.

As soon as the man appeared, flanked by Fazio and Pasanisi, Montalbano donned a broad, toothy smile. He stood up, went over to the man, and reached out and shook the man's hand vigorously. The other couldn't help but grimace in pain.

"I'm sorry, did I hurt you?"

Meriam translated at once, and the man replied.

"He says no. It's just that he has a wound on that hand, which he got during the journey."

"Oh, I'm so sorry! Let me see," said Montalbano, grabbing the man's hand again.

Between the thumb and forefinger, he could see the girl's tooth marks.

"Please sit down," said Montalbano, "and give me your personal particulars."

As the man gave him this information, Fazio wrote it down.

Montalbano asked him only one question:

"During the navigation, did you notice anything strange happening on board the barge?"

The man shook his head no.

"Do you intend to ask for political asylum?"

The man shook his head again, and then added a few comments.

Meriam translated.

"Not me. I'm only here for work."

For Montalbano, this answer meant that the man was fervently hoping to be sent back home as quickly as possible. It was the only way he could continue to ply his dirty trade.

"That's enough for me," said Montalbano. "I hope you'll soon make it to the processing center. Pasanisi, please escort the gentleman back to the holding cell, then bring me all the others."

When they came in, the inspector had them all stand facing his desk. The two that Fazio had seen sleeping were managing to remain upright only because they were leaning against each other. The man in the red down jacket, on the other hand, was pointing two intense eyes straight at the inspector and was so nervous that he couldn't refrain from tapping his left foot continuously against the floor.

"I want everyone's name and particulars."

Meriam translated for them, and Fazio took it all down.

"I will ask you the same thing I asked the others," the inspector went on. "During the journey, did any of you notice anything strange happening on board?"

The answer was a chorus of "no."

Montalbano then turned to the man in the down jacket.

"How did the boatmen treat you all?"

Before answering, the man grew more visibly nervous than ever, tapping his foot even faster than before, and sort of shrugged his shoulders.

Meriam translated what he said, which was that the boatmen behaved as they always did in these situations.

"One last question," said the inspector. "Do you intend to ask for political asylum?"

The answer of the two propping each other up was immediate, and in Italian:

"Yes!"

Apparently they knew what "political asylum" meant.

"And what about you?" Montalbano asked the man in the down jacket.

Meriam translated his answer.

"Not me. I'm only here for work."

Apparently the two boatmen had agreed on the answer they would give.

Montalbano ordered Pasanisi to take them all back to the holding cell. He glanced at his watch. Between one thing and another, it was now almost seven.

"If you don't need me anymore, I'd like to go back home and get ready to take Leena to the hospital."

"Thank you, Meriam. You've been a tremendous help, and I'm sure you'll be even more of a help to the girl. One last thing: Since you'll be needing to sleep, I can inform the tailor's that you won't be coming in today, if you want."

"Thank you, but I think I'll be able to go to work. Signora Elena is very understanding. I'm sure that when she finds out what happened, she'll be the first to give Leena a brand-new dress as a present."

"Okay, thanks again," said Montalbano, standing up and shaking her hand.

Meriam went out.

"And now," the inspector said to Fazio, "we start making some phone calls. You ring Sileci and explain the situation to him. The little girl is going to the hospital. Ask him to send a car to take the three migrants to the center. The other two will remain in detention here with us. And now I'm going to wake up the prosecutor and tell him the whole story."

Two hours later, the two boatmen were picked up and taken to prison in Montelusa. The matter was now out of the inspector's hands.

"Shall I set Pagliarello and Pasanisi free?" asked Fazio.

"Yes, and you, too, go and get a few hours of sleep."

"Why don't you do the same yourself?"

"Because I don't think I'd be able to sleep," said Montalbano.

"Suit yourself," said Fazio, going out.

But the inspector couldn't stand the thought of staying at the station any longer.

He felt the need to chase from his mind the scenes of the past few days: the drowned boy, the crucified flautist, the raped young girl, all those eyes staring at him from the motorboat . . .

His discipline as a cop allowed him to do what he had to do, but his soul as a man was having trouble bearing the weight of all this tragedy.

Going back to signing papers to distract himself just wouldn't cut it anymore, and walking along the dock of the port, where by this point he saw ghosts, wouldn't help him, either.

And so he did something he had never imagined he would do.

He left the station on foot and headed for the nearest church.

He went in.

It was completely empty.

He went and sat down on a bench and started looking at the statues of saints, which were all made of wood and had the faces of peasants and fishermen. The biggest of all was the statue of the black saint, San Calò. Who could say? It was possible that the saint, too, had arrived on these shores on a barge.

There was a sudden explosion of sound. Somebody had sat down at the organ.

He recognized the piece. It was the Toccata and Fugue in D Minor, by Bach.

He closed his eyes, leaned his head back, and breathed deeply, letting his chest and heart expand as the music carried him far, far away.

He waited for the organist to finish.

Then he left the same way he'd come in, and went to the Caffè Castiglione.

"A custard cream puff and a double espresso, please."

Now he could go back to the office and sign papers.

⬛

At the office he found Augello fresh as a rose in early morning. Feeling envious, he secretly hoped that Mimì's turn at the docks would be complicated and difficult.

He then told him in precise detail everything that had happened, and afterwards said he'd decided that, since he'd lost most of a night's sleep, Mimì should take his place that evening. Augello then asked if he could call him during the night if need be.

"Absolutely!" said Montalbano, thinking in his mind that not only would he unplug the land line, he would also turn off his cell phone.

Reassured, Mimì went back to his office. The inspector passed the time till lunch break by signing no fewer than two hundred different documents, then headed off to Enzo's trattoria. Despite the midmorning cream puff, he was even hungry.

"Inspector, would you like some migrants' soup?"

"Enzo, please, no. Don't talk to me about migrants. What've you got that's good, really good?"

"If you don't want fish as a first course, I've got a delicious *cannicciola*."

"And what's this *cannicciola*?"

"They're little Trapanese macaroni with cabbage and potatoes. My wife invented the dish."

"Well, I do always trust your wife's cooking."

The *cannicciola* was breathtaking.

He made up for his betrayal of the fish realm by ordering a dish of mullet cooked in salt for his second course. This, too, was excellent.

When leaving the restaurant he felt a little weighed down, thus necessitating a stroll along the jetty, despite what ghosts this might awaken.

Walking along at a slow pace, one lazy step at a time, he reached the lighthouse.

Sitting down beneath it, he fired up a cigarette and, looking around, he realized how much the port had changed.

Both the dock and the arm of the jetty he was on had been divided into so many sections marked by barriers. Seen from a distance, they looked like some kind of labyrinth. He quite logically thought that in any case, such temporary barriers were better than walls and barbed wire, as so many other European countries were contemplating.

"And what do *you* think of the European Union?" he asked a crab that was looking at him from the rock beside the one he was sitting on.

The crab did not reply.

"Would you rather not compromise yourself? All right, then, I will compromise myself instead. I think that after the great dream of this unified Europe got off the ground, we've done everything within our power to destroy its very foundations. We've blown off the lessons of history, politics, and basic economics. The only idea that seemed to remain intact was that of peace. Because after killing one another for centuries on end, we couldn't stand it any longer. But now we've forgotten that, too, and so we've come up with this fine excuse of migrants for putting old and new borders of barbed wire back up. They tell us there are terrorists hiding among these migrants instead of telling us that these poor bastards are fleeing from terrorists."

The crab, rather than state its opinion, slid into the water and disappeared.

When Montalbano returned to the station, Catarella informed him that Dr. Cosma had called. As soon as he sat down he gave him a ring.

"I just wanted to tell you," Dr. Osman began, "that I'm feeling better and I'm available if you need me tonight."

Fazio and Augello returned shortly thereafter.

Montalbano told Augello what Osman had just said.

"Dammit!" Mimì exclaimed.

"Why do you say that?"

"Because Fazio told me how beautiful and clever this Meriam is!"

"What, Mimì? Are you already licking your chops over her?"

At that moment Sileci butted in with his usual phone call.

"Tonight, round about midnight, as usual, we've got more than three hundred people coming in. I've already informed everyone. The more men you can send, the better. We'll all meet up at the port tonight."

"What's the greatest number of men we can muster?" Montalbano asked Fazio.

"What do you want me to say, Chief? If we squeeze really hard, we can come up with a dozen, half of whom, over the last week alone, have only managed to sleep every other night."

"Never mind, Fazio. We'll just grit our teeth and do our best."

"Okay, then, we'll leave it that if I need you, I'll give you a call," said Augello.

"I already told you that wouldn't be a problem, Mimì. Meanwhile you should think about informing Osman."

The meeting was adjourned.

━━━

As soon as he set foot in his house, Montalbano's first thought was to call Livia.

Livia wanted him to tell her, in full detail, the whole story of the girl who was raped.

Montalbano would have liked to have been spared this, but he knew that his girlfriend would never let him off the hook if he failed to tell her.

When they'd finished talking, he unplugged the phone and turned off his cell. Then he went into the kitchen to see what Adelina had cooked up for him.

He opened the refrigerator: empty.

Full of hope, he ran to the oven, opened it, and felt his heart sink.

Empty.

Had Adelina lost her mind?

Had she forgotten to make him dinner?

What was he going to do now?

He had no desire whatsoever to go out of the house and back to Enzo's. The only solution was to fry an egg and eat a little bread and tumazzo cheese.

It was only when he put a small frying pan with olive oil over the burner, frowning and cursing all the while, that he noticed a covered pot on the stove, giving off a pleasant aroma.

He froze, slowly reached out with one hand, seized the lid, and raised it a little.

The fragrance grew stronger.

A heartwarming scent of baccalà.

Removing the small skillet, he lifted the lid on the pot and looked inside.

Baccalà with passuluna olives.

He started to warm it on a low flame, then went and opened the French door to the veranda. Given the nice weather, he set the table outside.

Then, instead of putting the baccalà on a plate, he took the whole pot outside.

It took him quite a while to finish, because he savored every bite.

Then he cleared the table, went into the bathroom, then lay down in bed, closed his eyes, and immediately reopened them.

Something had occurred to him. He chased it from his thoughts at once and closed his eyes again.

But his eyelids seemed to have some kind of spring mechanism. They immediately came open again. And the worry of a moment before returned.

Changing position, he managed to close his eyes again.

One second later, they bugged open yet again, and he realized he would never be able to sleep until he did what he had to do.

Getting out of bed, he went into the dining room and plugged the phone back in.

Ten minutes later, he was in a deep sleep.

6

Entering headquarters, he immediately asked Catarella:

"Any news about last night's landing?"

"Nah, Chief. Ya know wha' they say: No nooz is goo' nooz."

"Who's on the premises?"

"Jess Fazio."

"Send him to me."

The phone seemed to have waited for him to open the door to his office to start ringing.

"Ahh, Chief, 'ere'd be the signura Marianna Ucrìa onna line an' she wants a talk t'yiz poissonally in—"

"Put her on," said Montalbano, cutting him off.

"Good morning, Meriam, what can I do for you?"

"Good morning, Inspector, I'm calling on behalf of Signora Elena. She would like you to confirm today's appointment."

"Confirmed. How is Leena?"

"I dropped in at the hospital to say hello to her this morning and they told me she'll be released at noon. Inspector Sileci will come and pick her up in his car and take her to the processing center."

"How did she seem to you?"

"Physically she's all right, but she'd had a bad night.

Apparently she had one nightmare after another and was unable to get any rest. I'll have a better sense of things this afternoon, since I promised I'd come back and see her before noon."

"Thank you, Meriam."

He hung up, and at that moment Fazio came in and sat down in the chair opposite the desk. Montalbano noticed he looked more run-down than usual.

"You look like someone who's lost a night's sleep. Insomnia?"

"What do you mean, 'insomnia'! I'd just fallen into a blissful sleep when Inspector Augello rang me to lend him a hand."

"Why, what happened?"

"Chief, that motorboat looked like a kindergarten. There were about fifteen little children aboard. Then, as soon as they began to disembark, the power went out. A couple of kids came down in the dark, while the others waited on the boat. When the lights came back on five minutes later and we were able to count the children, there was one missing, a four-year-old. His mother started wailing like the Virgin Mary at the foot of the Cross. So, while everyone was looking for him around the docks to no avail, Inspector Augello called me up to tell me to get there at once and lead a search team. Dr. Osman and me wasted a good hour without any result, when a sailor called out from the patrol boat and told us to stop the search because they'd found the boy, who'd somehow ended up in the engine room. By the time I got back home I couldn't fall asleep anymore."

"Well," said Montalbano, "at least everything turned out all right."

"But there's a huge problem, Chief!" Fazio continued.

"And what's that?"

"The problem is that our guys working on the disembarkments are starting to grumble. There's a lot of bad feeling going around, and they're not entirely wrong, 'cause you can't ask a guy who's spent a whole day on the job at the station to lose a night's sleep helping out Sileci."

"But," the inspector objected, "his own men are in the same situation."

"No, you're wrong there," said Fazio. "Sileci has twenty men at his disposal. One night ten of them work and ten of them sleep, and the next night they switch places. Sileci's men take turns. Our guys are always the same."

Montalbano sat there in silence.

Then he grabbed the receiver and told Catarella to ring Hizzoner the C'mishner for him.

"I, for one," Fazio went on, "at the present moment, just to give you an example, wouldn't be able to tell a corpse from a living man."

The phone rang.

"Montalbano! This is the commissioner. What can I do for you?"

"Excuse me just a second," said the inspector.

He set the phone down, stood up, and started shouting angrily.

"And no more arguing, for Christ's sake! I don't want to hear another word about this! All of you get out of here and close the door behind you!"

As Fazio was looking at him with his eyes popping out of his head, not understanding what was happening, Montalbano threw down his ace, slamming his hand on the desk and yelling:

"I said close the goddamn door!"

Then he sat back down, picked up the receiver, and said:

"I apologize, Mr. Commissioner, but—"

"What on earth is going on?" Bonetti-Alderighi asked in alarm, having heard the whole routine.

"What's going on is that my ten men lending support to Sileci are at the end of their rope. They haven't slept a wink in days, and so they came to my office to protest."

The word "protest" alarmed the commissioner even more.

"Listen, Montalbano, if you want, I can come to Vigàta myself to talk to—"

"No, no, Mr. Commissioner," the inspector interrupted him (all he needed now was Bonetti-Alderighi in his hair!), "please don't bother, it's something I can deal with myself. But I assure you, sir, we can't go on this way."

"I realize that," said the commissioner. "You have no idea how hard I am trying to get you some reinforcements, but at the ministry they just turn a deaf ear. All the same, there does lately seem to be a ray of hope."

"Meaning?"

"Apparently over the last few days the boatmen have changed routes. Now they seem to be aiming for the Greek islands. If this turns out to be true, there'll be a lot less pressure on us."

Poor Greeks, thought Montalbano. Like throwing a

drowning man a boulder. He kept that thought to himself and asked:

"And if it turns out not to be true?"

"If it's not, in three days we'll hold a meeting to work out what we can do. Carry on, Inspector."

And he hung up.

Fazio, who'd heard the whole conversation over the speakerphone, threw up his hands.

"Let's hope the guys can hold up for two more days . . . But if you ask me, it's always the same: The shears fly into the air and end up in the gardener's asshole . . ."

The inspector was about to get up and go to Enzo's for lunch when the goddamn telephone rang again.

"Ahh, Chief, 'at'd be yer goilfrenn, Miss Livia, 'oo—"

"Put her on."

He got worried. Normally Livia never called him at the office.

"Livia, what is it?"

"It's nothing, don't worry. I just wanted to remind you that today at three—"

"They've already reminded me, thanks," Montalbano retorted with irritation.

Livia made the mistake of insisting.

"So I needn't worry?"

Montalbano decided to make her pay for this phone call.

"At any rate there wasn't even any need for them to remind me. How could I forget a woman like Elena?"

"Just being an asshole, as usual," said Livia, who immediately understood his game.

When he got to Enzo's the place was almost empty.

"Inspector, my wife made some pasta that's really quite something . . ."

"No first course!" the inspector said firmly.

He immediately recoiled in shock. Why on earth had he said that? Then he realized that he'd said it out of pure and simple vanity. A burst of youth so silly that he was momentarily under the delusion that one less dish of pasta would be enough to let him show up at Elena's without his sixty-year-old paunch.

"So, what can I bring you?" asked Enzo.

"Your wife's pasta," said Montalbano, giving up.

Enzo smiled and said:

"And after the pasta?"

"Just some vegetables in season, with no sauce," said Montalbano, not giving up entirely.

Afterwards, since it was getting late, instead of taking his usual stroll along the jetty, he went to the bar, drank a double espresso, and then headed off, ever so slowly, for the tailor's.

Like the first time, the person to greet him was Meriam.

"Leena was so happy to see her parents again," she said as she led him down the corridor. "And you know what? Inspector Sileci told me that the two attackers, who were also the boatmen, just as you said, have been charged with rape of a minor and aiding and abetting illegal immigration. The boy's testimony was crucial."

The first thing Montalbano noticed upon entering the great room were two large parcels, which the old man and the youth were fussing around with.

Elena came up to him with a smile, wearing an ultramarine green dress.

"Good afternoon, Inspector. It's a pleasure to see you back here. I've brewed some tea for you."

"Thank you," he said, unsheathing a big, fake smile. "I was hoping you would." And he sat down in an armchair Elena had gestured towards.

The woman then sat down beside him and handed him his cup of tea.

Montalbano decided to use the same approach as the last time, and go one better. He emptied the cup in a single gulp.

Elena didn't understand.

"Would you like some more?"

"No, thank you. I'm good."

Then, just to make conversation, he gestured towards the two large parcels, which were now almost completely opened up, and asked:

"New arrivals?"

"Yes," said Elena, "and I'm curious to see if they've sent me everything."

"Why don't you check?" said Montalbano.

"Thank you," she replied, getting up and going over to the table.

From one package she started pulling out a great many bolts of fabric, which she lined up on the tabletop. Then one of her helpers grabbed the now empty boxes and took them out of the room.

Montalbano was spellbound by Elena's gestures. Lightly caressing the fabric with her hands, she didn't touch them so much as seem to feel them with all five of her senses. She would close her eyes and bring the material to her cheek, sniff it, set it back down, then pick it up again, rubbing it repeatedly between her thumb and forefinger.

All at once she stopped.

Then she said:

"Hey! Look at this beautiful gray. If it had come sooner, it would have been perfect for your suit." She picked up the roll, approached Montalbano, and had him look at it and touch it. "Don't you think?" she asked.

But before the inspector could answer, she continued:

"On the other hand, maybe not. Actually, I think you'll like the rust-colored light wool."

She went back to unrolling and rerolling the different bolts.

At a certain point her eyes lit up even more.

"Finally! I'd been trying to find this cotton for years!" Then, raising her voice, she called out: "Meriam, come quick, this is the muslin I was talking to you about."

Meriam approached, her curiosity aroused.

"Touch it," Elena continued, still holding the fabric. "It feels just like raw cotton or, better yet, like a cotton plant moving in the sunlight."

Then there occurred a sort of freeze-frame of her person, while everything around her kept on moving. In the middle stood Elena, completely still, eyes faraway in thought.

Afterwards, as if her image were set back in motion, Elena shook herself and started opening the bolts of fabric one after another until they covered everything that was on the table.

They had all the colors of the desert: sandy beiges, luminous oasis greens, boundless sky-blues, and the midnight blue of Tuareg turbans.

Meriam meanwhile was touching the fabrics ever so lightly, as though afraid to damage them.

"These are so wonderful, Elena! They remind me of the bands my mother used to use to swaddle infants. We should be careful. It's a rather treacherous fabric, very delicate, and tears easily."

And she began to fold them up again ever so gently.

"Come and see, Salvo," said Elena.

Montalbano got up and went over to her.

"Feel how soft this is. I have no idea how this muslin can be so light and have such a dense, complicated weave, unlike all the other similar kinds of cotton."

Despite not knowing the first thing about these matters, Montalbano touched the fabric. And indeed it was like having air between one's fingers, but not just any air: an air of effervescence and beauty.

"You have no idea how long I've been looking for this fabric. I had two rolls of it in a prior life, when I had my tailor's shop in the north. It's Lebanese cotton, and you won't believe what it's called: 'Princess Sicilia.'"

"Why's that?" the inspector asked with a smile.

"I don't quite remember the whole story, but apparently there was once a Lebanese princess named Sicilia, who was forced to sail long and far to reach these shores, which were deserted at the time."

"I've never heard of her," said Montalbano.

"Here, feel this," Elena continued. Then she stopped, looked at the inspector, and suddenly seemed very rushed. "I'm taking too much of your time," she said.

"No, not at all."

"Nicola, let's start the fitting, if you don't mind."

And with a quick step, she preceded Montalbano down the corridor towards the fitting room, followed by the old tailor holding a hanger with clothes on it.

By now familiar with the routine, Montalbano took off his jacket as the tailor had him put on the left side of half a jacket. He adjusted it well on the inspector's shoulder, then stepped aside for Elena.

Elena started looking at how the garment hung on the inspector's body. Drawing close to him, she grabbed the lower hem and jerked it down, then took a few steps back to have another look. Then she approached again and folded the hem of the sleeve back a little, after which she asked Montalbano to raise and lower his arm. She asked her assistant for the chalk and started making marks, in a kind of circle, around the sleeve. Then she started carefully studying the sleeve join, made a face, raised the sleeve two or three times, and made another chalk mark on the shoulder. Finally, with a quick jerk, she yanked the sleeve off of him and started looking at the inside of the sort of half vest that remained on Montalbano's body.

Here, too, she made two or three mysterious marks, and said:

"Nicola, please help the inspector take it off. We're all done."

The tailor also helped him put his jacket back on.

"Nicola, in your opinion, when will we be ready for our final appointment with the inspector?" asked Elena.

"In three days," the assistant said.

"Then we'll be expecting you at the same time, Inspector. And we'll have you try on the full suit, trousers included."

They left the room and headed back towards the big hall.

Montalbano approached the table where Meriam was folding all the bolts back up.

"Meriam, I wanted to thank you again for your help. And thank you, too, Elena, for being so understanding."

His left hand was resting on the table as he spoke, and all at once he felt something scratch the back of his hand and saw a white cloud moving across the table.

"Ouch!" he exclaimed, more out of surprise than pain.

"Did he scratch you?" asked Elena.

"No," said Montalbano. "It's nothing. Just a little superficial scratch."

"Naughty boy!" Elena said to the white cloud, which had meanwhile turned into a cat.

"I'm sorry, but Rinaldo has been acting strangely all day and bothering everybody. He won't stop sticking to me. Maybe he senses an earthquake on the way."

"Or maybe he just doesn't like me," said Montalbano, about to leave the big room after saying good-bye to Elena's assistants.

Elena followed him out with the cat in her arms and,

opposite the fitting room, opened a small door through which he could see some stairs.

She set the cat down and tapped him lightly on the rump.

"Go back upstairs, Rinaldo," she said, pushing him towards the first stair. "As you can see," she said, closing the door, "I work at home. I live upstairs from my shop."

They'd barely taken three steps down the corridor when Montalbano nearly tripped over something. He looked down and saw that it was Rinaldo.

"But is it your cat?" he asked. "How did he manage to open the door?"

Elena smiled.

"He's a very smart cat. He just jumps up, hangs from the handle, and opens the door!"

She bent down to pick him up again.

"Be a good kitty, Rinaldo. What's got into you today? Mamma is not going out; she'll be here with you all day. She's not going anywhere."

Then, turning to Montalbano:

"I really don't know what's got into his head. He's so restless, he's just adding to my agitation."

"Why, is there anything wrong?" asked the inspector.

"Oh, no, never mind."

For a brief moment her face was transformed. A small dark cloud had momentarily obscured the light in her eyes.

Elena then showed him out and gave him a peck on the cheek by way of good-bye, but it seemed to Montalbano that her head was elsewhere.

He'd just stepped out of the tailor's shop when a man came up to him and stood before him.

"Hello, Inspector! What a lucky coincidence! I was just thinking I needed to have a few words with you."

Though he'd recognized him at once, Montalbano made a puzzled face, because the man was someone he really didn't like.

"I'm sorry, but who are you?" he asked brusquely.

"I'm Filippo Zirafa," said the man. "I work for the *Gazzettino Siciliano*. We've spoken to each other before . . ."

Zirafa was known for his particularly vehement anti-migrant articles. That was the main reason the inspector couldn't stand him.

"I don't remember. What do you want?"

"I would like to ask you a few questions about—"

"I don't grant interviews," said Montalbano, cutting him off.

But the man would not give up.

"All right, then allow me to make a comment. I've gotten wind of the fact that a young migrant girl has been admitted to Montelusa Hospital after she was raped during the crossing."

"Oh, really?!" said Montalbano, feigning surprise.

"Yes. So I would like to know what you think of these so-called migrants who pretend to be desperate wretches seeking safety and instead end up raping a young girl. It seems clear to me that they're just crooks, terrorists who come first to steal jobs from our working people and then to rape our women. Don't you agree?"

"Totally," said Montalbano. "And I'll tell you something else. But you have to promise me not to reveal your source."

"Of course. I promise."

"Apparently while out at sea these migrants engage in veritable orgies. I was told that one time they actually organized a birthday party replete with music, singing, Chinese lanterns, and dancing."

The journalist gawked, slack-jawed, but immediately recovered.

"Are you pulling my leg?"

"I wouldn't dream of it," said the inspector. "I have nothing but the greatest respect for the press."

And he reached out, moved Zirafa to one side, and resumed walking, as the man stood there speechless, watching him.

At the usual four o'clock meeting with Augello and Fazio, Mimì told them, in full detail, about the case of the little boy who'd disappeared the previous night, before he was later found in the engine room.

"The problem," said Montalbano, "is that we must try in every way possible to prevent these kinds of mishaps during the landings."

"And how can we do that?" asked Fazio.

"I think I have an inkling."

At that moment Sileci came in. Fazio vacated his chair for him.

"So, what can we expect this evening?" the inspector asked him.

"The situation's looking pretty serious."

"Meaning?"

"Meaning that two boats are expected around one o'clock,

with a total of four hundred and twenty migrants, including at least four dead and ten with grave injuries."

"Jesus Christ!" exclaimed Fazio. "I'll inform Dr. Osman at once."

"How many men do you have available?" Montalbano asked Sileci.

"The usual ten."

"Come on!" said Montalbano. "Tonight you have to bring at least fifteen. My guys are totally exhausted and I can't give you any more than ten men."

Sileci, who realized he'd been pushing his luck, threw up his hands and gave in.

"And there's another thing," said Montalbano. "The buses are too far from the boat. The migrants disembark in groups of forty. From now on let's arrange it so that the bus is at the foot of the gangway, on the dock, as soon as they come down, so that there will be little room for escape. I also wanted to request that you have all the bus drivers remain at the wheel and have their vehicles arranged in a semicircle so that, if the lights go out, they can turn on their headlights and enable us to see. Got that?"

"Got it," said Sileci.

The meeting broke up. Montalbano lingered a bit in his office. Before going out he rang Livia and told her he'd gone for a fitting and would be busy all night at the docks. Then he left and headed home.

In the fridge he found a platter of marinated sardines in a sauce of olive oil and oranges. Montalbano ate them cold while watching TV.

That evening the program *Chi l'ha visto?* was on. It was

a show he found interesting, because a strange thing often happened: In certain cases of disappearance or murder, he would immediately think of what would be the best lead to follow, whereas his colleagues, without fail, would always choose a different one.

Why, moreover, even though extremely advanced technologies were now available that previously only James Bond had possessed, did these new means always end up complicating things instead of making them easier?

It was the same with medicine. Doctors had lost their "clinical eye" and relied only on test results. Meanwhile the police were losing their intuition and passively accepting scientific findings.

This, in a country where everyone suddenly turns into cops, coroners, judges, and prosecutors for every case, splitting up into "guilty" and "innocent" camps with the same intensity with which they root for their favorite soccer teams.

It was time. He turned off the television set and started getting ready for the night ahead.

7

The first thing he did was take a pair of old jeans out of the armoire. He didn't want to ruin another good pair of trousers. But he had some trouble actually fitting into the jeans, and so he lay down on the bed, sucked in his gut, held his breath, and, counting one, two, three in his mind, was finally able to zip them up.

The second thing he did was drink a double mug of espresso with a dash of whisky thrown in to balance things out.

Then he put on the usual jacket, went out, locked the door, and drove off.

Once he was on the dock, he realized at once that Sileci had taken his advice. The buses were parked in a semicircle and the drivers were all in their seats.

This time, in addition to the ambulances, there were also some small vans with body bags.

Dr. Osman and Sileci came over to the inspector.

"Naturally," said the doctor, "we're in agreement that the injured should disembark first, then the migrants, and then we'll have the dead brought down."

"That's fine with me," said Montalbano.

"How far from the gangway should the first bus pull up?" asked Sileci.

"Let's put three men on each side of the gangway to

form a kind of corridor leading the migrants directly to the bus's entrance. If that approach works, then clearly we'll be able, in the future, to reduce considerably the number of men needed for these landings. What do you think?"

"It's worth a try," replied Sileci, who looked dead tired.

Then his cell phone rang. Sileci answered, listened, ended the exchange, and said:

"The first ship is stopped at the entrance to the harbor."

"And where's the pilot boat?" asked Montalbano.

"It's waiting at the usual place."

"Then let's go," the inspector said to Osman.

He had barely taken three steps when he heard a car pull up at high speed and come to a screeching halt.

The bus drivers, for whatever reason, all turned their headlights on at the same time.

Out of the car popped Catarella, completely dazed by the lights; shielding his eyes with his hands, he yelled:

"Inspector Montalbano! Inspector Montalbano! Stop, fer peetie's sake! Don' get onna boat, fer peetie's sake!"

Montalbano balked. What the hell was going on?

"Turn off those lights," he shouted as he ran towards Catarella. "I'm over here, Cat. What's happened?"

"Ahh, Chief, Chief! A terrible moider's wha' happened!"

The inspector felt lost.

He started fumbling for the cell phone in the pocket of his jeans, which were still too tight. Hurling a curse, he managed to extract the phone and give an order to Catarella:

"Wake up Fazio and tell him to go to the scene."

Meanwhile Montalbano had dialed Augello's number:

"Mimì, you must come to the port at once."

"I'm in my underpants."

"Then come in your underpants. I have to go, and you're going to have to oversee the disembarkment. There are already four dead aboard the ship, and if you're not here in three minutes, there'll be a fifth fatality. Got that?"

"Just tell me one thing," said Mimì. "Why are you leaving?"

"I suddenly feel very hungry," said Montalbano, hanging up, thus interrupting the litany of curses Mimì had started hurling at him.

"So what happened?" he asked, turning to Catarella.

"Chief, I gotta tiliphone call onna tiliphone from a night watchman woikin' at night, an' 'e said 'e discovered a terrible crime whilse 'e was doin' 'is night watchin' an' 'e said 'e wou' wait onna premisses for us to get there."

"Do you know the address?"

"Yeah, Chief. Via Calibardo, 62."

"I'm gonna go there now," said Montalbano, "and you get yourself back to the station."

Dr. Osman intercepted him on his way back to the car.

"Could you please tell me—"

"Yes, Doctor. There's been a serious crime committed. Inspector Augello's on his way to take my place. I'm very sorry, but I really must go now."

He shook the doctor's hand and drove off to Via *Garibaldi*, which ran parallel to Via Roma.

He immediately spotted the night watchman, who was standing outside the half-open entrance to a building. He got out of the car.

"I'm Montalbano. What happened?"

"Inspector, I was making my usual rounds when I noticed that this doorway, which is usually closed, was still open. So I poked my head inside and, from the stairwell, I saw the door to the apartment wide open, with all the lights on inside. I got worried and went into the place. I asked out loud if anyone was at home, but there was no answer. Then I looked in the different rooms, and I noticed some towels thrown on the bathroom floor. Then I noticed a small staircase at the end of the corridor. I went down and . . . I'm sorry, Inspector . . . it's hard for me to talk . . . That's where I saw . . . the horror . . ."

But Montalbano was no longer listening. His legs had suddenly turned to mush, and he was overcome by a bout of dizziness that forced him to brace himself against the wall with one hand. Then he asked:

"But . . . is this . . . the tailor's shop . . . the tailor . . . Elena?"

"Yes, yes, Inspector. They killed her in the big room. But, sir, you can't imagine . . . the butchery!"

At that moment Fazio pulled up in his car. When he got out he immediately noticed the state Montalbano was in.

"What's wrong, Chief? Are you okay?"

Montalbano gestured for him to wait a minute. He needed to catch his breath.

At last he was able to speak.

"Elena's been killed. The tailor."

He was slowly beginning to regain some self-control, and so he turned to the night guard:

"Please leave your name and telephone number with Inspector Fazio," he said. And, still supporting himself against the wall, he went into the building and started climbing the stairs, gripping the bannister tight.

If his legs were mush, his feet had turned to cement.

Fazio caught up to him on the landing.

"Should I summon the circus, Chief?"

"No, let's us have a look first."

He entered the apartment but did not stop to look in the rooms.

Reaching the end of the corridor, he started descending the staircase leading to the floor below. At the bottom was the small fitting room. He headed for the big room, but then stopped in the doorway.

He needed a moment of preparation before he could confront the horror, as the guard had called it. For him, however, the horror was twofold.

He felt an absurd sort of intimacy with the place. He'd met Elena only twice in his life, and yet it was as if she'd already become a friend. It had taken little for her to seem almost like family.

Then, making up his mind, he took two steps forward, went in, and stopped again. Elena's body lay on the floor, next to the large table. She was wearing a different dress from the one she'd had on that afternoon. It apparently had once been light in color, but now it was anyone's guess what the original hue was, as it was entirely drenched in blood.

There also was blood all around on the coir rugs, and a few spatterings had ended up on the fabric stored on the shelves.

Elena lay supine, left hand on her belly, right arm

extended under the table. Montalbano managed to take another three steps forward, with a silent Fazio still behind him.

He bent down to get a better look.

She'd been stabbed to death, the knife thrust into her body over and over. But then he suddenly realized that the murder weapon may have been a large, long pair of tailoring scissors, which was on the table but seemed to have no traces of blood on it.

At this point he couldn't take it anymore, and felt the need to go and sit down in the armchair.

He stayed that way, in silence, until Fazio repeated his question:

"Chief, can I summon—"

"Yes."

Fazio pulled out his cell phone and went into the corridor. As soon as Montalbano was alone, he started looking around, while remaining seated.

The first question that popped into his mind was:

How is it that, with all this blood around, the killer left no footprints?

Then he stood up, came across Fazio in the corridor, who was still talking, and went and checked everything. The glass door was locked from the inside. He opened it. The metal shutter was down and secured with a padlock. He reclosed the door and returned to the great room.

To leave the building, the killer must necessarily have gone back up to the apartment. But how? By flying?

"I've informed everyone," Fazio said as Montalbano was sitting back down in the armchair.

Fazio approached the victim, being careful about where

he stepped. He crouched down and started studying her from up close.

Then he stood back up and went and sat in the armchair next to Montalbano, who was sitting with his head in his hands.

"Chief," he said in a soft voice. "What are you doing? Did you know her, by any chance?"

"Yes, she was a friend. I saw her just today."

Noticing that the inspector seemed particularly upset, Fazio ventured to ask:

"But was she a friend friend or just a friend?"

"She was a friend. And she was also my tailor. Just this afternoon she had me try on a suit."

Fazio realized that one word wouldn't be enough and two would have been too much.

So he changed the subject.

"Did you also notice something strange?"

"What?" asked Montalbano, lost in thought.

"The body was lacerated all over—the neck, the stomach, the face, the arms, but her chest was untouched."

"It's probably just a coincidence," said the inspector.

"I don't think so, Chief. If the murder weapon was that pair of scissors on the table, then it wasn't a premeditated crime but some kind of fit of rage. And how do you explain that someone stabbing wildly like that never manages, not even by chance, to strike the broadest part of the victim's body?"

"Fazio, do me a favor. Let's talk about this later. Right now I can't deal with it."

He suddenly remembered the cat.

"Rinaldo!"

Fazio's eyes opened wide.

"Who's Rinaldo?"

"The cat," said Montalbano. "Listen, please go back up into the apartment and see if the cat is in there. He's a white cat, with long hair."

Fazio went out.

Montalbano couldn't resist the urge to smoke a cigarette.

He raised his eyes slowly and let them rest on Elena's corpse.

For an instant, but only an instant, he saw her standing again, smiling, softly rubbing that special fabric against her cheek . . . what was it called again? Princess? Princess of Sicily!

And at that exact moment he spotted, right beside the scissors, a bloodied piece of fabric. He sprang to his feet and went over to look at it without, however, touching it, and he realized it was a large remnant of the fabric that Elena had had him feel. Except that it was folded in two as if it had been used as some sort of neck band and then violently yanked to the point that it was half-torn.

The smoke from the cigarette bothered him, and so he extinguished it with his hand and put the butt in his jacket pocket.

He went and sat back down.

"I looked for the cat, Chief, but couldn't find him," said Fazio. "It's anybody's guess where he's gone to hide. He's probably on top of an armoire, or maybe he went out of the house."

He hadn't finished speaking when Montalbano noticed

the slightest of movements on the set of fabric-stacked shelves behind the table. Then everything became motionless again. But the inspector didn't take his eyes off the spot. And his patience was rewarded, because moments later the movement resumed.

He was positive it was Rinaldo. At the risk of getting scratched again, he got up, went over to the shelving, and called in a soft voice:

"Rinaldo."

Then a sort of miracle occurred. At the very back of the shelving, the cat's face popped out, eyeing him.

"Come, Rinaldo."

The cat came out a little farther.

Without saying a word, Montalbano reached out and laid a hand on the wooden tabletop. Rinaldo came slowly forward until he was close enough to sniff his hand. Then he lightly licked one of the inspector's fingers.

Montalbano picked him up with both hands. The cat put up no resistance. And at that moment he realized that all the cat's white fur had become pink with its mistress's blood. He also noticed that the cat's paws were all redder than its fur. It was possible that the cat had attacked the killer. He set the animal back down gently on the shelf, scratching its nose and saying:

"Be a good kitty now, Rinà, and stay right there."

The sound of police sirens began to fill the air.

"That must be Forensics," said Fazio.

"Go and meet them. I'm going upstairs to have a look."

He wanted to see the layout of the apartment, and so he opened the first door on the right.

There was a large kitchen, reminiscent of those old-fashioned Sicilian kitchens with colored terra-cotta tiles over the oven. Past it was a door leading to a spacious dining room.

He turned around, went back into the corridor, and headed for the last room on the right. It was a large, elegant salon full of books.

Going to open the door opposite, he found a small guest room with a single bed; next to it was a large, colorful bathroom. Beyond that was Elena's bedroom, which had a small door leading to a personal bathroom. As the night watchman had said, there were towels thrown on the floor.

Montalbano heard the forensics team coming up the stairs and raced into the kitchen and pushed the door to, with the tip of his toes.

He didn't want to see anyone.

He started looking around.

The kitchen was in perfect order. He opened the garbage pail and was convinced that Elena had had somebody over for dinner.

At this point he heard Dr. Pasquano walk past in the hallway, cursing for having been woken up in the middle of the night. Montalbano hid behind the door.

After Pasquano had passed, he went into the far room at the end of the hall.

It was an enormous, meticulously outfitted salon: precious rugs on the floor, an antique chaise longue reupholstered in the Oriental style, a small opium-smoker's cot transformed into a little couch, and a great many large cushions to sit down on. The walls to both left and right were covered with shelves teeming with books and statuettes.

Books, but also Caltagirone pottery, a series of small objets d'art, all gold, little Greek houses, Maghreb terra-cotta, Tunisian ceramics . . . It was like a little Mediterranean bazaar.

A small glass showcase, similar to those one finds in doctors' offices, featured a great many men's fashion magazines.

He went back out into the corridor and into the guest room, which had a small armoire and a single bed that had been made up for the night.

On top of the bed were some folded towels.

Then the spacious, immaculately clean bathroom.

Finally he went into the room where Elena slept. It was huge, all white, and her bed, wide enough for three, was covered in white linen.

Instead of the usual table lamps on the nightstands, there were two standing lamps with broad shades beside them, also white. A colossal armoire, also the color of the moon, covered an entire wall. The only note of color in the room was a midnight blue desk with three drawers on the right and three drawers on the left. Next to the desk was the entrance to the bathroom, which had a modern shower all made of glass, as well as a renovated old bathtub with little lion's feet.

Montalbano bent down to feel the two towels that were on the floor between the tub and the shower. They were still damp.

He slid open the door to the shower..

He noticed that it had been recently used, because there were still a few droplets of water on the glass walls.

Apparently Elena, either before or after dinner, had taken a shower and changed her clothes to meet the person who would then kill her.

And it could not, moreover, have been the dinner guest who used the shower, since he would have used the guest bathroom.

Still struggling, he extracted his cell phone from his pocket and rang Fazio.

"How far along is Dr. Pasquano?" he asked in a soft voice.

"He's almost done, Chief."

"Then, when he's about to leave, bring him to me upstairs. Take him into the first room on the right, just past the staircase. But don't tell him I want to see him."

"Okay, Chief."

He went back into the kitchen, and as he was sitting down his cell phone rang.

Good thing the door was half-closed.

"Salvo." It was Augello, talking in a whiny voice. "The scene here is a total madhouse. Couldn't you take five minutes and come—"

"No," said Montalbano, cutting him off.

Then he heard Pasquano's voice in the stairwell.

"So, to what do we owe the fact that the illustrious inspector is out of our hair for once? Is he having trouble getting out of bed, considering his age?"

"Here I am," said Montalbano, opening the door and appearing in front of the doctor.

Pasquano recoiled in surprise, took a step back, and collided with Fazio.

"What? So you managed to rise from the dead?"

"I need to ask you some questions," said Montalbano, turning and going back into the kitchen.

Pasquano and Fazio followed him.

"So, how long has she been dead, in your opinion?"

"Let's make a preliminary agreement: only three questions, because I'm so sleepy I could die."

"Okay."

"In my opinion, not more than three hours. Let's say she died sometime after eleven o'clock."

"My second question is yes or no. Was she killed with the scissors?"

"I think so. The wounds are too wide and deep. It's consistent with the tailor's scissors. I counted twenty-two, at least four of which were fatal. Okay, let's have the last question."

"How much did you lose at poker?"

"Good night," said Pasquano, casting a disdainful glance at him, turning around, and heading out.

"Go see him out, Fazio," said the inspector.

"I don't need anyone to see me out. Unlike you, I can still find my way," said Pasquano, walking away, teetering down the corridor.

Fazio and Montalbano looked at each other.

"Is Prosecutor Tommaseo here yet?"

"Not yet, Chief. He probably went and crashed into a tree somewhere. Forensics says this is gonna take a while. And you know what else? They grabbed the cat and put him in a sack."

"Why'd they do that?"

"Because they said the cat's claws are covered in blood, and it's probably not just the victim's blood. He may have scratched the killer."

"Tell you what," said Montalbano. "There's nothing left for me to do here. I'm going to go to the station. As soon as they've finished here, you come and join me at the office. We have to inform the family. Could you look into that?"

"Okay," said Fazio.

The inspector got in his car, but instead of heading for the station, he turned in the direction of the port. Upon arriving he noticed that everyone was already gone.

Then he spotted Mimì Augello in the distance, walking back to his car, alone.

He started flashing his headlights and honking his horn.

Mimì stopped and turned.

Recognizing Montalbano's car, he tapped his right hand against his watch, as if to say:

So you decide to show up now?

Montalbano stopped the car and got out.

"Mimì, don't give me any guff. Do you know who was killed? Elena. The tailor."

Augello seemed to turn into a pillar of salt.

"The beautiful Elena . . ." he whispered.

"But what happened during the landing?" Montalbano asked.

"And you don't give me any guff, either! How was Elena killed? What the hell happened? Eh? Did they shoot her? Was it an accident? How the fuck is that possible?"

"Mimì, I have no idea. They found her in her shop, carved up with at least twenty-two scissor wounds."

"She was killed with a pair of scissors?"

"Yes. Tailor's scissors, the long, fat kind."

"It was probably some jilted lover. Losing a woman like that would be hard to swallow."

"I don't know, Mimì. All I know is that whoever did

it, did it with as much hatred and ferocity as he could muster. But are you going to tell me what happened here or aren't you?"

Mimì seemed to have lost all interest in what had happened during the landing.

"What can I say, Salvo? Your plan worked like a dream. But all hell broke loose when the families of the four dead people refused to get on the bus. They wanted to stay with their dead. The only problem was, Sileci was against it, and that triggered a nice little scuffle. Three or four migrants took advantage of the confusion to try and run away. That was when I rang you."

"And then what?" asked Montalbano.

"And then Dr. Osman was finally able to make peace. And now I'm outta here. I'm going home to get some sleep."

"Godspeed!" said Montalbano, raising his head and starting back towards his car.

8

He reached for the handle to open the door, but then changed his mind. His head felt heavy, as if all the thoughts in his brain were tied up in knots. Maybe a bit of sea air would do him good.

He started walking and came to the edge of the dock.

And here he stopped, and started breathing deeply. With each mouthful of night-scented air that entered his lungs, he could feel his thoughts disentangling, his brain becoming light and alert again.

He got back in the car, turned on the engine, but did not drive away.

Twisting and turning his entire body, and cursing the saints all the while, he managed to extract his cell phone from his jeans pocket.

He rang Fazio.

"How far along are you guys?"

"We've got enough to keep us busy for another hour, hour and a half, Chief."

"Okay. Have you got Meriam's number within reach?"

"Yeah, Chief. Both the cell phone and the land line."

"Gimme both."

He set the phone down on the passenger's seat and, unable

to find a clean piece of paper, wrote the numbers on the back of the car registration.

Finally he drove off, straight to Via Alloro.

He pulled up outside number 14. Grabbing his cell phone, he rang Meriam's land line. The phone rang a long time before the woman's sleepy voice replied:

"Hello! Who is this?"

"It's Inspector Montalbano."

He clearly heard her hold her breath. Then she asked, alarmed:

"Has something happened to Leena?"

"No."

"Do you want me to come to the port?"

"No. I need to talk to you."

"All right. In half an hour I—"

"I'm right outside your place," Montalbano interrupted her. "As soon as you're ready, please buzz me in."

He got out of the car and locked it. Firing up a cigarette, he approached the main door.

A short while later, he heard her voice over the speaker:

"Are you there, Inspector?"

"Yes, I'm here."

The front door clicked, and Montalbano pushed it open, went inside, and climbed the stairs slowly, trying to think of what words to use to break the terrible news to Meriam.

She was waiting for him outside her open door.

Her eyes met Montalbano's at once, and it was as though she'd read his mind, because her face suddenly changed expression. But she said nothing. She stepped aside just enough to let the inspector in. Closing the door, she led him into a small sitting room and gestured for him to sit down.

She, on the other hand, remained standing in silence, not once taking her eyes off him.

Then she asked:

"Shall I make you some coffee?"

"That would be wonderful," said the inspector, who still hadn't figured out where to begin.

Meriam raced out of the room as if feeling relieved not to have to remain in the same room with him. Or, at least, that was Montalbano's impression.

Too many times he'd felt like the bird of ill omen, too many times he'd been forced to enter people's lives with bad news that would in turn destroy those same lives.

And yet, despite all that experience, he still had never found a proper way to bear such news, or at least to make it seem a little less harsh, even to himself.

Meriam took a good while to return with a tray and coffee, and Montalbano noticed, upon seeing her, that her eyes were red, and that she'd washed her face in the meantime.

The woman sat down without speaking.

Montalbano sipped his coffee, and was about to open his mouth when Meriam beat him to it.

"It's about Elena, isn't it?" she asked.

He very nearly choked on his coffee. How did she know?

He felt puzzled, but at the same time relieved, because Meriam was sparing him the hardest part of his task.

"Yes," he said.

She buried her face in her hands and started crying in silence, her body shaking with sobs she tried to suppress. Then she said, "Excuse me," and she got up and left the room again.

A few minutes later she returned and sat back down. This time Montalbano was the first to speak.

"She was murdered," he said.

"When?" asked Meriam, though it was not so much by her voice but by the movement of her lips that Montalbano understood the question.

"Around eleven p.m."

"How?"

"With a large pair of tailoring scissors."

"But who would do such a thing?" Meriam asked, more to herself than to the inspector.

"I don't know the answer. But now you must tell me why you immediately thought of Elena."

"I really don't know, Inspector . . . Yesterday afternoon, when we left, I . . . I had a strange feeling. Actually, shortly after you'd done your fitting, Signora Elena literally chased us out of the shop. She said she needed to be alone. But she was clearly upset, very upset, to the point that she started tearing up, with her own hands, some of the fabrics that had just arrived. I'd never seen her act that way. She was impolite, almost rude. Even with Nicola."

"Why with Nicola?"

"Well, Inspector, Nicola sees himself as a kind of father to Elena. His wife died some years ago, and his children live up north. He spends much of his day in the shop, and often, when Elena closes up, he stays behind, working, tidying up, cleaning . . . The shop is sort of his home. And yesterday evening Elena practically had to shout at him to leave, because Nicola wanted to stay."

"Do you have any idea why Elena might have been so upset? Any suspicions?"

"Elena is very reserved. She really doesn't talk much about her private life."

"Do you know if she has any relatives?"

"Her parents are both dead, and she was an only child. I don't know if she has any close relatives, but I know her sister-in-law, who lives here in town."

"So Elena's married?"

"Yes, or she was, to a man from Vigàta, but he died many years ago, when she was still very young, and so she decided to come and live here, because she gets along very well with Teresa, her sister-in-law."

"Could you give me her address?"

"Of course. Via della Regione, number 18. But I'd like to be there when you go. I'm afraid Teresa won't be able—"

"Yes, of course you can come. I'll get in touch with you tomorrow morning, before I go."

"All right, thank you."

Silence descended. Then Meriam, as though embarrassed, asked:

"Where is she now?"

"I think she's still in the big room at the shop. That's where we found her."

Meriam looked bewildered.

116

"I would have thought," she said, "that she'd be . . . in her apartment."

"Why?"

"I don't know. The shop is . . . you know, just for customers . . . When she chased us out I had the feeling she was waiting for someone she didn't want us to meet."

"You may be right. It appears that Elena didn't eat alone last night. Why she then went downstairs with her killer, I can't say. They must have had an argument . . ."

At this point Meriam couldn't take it any longer.

She started rocking back and forth, still from a sitting position, while from her lips came a sort of wailing lament. The words were in Arabic, but it sounded exactly like what one hears during the Good Friday processions.

"Meriam . . ." he called to her softly.

But she didn't even hear him.

So Montalbano stood up, went over to her, stroked her head gently, left the room, descended the stairs, opened the front door, got back in his car, and headed off in the direction of the police station. But then he merely drove past it, because he'd already decided to go home and take off those goddamn jeans, which made him feel as though he was trapped in a cage.

Entering his house, he dashed straight into the bedroom.

He lay down on the bed. This time he counted to five, sucked in his belly, and was finally able to pull down his jeans, which remained stuck, however, around his shoes. He took these off and, cursing to high heaven while executing a move worthy of a fakir, managed to pull one leg of the jeans off by turning it inside out, and with his free foot he seized the hem of the other jeans leg and pulled as though in a tug-of-war.

Free at last, he went and selected, following the law of opposites, a pair of trousers that were way too big for him. He put these on and raced out of the house.

In Catarella's place was another officer he was unfamiliar with. He walked past him, not bothering to wake him up, and went into Fazio's office.

Fazio, too, was in a deep sleep, head cradled in his arms, which were folded on his desk. The inspector put a hand on his shoulder and shook him.

"Whaaa . . . !" said Fazio, opening his eyes.

"Come with me."

In the twinkling of an eye, Fazio shook off his sleepiness and fatigue and followed him into his office.

"Chief, before anything else, I need to tell you about something weird that happened to me."

"So tell me."

"After the traveling circus had left and put seals over the door, an old man suddenly came up holding a packet, and when he asked me what had happened, I told him the whole story. *Matre santa*, Chief! You wouldn't believe his reaction! He immediately started crying like a baby. I was afraid he was gonna fall, so I grabbed him, and since he couldn't stand on his own two feet, I brought him over to my car and sat him down. When he finally managed to calm down a little, he explained that he worked at the tailor's shop and that he'd baked a *ciambella* for Signora Elena during the night. And since I realized he might be able to tell us something, I brought him back with me here. He's in the waiting room."

"It must be Nicola. Go and get him."

The little old man came in, practically held up by Fazio, and when Montalbano approached him, he nearly threw himself in the inspector's arms.

"Now, now, Nicola!" said Montalbano, sitting him down.

Nicola set the packet on the table.

"Was this something you did every morning?" asked Montalbano.

"Did what?"

"Bring her breakfast."

"No, sir. Not every morning. Just every so often."

"Did Elena always wake up so early?"

"No, Inspector. Usually around seven. But I . . ."

He stopped.

"Go on."

"But I had a bad night."

"Why?"

"Because I couldn't stop thinking about what happened yesterday afternoon."

"Why, what happened? Can you tell me about it?"

"Okay. Right after we did your fitting, Elena wanted us all out of the shop. And since I wanted to stay, because there was still a lot of stuff that had to be done, she started yelling at me and insulting me. She'd never done that before. She reminded me that I was nothing but a simple hired hand and that she was the one who gave the orders. The thing is, Inspector, I know she didn't really think those things; she was just saying them to make me mad and leave. So, even

119

though I knew it wasn't true, I put the fabrics back on the shelves, I got the others to help me clear the big worktable, and then we all left. And I went home feeling really, really worried."

"Do you have any idea why Elena was so agitated?"

"No, sir, no idea at all. Don't you remember how she was when we were doing the fitting? All smiling as usual, cheerful and calm. Then all of a sudden she changed. She wanted us all to leave, 'cause it was clear she wanted to be alone. But . . ."

"Go on."

"But thing is, Inspector, I was scared. So, after Elena closed up the shop and pulled down the shutter, I went back to Via Garibaldi and hung around in view of her front door. I was convinced she was waiting for someone and that this visitor was the reason she got so upset. I stayed there for about an hour, but I didn't see anyone go in or come out, and so I went home."

"Listen to me carefully, Nicola," said Montalbano. "After I left, did Elena go upstairs into her apartment?"

"No, sir. She went straight back into the big room."

"Another question: Just before telling you all to leave the shop, did she by any chance receive a phone call, on her cell phone or land line?"

"No, sir. There weren't any phone calls. You have to believe me, Inspector. Nothing out of the ordinary happened yesterday. If anything happened it was only inside her head. And I can't get any rest over it."

"Nicola, Meriam mentioned to me that Elena has a

sister-in-law, but didn't tell me anything else. Do you know this woman?"

"Of course. Teresa Messina! They're really more than sisters-in-law, you know. They're just like real sisters. Teresa's got two little kids who just adore Elena. Oh, but, Jesus! Jesus Christ! And who's gonna tell *her* now? Teresa's already lost her brother, her father, and her mother, and now Elena! It's just not right, Inspector! Who could ever wish any harm to such a good, generous, bighearted woman! It's really true that the best are the first to go!"

Nicola started crying again.

Montalbano let him get it out of his system, then said:

"Listen, Nicola. I am definitely going to be needing you—"

Fazio interrupted him.

"I've already got his address and phone number."

Nicola stood up. Montalbano shook his hand, then pulled him towards himself and hugged him.

"Try to be strong," he said.

Nicola looked him in the eyes and said:

"What for?"

"Because life, unfortunately, goes on," said Montalbano. Then, turning to Fazio: "Have somebody drive him home."

Fazio returned almost immediately.

"Tell me what Forensics said," the inspector ordered him.

"Since the killer would have been covered in blood, he must have taken care to remove his shoes, meticulously avoided leaving any traces, then went upstairs, into Signora Elena's bathroom, and took a shower. Forensics found blood in the shower stall. Almost certainly the victim's. They took a sampling of it for testing. And another thing: There are no fingerprints on the shower's sliding glass door, and not even on the taps. Which means the killer wiped them away with the towels. There are no traces anywhere, not even on the scissors. He probably wiped them down with the piece of fabric they found beside them."

"And what do you yourself think?" asked the inspector.

"Chief, if you ask me, we're looking at a crime of passion. Some kind of rash act, probably triggered by an argument. The fact remains, however, that the killer spared her chest."

"And what does Forensics say about that?"

"They say it's almost impossible it was an accident. That there was clear intentionality in avoiding her breasts."

"And what does that mean?"

"How should I know!"

"You know what you need to do, starting this very morning?"

"Yeah, Chief."

"And what's that?"

"A woman like that had to have a man around."

"I agree. Good luck in your endeavors," said the inspector.

"Thanks," Fazio replied, getting up and leaving the room.

Montalbano glanced at his watch. It was already almost seven.

By now Livia must already be drinking her first morning coffee. He dialed her number at home.

"Livia?"

"Salvo, what is it?" she replied with surprise and concern.

"I have some bad news. Elena, the tailor, was murdered last night."

"You are such an asshole!" Livia yelled, hanging up.

Montalbano got angry.

Did she really think he was so cynical as to joke about something like death?

He felt so upset he dialed the wrong number twice.

Then he heard her voice again.

"Listen, Salvo, I really wouldn't have thought you could ever be so stupid as to—"

"Wait a second, Livia. I meant it."

From the tone of his voice she could tell he meant it.

"Oh, my God! So it's true?"

"Unfortunately, all too true. She was found murdered in her shop."

He heard Livia start crying.

"I'm so sorry, Livia. I'll call you back this evening," said Montalbano.

And now came the hardest part. The bird of ill omen had to perform its task again. But maybe its flight could be made a little gentler. So he rang Meriam.

"How are you feeling?"

"So-so. Do you want me to go to Teresa's?"

"Yes. But I'm told she has children. Are they still small? Do they go to school?"

"Yes, she takes them there herself every morning."

"Then she goes to work?"

"Yes. But she works out of her home."

"How would you feel if we went there around nine o'clock?"

"That's fine," said Meriam. "If you like, I can come to you at the station. I don't think I can stand to wait here at home any longer."

"All right."

The last thing he expected was to see Mimì Augello appear before him.

"Weren't you dying from lack of sleep? What happened? Did it pass?"

"Yeah, it passed."

"How's that?"

"Two reasons. First of all because I realized that if you throw yourself whole hog into this investigation, dragging Fazio along behind you, it means I'm left alone, like an idiot, to handle the inevitable landings at the port every night. Is that fair?"

"No, Mimì, it's not fair. But does it seem fair to you to kill a defenseless woman with a pair of scissors?"

"No. And that's the second reason, which we'll get to in a minute."

"Then tell me now how we should resolve this situation."

"Call the commissioner and tell him we simply cannot work this way any longer. It's impossible."

Montalbano thought this was a good idea.

He picked up the receiver and said to Catarella:

"Get me Hizzoner the C'mishner, Cat, and put him through as soon as you've got him on the line."

The call came through at once.

The commissioner normally went to his office early in

the morning, and this was a good time of day to catch him still in a conciliatory mood towards the outside world. Montalbano turned on the speakerphone.

The commissioner's first question was:

"Montalbano, how are you?"

"Well, thank you, and yourself?"

"I can't complain. I've just been told about last night's murder."

"Well, that's exactly what I wanted to talk to you about, sir. I don't think it's going to be an easy case. As you were probably informed, initial tests seem to show that the killer left no trace of himself whatsoever. Inspector Fazio and I are going to have our hands full with this investigation."

"And so?" asked the commissioner.

"And so that leaves Inspector Augello alone to deal with the migrant landings. You do realize that, if the situation before was intolerable, then now . . . In theory, Augello's supposed to be present every night at the docks for the disembarkations, and then be at the office again the following day."

"And so?" the commissioner asked again.

"And so I'm calling you to ask if we can be relieved of that particular duty."

"It's not possible," the commissioner said decisively.

"But, Mr. Commissioner, Augello is a human being, not a robot . . ."

"Just do as Sileci does, Montalbano."

"And what does Sileci do?"

"He's been relieved of his daytime duties. Submit a request to me concerning Augello, and I'll sign it."

"Thank you, sir. Have a good day."

"You're welcome, Inspector. I'll be hearing from you, then," said the commissioner, hanging up.

Mimì seemed to have his knickers in a knot.

"So, what am I, anyway? Some kind of night watchman? And, besides, I can't help it, but I'm simply unable to sleep during the day. It's just the way I am."

"Mimì, what can I say? It just means you won't sleep either in the day or at night."

"You're just a son of a bitch. You know what I say? That, starting this evening, if you want to tell me anything, you can find me after midnight on the dock," said Mimì, after which he got up and headed for the door.

Montalbano stopped him.

"Wait, before you go, tell me what was the second reason you couldn't fall asleep."

"I was thinking about Elena's murder. She was a woman who had a gift for being liked by everyone. She'd given work to so many people in town. She wasn't a home-wrecker, didn't make married women jealous, or bust anyone's chops. And yet, it's also clear that this was a crime of passion. And I, if you don't mind, am the person in the best position to judge how these sorts of things go. I know more about these kinds of love affairs than anyone. Of course, that's all over for me. So I guess I'll go and be a night watchman. Good-bye."

Montalbano didn't stop him this time.

Mimì opened the door and went out into the hallway.

Less than two minutes later, the door opened again and Mimì reappeared, arm linked with a man the inspector didn't know.

"It is my honor to introduce to you the illustrious Salvo Montalbano," said Augello. "Inspector, this is my dear friend Diego Trupia."

But Diego Trupia didn't smile. He just stood in the doorway without moving.

Augello let go of the man's arm and looked at him.

"But what are you doing here, anyway, Diego?"

Trupia, a tall man with all his hair and sporting a short, well-groomed beard, looked about forty, perhaps less. Dressed like a young person and clearly in excellent physical condition, he replied in a faint voice.

"I need to speak to the inspector."

"Why on earth, Decù? What happened? Did you kill someone?"

"No, *I* didn't. But someone killed my Elena."

9

Upon hearing these words, Augello sidestepped like a horse. Then he sort of whinnied and looked at his friend with saucer eyes:

"What do you mean, *your* Elena?" he asked.

"I mean just that."

Montalbano immediately realized that Trupia had no desire to talk in front of Augello. And so he said:

"Mimì, do me a favor and let me speak with Signor Trupia alone."

Augello cast a scornful glance at Trupia and left the room, closing the door behind him.

Trupia sat down. He looked neither nervous nor afraid. He probably felt terribly uneasy, and in fact he looked Montalbano in the eye and said:

"I don't know where to begin."

"Then I'll begin," said the inspector. "How did you learn what happened?"

"Inspector, I live alone and am in the habit of having my breakfast in a bar next door, and when I was there this morning I heard two people saying that Elena had been murdered. I very nearly fainted. Then, after mustering up the courage, I raced over to Via Garibaldi and saw the seals outside her door. So I raced back home. I needed to be alone for a while, to think, to figure out the best way to . . ."

He stopped, unable to continue.

"To come here and tell us your situation?"

"Yes."

"So you and Elena were a couple?"

"Yes."

"Since when?"

"A little less than two years. It wasn't something that was out in the open, but I figured it was best if I came here on my own, since sooner or later my name would have turned up."

"You did the right thing."

"I want to declare straightaway that I did not kill Elena."

"Did the people in the bar say how she was killed?"

"No."

"Stabbed to death with a pair of scissors."

Trupia gave a start. He made a pained, troubled face, then brought a hand to his mouth but said nothing.

"When was the last time you saw her?" asked Montalbano.

"Three days ago, Inspector. I didn't hear from her or see her after that," replied the man, trying to regain his composure.

"Why not?"

"We'd had a quarrel."

"What about?"

"I asked her to marry me."

"And Elena said no?"

"Not only. She was very angry, and felt offended. And

she said that if I kept insisting, our relationship would end right then and there."

"Did she give you any explanation for refusing?"

"No, she only said she'd been married once and that was enough for her."

"So when you said that your affair was not out in the open, did you mean that Elena wanted to keep it a secret?"

"No, actually, I myself had no problem with the arrangement. When I first met her I wasn't with anyone else, and she wasn't, either, or at least I hope she wasn't. We enjoyed spending time together, and we always made sure that our encounters were something special. We were both worried about falling into a routine and taking things for granted."

"So then why did you ask her to marry you?" queried Montalbano, who knew that kind of fear well.

"Now, this will sound ridiculous, but at first I didn't want to get married. Lately, though, on several occasions, I sort of sensed that our fleeting nighttime encounters were no longer enough for Elena. I felt that she needed, well, a constant, committed presence, a sense of protection, reassurance. She was an extremely generous woman who never asked anyone for anything; she was always ready to give freely without expecting anything in return. But she was tired. I sensed that she could no longer bear the burden of life all alone, and so it seemed right to me to ask her to share this burden. Believe me, my marriage proposal came from what I perceived to be a need of hers, and not from any desire of my own to settle down."

"Perhaps you were wrong, considering Elena's refusal."

"Inspector, I don't want to seem presumptuous, but I believe her refusal was prompted by her inability to open herself up entirely. That was why she threw me out of her house so brusquely, and that was why I made a point of not calling her on the phone. But I don't think I could have held out much longer. Already this morning when I woke up, she was very much on my mind. But never would I have imagined that that thought was so strong because she was dead."

Montalbano liked the way this man reasoned.

At first he looked a bit like a gussied-up rich kid, but in fact he had a heart and a brain, and both seemed to work well.

"What do you do for a living?"

"I have a small publishing house. My grandfather left me a lot of money, and I'd just finished university with a degree in literature. I could have traveled round the world, and in fact I could have lived on that inheritance without ever having to work, but instead I put into practice what my grandfather had taught me: share everything with everyone. So, since he'd been a tremendous reader, and I a great admirer of contemporary literature, I decided to make books. A limited number, of very high quality, and fine editions. It's not as if they bring in much money, but my hope is that they'll give pleasure to those who buy them."

Montalbano's esteem of Trupia rose vertiginously. But there was still one gray area:

"I'm sorry, but how is it you're friends with Augello?"

"I feel like I've known Mimì all my life. Just think, he even helped me distribute my first publications among the relatively limited number of Sicilian bookshops."

"To get back to the subject," said Montalbano, "unfortunately, I have to ask you a routine question."

"You want to know where I was last night?" Trupia cut in.

"Yes, please tell me."

"It's a bit of a problem. Yesterday evening I went to eat at my usual restaurant. It was probably around nine. I came out at ten-thirty and went home to watch TV. Were you able to determine at what time Elena was murdered?"

Up to this point, the man had been cool and calm, but when he pronounced Elena's name, tears welled up in his eyes.

Montalbano got up, went to get some water, filled up the glass, handed it to him, and said: "No later than midnight."

Trupia drank the water. Setting the glass down, he threw up his hands.

"Then I have no alibi," he said.

The telephone rang.

"Chief, Chief, the signura Marianna Ucrìa'd a happen a be—"

"All right, show her in."

"Chief, I can't show 'er in t'yiz insomuch as she in't onna premisses but onna line."

"Then put her on."

Montalbano turned to Trupia, excusing himself for the interruption.

Then he heard Meriam's voice.

"Inspector, I just got a call from Stefano, Teresa's husband, asking me to come immediately to his house because he needs help."

"Why, what happened?" Montalbano asked in alarm.

"Teresa went to the market after driving the kids to school and found out everything . . ."

Montalbano felt very bad that Teresa had learned of her sister-in-law's death in such a fashion, but, deep down, he thanked fate for having spared him just this once the need to play the bird of ill omen.

"When do you think I could see her?"

"I'll call you as soon as I get to their place."

"Okay, I'll wait for your call."

Montalbano set down the receiver and said:

"Back to us. Had Elena been particularly agitated lately?"

"No. But as I said, I didn't see her during her last three days. But up to that point she'd seemed normal, the way she always was."

"Do you know whether she'd quarreled with anyone or had some unpleasant disagreement?"

"To my knowledge, no. Elena was extremely reserved, Inspector. Did you ever get a chance to meet her?"

"Yes. I think I was her very last customer," said Montalbano.

"Then you probably noticed that she was very sociable and immediately friendly. But, in spite of this apparent openness, she was quite discreet and had trouble forming intimate relationships. She never really confided even in me."

"Strange. I had the opposite impression."

"It was probably just a façade. The apparent sociability was her way of protecting her real nature, which was solitary and bashful."

"I've been told she had a close relationship with her sister-in-law, Teresa. Do you know her?"

"Yes, I do, I saw her a number of times at dinner parties with other friends, but I don't think Teresa knew about my relationship with Elena."

"Could you tell me the names of these friends of Elena?"

"Of course, Inspector. I don't think they'll know any more than me, but I can give you some names."

"Did Elena ever talk to you about her marriage? Her family? Or her husband's death?"

"Would you believe I only learned about her husband a few months ago?"

"What did she tell you?"

"Very little. She said they were two young fashion designers in the Veneto, if I recall. Who met at the Accademia della Moda, got married almost immediately, and then the husband died shortly thereafter. Maybe an illness. I didn't have the courage to ask her, Inspector. She already seemed rather shaken for having told me the little she did."

"Thank you," said Montalbano. "For me, that's enough for now."

He stood up, went over to the door, said something, then sat back down.

Fazio immediately appeared.

"Signor Trupia, please go with Inspector Fazio, who will take down everything you have just said. And give him also the names and addresses of Elena's friends, and tell him how and when you met her. Also, I would like you please to remain reachable at any moment, and therefore not to leave Vigàta for any reason."

He held out his hand; Trupia shook it and then turned and followed Fazio.

The moment the door closed, the inspector felt overwhelmed by a sudden feeling of weariness.

A dark, dense cloud descended inside his head, which he laid down on his folded arms on the desk.

Closing his eyes, he began to slip slowly into a kind of tube stuffed full of jet-black cotton. Soon all movement ceased. He'd sunk into the Great Nothing . . .

Then, out of the silence of that Nothing, faint echoes began to reach his ears, first distant, then closer and closer, human sounds that little by little became fragments of words.

". . . ief . . . ief! . . . 'oo? . . . Jesus! . . . alp! . . . ief . . . ief . . . wha'ss goin' on?"

Montalbano realized that someone was violently shaking his shoulders. Finally, after repeated shakes, he managed with effort to resurface from the darkness.

One shake even more violent than the others made him strike his head on the wooden desktop.

He cursed the saints, opened his eyes, sat up, and saw Catarella standing beside him, pale and terrified.

"Cool it, Cat!" he managed to say.

"So you's alive! My Gah! Whatta scare! My legs is all tremmlin'. I tought you was dead, Chief!"

"What the hell is going on?" said Montalbano. "All I did was doze off, Cat. What happened? What did you want?"

"Well, insomuch as the signura Marianna Ucrìa called onna tiliphone line ann'en I called yiz an' ya din't anser, I tol' Signura Ucrìa to call later. So I came to yer premisses an' when ya din't anser me, I started shakin' yiz all over an' ya still wou'n't anser. Jesus, I's so scared!"

"Okay, okay," said Montalbano. "What time is it, anyway?"

"Past ten, Chief."

He'd slept for an hour and a half!

"I'm gonna go wash my face. You go back to the switchboard," he said to Catarella.

He went into the bathroom, took off his jacket and shirt, leaving himself bare-chested, and washed himself all over. Then he dried himself off, put his clothes back on, and went to tell Catarella to make him a triple espresso. But he already felt quite a bit better, and so he called Meriam on her cell phone.

"Sorry about just now, I was out of the room. Where are you?"

"I'm at Teresa's."

"Can I come there?"

"Yes, Inspector, but I don't know whether Teresa . . ."

"All right, I'm going to try anyway."

He drank his triple espresso, got in his car, and was soon pulling up in Via della Regione.

The person who opened the door was a handsome man of about fifty.

"I'm Stefano Messina. Pleased to meet you."

He showed the inspector into a small sitting room.

Montalbano summoned his courage and asked him whether, if need be, he could go and identify Elena's body.

"Of course."

"How is Signora Teresa?"

"What can I say, Inspector. For Teresa it's as if Franco has died a second time."

Franco must have been Elena's husband's name.

"Could I see her?"

"Excuse me just a second," said the man, getting up and leaving the room.

He returned a few minutes later.

"Please follow me."

In the bedroom Montalbano saw Teresa lying on the bed looking like an empty sack thrown down on the blanket.

She was all dressed up and wearing an overcoat and even shoes on her feet, her right hand still clutching the purse she'd taken to go shopping. Her eyes were closed.

Meriam was sitting beside her in a chair.

"Is she asleep?" the inspector asked softly.

"She's sedated," said Stefano.

The inspector realized it was all for naught.

Without a word, he turned around and went back into the sitting room.

Moments later, Stefano came in. He looked at the inspector and said:

"Thank you for understanding."

Moments later Meriam came in as well.

"I think that even if we'd woken her up she wouldn't have been in any condition to answer my questions. That only happens in movies."

"Let's do this," said Meriam with a hint of a smile. "If Teresa has recovered by this afternoon, I'll give you a call. Okay?"

"Okay, thanks, Meriam. You're a rare jewel."

He shook both their hands and headed back to the station.

He'd just gone into his office when Mimì Augello shot in like a rocket.

"I was reading Fazio's transcript of Trupia's statement," he said, sitting down.

"And so?"

"What an asshole!"

"Mind telling me why?"

"Don't you realize that it was I who introduced him to Elena? And I even told him I had my eye on her. And he betrayed me. He stole her from me, said nothing to me, and he may even have killed her!"

"Cut the shit, Mimì."

"But why are you so certain he's innocent?"

"At the moment I don't know whether he's innocent or guilty, but it's not as if everyone who's ever snatched a girl away from you has become a killer. And, anyway, wasn't this Trupia a close friend of yours?"

"You said it right. He *was* a friend of mine. Anyone who betrays his friends in this fashion is capable of anything."

"Do you realize you're talking nonsense?"

"No, Salvo. Just think about it for a minute. He was her last lover. He comes here on his own initiative to tell us that they'd had a quarrel three days earlier. And the crime was one of passion. I'm totally convinced that Trupia went out to eat, then dropped by Elena's, where they had a fight that ended the way it ended."

"Well, so much for friendship, Mimì! Sure, that's one possible hypothesis, even though in my opinion the killer dined with Elena. But do you know this Trupia to be a violent man?"

"No, but it's you who taught me that it's the opportunity that makes the thief. If I was in your shoes, there's something I would do."

"And what's that?"

"All you need to do is check whether Elena received any phone calls from Trupia, or vice versa, on the day she was murdered."

It wasn't a bad idea. Montalbano picked up the phone and said to Catarella:

"Send me Fazio, would you, Cat?"

Fazio came in.

"Has Forensics got Elena's cell phone?" Montalbano asked him.

"No, Chief, they haven't got it 'cause they couldn't find it. We looked everywhere for it, even inside the freezer. In my opinion—and Forensics agrees—the killer took it."

"Wha'd I say?" Mimì said triumphantly. "So apparently Trupia did call her, and therefore he had to get rid of the phone."

"Fazio, try, as soon as you can, to get a printout of Trupia's phone records. But I have to tell you, there's no doubt in my mind that this is the wrong track."

Mimì stood up angrily.

"And now you're gonna tell me I'm biased. Well, I'm outta here."

He left the room, slamming the door behind him.

The echo of the crash segued into the ringing of the telephone.

"Chief, 'at'd be Dacter Pasquano onna line."

Montalbano couldn't believe his ears. Was it possible Pasquano had already performed the autopsy? And that he was being so kind as to take the trouble of phoning him to tell him the results? Whatever the case, the inspector turned on the speakerphone so that Fazio could also hear their conversation.

"Good morning, Doctor. I'm at your service. Do you need a poker partner?"

"From you I need nothing at all. It's the other way around. It's you who need something from me."

"Then to what do I owe the pleasure of hearing your voice?"

"I thought you might be interested in the murder of the beautiful seamstress."

"Of course I'm interested."

"And don't you want to know about the autopsy?"

So the world really was turning upside down.

"Well, yes . . . th-thanks," Montalbano stammered, trying to recover from the shock.

"First of all, the lady had just eaten dinner and was murdered before her digestive processes had even begun."

"Which confirms what I was already thinking."

"Then your mind must be so farsighted, so razor-sharp,

that I have no words, and so I'll stop talking and you can feel free to listen to your own thoughts."

"I'm sorry, Doctor, but did you by any chance get up on the wrong side of the bed this morning? I promise I won't interrupt you again. I'm all ears."

"The murder weapon," Pasquano resumed, "was that pair of scissors that was found on the table. The wounds were perfectly consistent with that. And I should add that it would take great strength to plunge a pair of scissors like that so deeply into a body the way the killer did."

Montalbano couldn't restrain himself.

"So you think the killer was a rather powerful man?"

"No, no, there you go again. You're not abiding by the rules. You're doing the thinking instead of me. I swear that if you interrupt me again—"

"Sorry, sorry . . ."

"The first stab apparently caught her entirely by surprise. There's no sign of any wounds on her hands from self-defense. The killer, who was standing behind her, aimed for her neck and cleanly severed her jugular, wounding her fatally. The woman should theoretically have fallen down face-forward, but she must have made some kind of movement to make her fall on her back. And now I beg your pardon, but I can't help but ask: Given your advanced age, can I go on talking? Have you grasped everything I've said so far?"

He was clearly trying to provoke him, but Montalbano let it slide and played along.

"I hope so. Go on."

"At this point the killer bent down and started stabbing the body wildly. This was how, given the close distance, he was able to avoid striking the breasts."

"And so," said Montalbano, "the fact that he spared the entire area of the breasts was not an accident?"

"No! Certainly not. It was clearly intentional."

"And why do you think he acted that way?"

"You can finally start thinking again now, and you'll see that with a little mental effort you, too, will, ever so slowly, manage to come up with an answer to that question."

"Why, do you have an idea yourself?"

"Me, no. But the poets, yes. You've got an embarrassment of riches there. We could begin with Ariosto: *her rotund bosoms were like milk* . . . And surely you'll recall the amorous sorrow of D'Annunzio when he wrote: *Oh, but to seek, in the shadow that lay across her breast, as at the bottom of a tomb, Infinity* . . . And how could we forget Cardarelli? *Wretched woman of turgid breast, your only richness is your milk* . . ."

Montalbano was slack-jawed, spellbound. He could never have imagined Pasquano would be a connoisseur of poetry.

"Mind putting that in plain language?" he ventured.

"No," said Pasquano, hanging up.

"Shit!" said Fazio. "I wanna know if the doctor's knowledge of poetry stops at the breasts or includes some of the other parts of the female body."

"Fazio, what can I tell you? All I can say is that this blast of poetry has stirred up a hunger in me so powerful I can barely stand it any longer."

And for once, perhaps owing to his fatigue, or his advanced age, or his fear of falling asleep while eating, he invited Fazio to come and have lunch with him at Enzo's.

"But on one condition," he added. "That we don't talk about the case while we're eating. Better yet, let's not talk at all."

10

As the inspector's car was crossing the Corso, Fazio said:

"Pull over for a second so I can get out."

"Okay, I'll wait for you. Did you forget something?"

"No, I just want to check something. You go on ahead, I'll join you in a minute."

Montalbano continued on to the restaurant, parked, went inside, and said to Enzo:

"Set a table for two."

"Who is it? A man or a woman?" Enzo asked.

"It's just Fazio."

Enzo walked away a little disappointed, but after taking three steps he turned around and came back to Montalbano.

"Forgive me for asking, Inspector, but what can you tell me about the murder of poor Elena?"

"Did you know her?"

"I did, Inspector. If only there were more women like her!"

"In what sense?"

"First of all, she was so cheerful and open, and always smiling. And so friendly. And what an appetite! You know, Inspector, nowadays women don't eat anymore. A little salad here, a bit of chicory with oil and lemon there. But not

Signora Elena. She would sit down and order antipasto, first course, second course, dessert, and you have no idea how much coffee. All of it nicely sprinkled with good wine. And since she would sometimes come alone but didn't like to eat alone, she would ask me to sit down with her and we would chat. And you know what? Often, when she would come late in the evening and all the other customers had left and I was starting to close up, we would play *tressette* when she was done eating. And if she won, she didn't have to pay."

"What can I say?" said Montalbano. "Unfortunately, we're still at the initial stages. But I'll keep you informed."

At that moment Fazio came in and sat down.

"What do you want to eat?" the inspector asked him.

"You know what? I feel like some pasta with *bottarga*."

Just hearing the word stirred a fervent desire for *bottarga* in Montalbano.

At their request Enzo said that wouldn't be a problem, and he would add a little grated lemon rind from his own tree.

During the entire meal, which included, aside from the *bottarga*, some fried mullet with onions, Fazio kept his word and never once opened his mouth except to express appreciation and wonderment at the excellence of the dishes. Only after drinking his coffee did he pull a folded magazine out of his jacket pocket.

He set it down on the table and then covered it with one hand so that the inspector couldn't see the cover.

He had a sly, smug little smile on his face, which immediately got on Montalbano's nerves.

Determined not to give him any satisfaction, the inspector got up without saying a word and went to the bathroom.

He managed in time to see the smile vanish from Fazio's face.

When he returned, he remained standing and said hurriedly:

"Let's go."

Whereupon Fazio said:

"Excuse me, Chief, but would you just listen to me for a second? I have to show you something."

"Well, then, let's see it!" the inspector said rudely, sitting down in a huff.

"As we were passing by in the car, I spotted this magazine on display and thought I'd caught one of its headlines."

Without a word, Montalbano reached out with one hand and pulled the magazine out from under Fazio's hand to where he could read it.

On the cover was an image of a beautiful pair of female breasts, with, beneath it, the title: THE FEMALE BREAST IN ITALIAN POETRY.

"That's where Dr. Pasquano got all his knowledge of poetry!"

"The son of a bitch!" the inspector exclaimed.

He felt so reassured, however, that he said to Fazio:

"Thank you. Because it's very likely that I would never have been able to sleep tonight, thinking about all of Pasquano's quotations. I'll drive you back to the station."

"There's no need," said Fazio. "I'm happy to go on foot if you feel like taking your usual walk along the jetty."

He'd just started walking along the jetty on his way to the flat rock when his cell phone rang. Since at that very moment he'd been thinking of how to get back at Pasquano for tricking him, he had confirmation that not only was it enough to speak of the devil for him to appear, one only had to think of him.

For it was none other than the doctor calling.

"Montalbano, I'm so sorry to wake you during your postprandial siesta."

"Who says I'm sleeping? You're the one who needs to sleep, not me. I feel just fine and am enjoying the sea air. So, tell me instead, what winds are blowing at the morgue?"

"Well, that's just it. Inside the morgue, and in my room, the usual fetid air is putrescent, but out in the hallway it's even worse."

"Why do you say that?"

"Because for the last two hours there's been a gentleman sitting on the floor out there, without any shoes on his feet, wailing, crying, singing, praying, and saying he wants to see the victim's corpse."

"And what's that got to do with me?"

"The man says he's a friend of yours. And if you don't come and get him, I'm going to kill the guy and put him directly in bed with Signora Elena. That way he can see her all he wants."

"What's his name?"

"He's got some kind of Turkish name: Ossiman, Os-man, something like that . . . Hello? Hello! . . ."

But Montalbano had already hung up and was running towards his car.

While speeding along the road to Montelusa, he was unable to string together any thoughts with even the slightest logical connection between them.

It felt as if a vast forest of question marks had sprouted inside his brain, and he was trying blindly to wend his way through them, crashing into one after another, as though in a labyrinth with no way out.

All he could manage to formulate were a few fragments of questions.

Osman? What did he have to do with anything? What was he doing at the morgue? Why was he crying? Why was he barefoot? Had he heard right? Might it not be some Turk by the name of Osman? But the man had said he was a friend of his . . . and so . . .

And then, given the man that he, the inspector, knew, who was always so soft-spoken, reserved, and self-contained, how had Osman been reduced to such a state?

At last he pulled up in the lot of the Institute for Forensic Medicine, got out of the car, raced inside, and found the corridor completely deserted.

Halfway down the hall, however, was a sort of large ball of rolled-up rags that didn't even look human, and yet it was emitting a sort of melodious lament.

He drew near to it and stopped.

The doctor was scarcely recognizable, sitting as he was

on the floor, shoulders against the wall, head buried between his legs, arms wrapped around his knees . . . But the inspector clearly heard, in the faint, stifled breath emitted by that human ball, the sound of the name "Elena."

He knelt down in front of him, lowering himself to the point where his face was almost touching the doctor's hair. He started calling to him in a low voice.

"Osman, Osman . . . It's Montalbano here. Come on, Osman, buck up. I'm here for you."

There was no reaction.

Montalbano kept repeating his name, almost in tune with the man's lament.

And it worked. The wailing stopped.

Osman raised his head very slowly.

Upon seeing his face, Montalbano felt a cold shudder snaking up his spine. The expression in the doctor's eyes seemed to belong to someone much older than him. Osman's features looked transformed.

He muttered something the inspector didn't understand.

"What?" Montalbano asked.

"I want to see Elena."

"I'll do everything within my power, I promise. Meanwhile, let me help you up."

With the inspector's support, Osman managed first to get on his knees, and then, with some effort, he was able to slide his back up against the wall until he was standing.

"Think you can manage to stay on your feet?"

"Yes," said Osman.

Montalbano went and picked up the pair of shoes lying

a short distance down the hall, then came back and, kneeling down, put them on the doctor, one after the other, with all the patience of a mother.

He then led him to the nearest chair.

"Wait for me here. Don't move for any reason."

He rushed off towards Pasquano's office, opened the door, and dashed in.

The doctor leapt up in his chair.

"What fucking way of entering is that?"

"I haven't got any time to waste," said Montalbano. "Just tell me one thing: Is it strictly forbidden for nonrelatives to see the body?"

"Absolutely. You would need a court order. Why, don't you think that I would otherwise have let your friend in? He's been busting my chops for the last two hours with his little song, which, if you ask me, is going to bring bad luck."

"And what if I told you my friend is the victim's brother?"

"I would reply that you're lying through your teeth. But since you're such a good liar, I'll pretend to believe you. So you will take full responsibility for this?"

"Yes. You have my word."

"All right, then, follow me."

As they were walking down the hall towards Osman, Pasquano said under his breath:

"You two wait for me here. It's better if I go in first. I'll cover the poor woman up with a sheet and leave just the head exposed. Luckily, her face was unmarred."

He moved towards the door, opened it, and went inside, leaving it open behind him.

Montalbano went over to Osman.

"Just another minute or two, and you'll be able to see her."

"Thank you," Osman managed to say.

Moments later, Pasquano poked his head out.

"Come," he said.

Osman stood up. Montalbano put his arm around his shoulders and guided him into the room. One of the freezer doors was open. Pasquano had wheeled out Elena's stretcher and was standing beside it, holding one end of the sheet up.

At this point Osman came abruptly out from under Montalbano's arm and said:

"I can manage on my own."

Montalbano was certain the man would stagger as he walked, but in fact Dr. Osman took those five steps with assurance and precision.

When he reached Pasquano, he stopped and looked at the victim's face.

Osman no longer wore any expression at all. His lips were moving, but no sound came out of his mouth. Then he slowly bent down until his lips were touching Elena's forehead. He stayed that way for a few seconds, then stood back up and headed out of the room as though sleepwalking.

"Thank you," Montalbano said to Pasquano.

Osman was now making straight for the exit.

As soon as he was outside, he said:

"Thank you for everything."

"But do you intend to drive back to Vigàta in your own car?"

"Yes," said Osman.

"Get that idea out of your head. You can come and fetch

your car another time. I'll drive you home. But, come to think of it, would you like to come to my house in Marinella?"

"Yes," the man repeated.

As they were getting in the car, Montalbano's cell phone rang.

"Hello!"

"Inspector, I'm sorry. This is Meriam. I'm calling you because I'm very worried. I'll explain. You don't know . . . but Elena . . . I'm sorry, but . . . I haven't been able to get in touch with Dr. Osman since this morning . . ."

Before replying, Montalbano got out of the car so that the doctor couldn't hear.

"He's here with me."

"How is he?"

"He's in a bad way."

"Are you at the police station?"

"No. I thought I would take him back to my place to give him a little time to recover."

"Wouldn't it be better just to take him home?"

"I wouldn't feel right leaving him alone."

"Don't worry about that. I'm already at his place, just outside. I'll wait for you."

"All right," said the inspector, getting back in the car.

He told the doctor he was taking him home. Osman was still so disoriented that he didn't even bother to ask the reason for the change in plan.

As soon as Osman saw Meriam outside his front door,

he opened the car door, got out, ran towards her, and embraced her.

Montalbano put the car in gear and drove off.

He wanted to head home to Marinella, but suddenly found himself, for no apparent reason, outside the police station.

By this point he was so tired that he could no longer think on his own, and so he let his car decide. He parked and went into the building.

"Ahh, Chief! F'rensix called jess now 'cuz 'ey wannit a know from yiz poissonally in poisson 'oo was asposta pay fer the Vissikassi."

"And what the hell is a Vissikassi?"

"Wha', Chief? Ya never hoid a Vissikassi? 'Ey show it alla time on TV."

"And what do they show, Cat?"

"'Ey show cats all happy an' smilin' an' stuff 'cuzza Vissikassi."

"So this Vissikassi is something that makes cats happy and we're supposed to pay to make Forensics happy?"

"'A'ss right, Chief. Assolutely right. Vissikassi's a cat food 'at makes cats rilly 'appy."

"I get it, Cat. But now explain to me why we should pay for this Vissikassi and, more important, who's it for."

"Iss fer the cat o' the tailor lady. The witness cat, in utter woids."

"Rinaldo!" Montalbano exclaimed. "Okay, tell Forensics that I'll pay the bill myself but only if they bring me the cat here after it testifies. I'm afraid they'll just let it starve to death, because they'll end up eating the Vissikassi themselves."

"Y'er right, Chief! Man, ya know so many tings! I'll call 'em now straightaways!"

Montalbano went into his office and found Fazio sitting straight up in a chair, immobile, eyes popping out of his head. He was clearly daydreaming.

"Fazio!" the inspector yelled.

His assistant gave a start.

"Yessir!" he replied. He then managed to take a breath and said: "But what ever happened to you?"

"I'll tell you later. You got any news?"

"Yeah, Chief," said Fazio, immediately thrilled. "I learned something of tremendous importance."

"So tell me."

Fazio assumed a conspiratorial air.

"Apparently, I'm told—now pay attention—that Dr. Osman and Elena used to be . . . know what I mean?"

"No," said Montalbano, who was starting to enjoy himself.

"Well, in short, apparently they were a little more than just friends."

Montalbano almost felt touched. How could someone like Fazio, who'd seen so many nasty things in his life, still feel embarrassed to talk about love?

But the inspector's emotion didn't prevent him from twisting the knife just a wee bit in the wound.

"And so?" he persisted.

"And so I think it might be useful to find out whether this story is true or not."

"It's true. Already known," said Montalbano, in the

same tone that Fazio always used when he said "already taken care of."

Fazio opened his eyes wide.

"How'd you know?"

"I just dropped Dr. Osman off five minutes ago outside his front door."

And he told him everything that had happened after they'd parted ways at the trattoria.

"So you weren't able to question him?" asked Fazio.

"No. In an hour or so I want you to call him at home and tell him I'll be waiting for him at the station tomorrow morning around nine-thirty. And I want you there, too, of course. But now I have to tell you that I'm dead tired and need to go home and get some rest. Have a good evening. I'll see you in the morning."

When passing by Catarella, he said:

"Cat, I'm going home and don't want to be disturbed by anyone, even if Hizzoner the minister of justice calls."

"Yessir, Chief! I wannit a tell yiz 'at F'rensix axed me t'ax yiz if y'er also gonna pay for the cat's letter."

"Letter? What letter?"

"Chief, I swear, I tried a ax 'em, but I din't unnastand. 'Ey jess said sum'n 'at sounded like a 'cat letter.'"

"Was it cat litter?"

"Yeah, 'a'ss it, Chief! 'A'ss azackly right!"

"Tell 'em not to get all bent out of shape over it. I'll pay for it myself. And tell 'em I'll pay for the sand, too."

"Don't botter 'bout 'at, Chief. I c'n go an' shovel up some sand at the beach if we need any. 'Ere's so much roun' here, nobody's gotta pay for it."

When he got home it was almost six p.m. There was a gorgeous sunset. Montalbano felt his nervous tension let up the moment he sat down on the veranda.

He just stayed there motionless, breathing in the air, too weak even to stick his hand in his pocket and pull out the pack of cigarettes. He was sitting so still, in fact, that a dove came and perched on the railing of the veranda. It started pacing back and forth, and then stopped and looked at him.

"I don't feel like talking," said Montalbano, feeling his eyelids beginning to droop.

The dove flew away.

Montalbano closed his eyes.

When he reopened them, it was pitch-dark outside. He got scared. He flicked his lighter and looked at his watch. Nine p.m.

He went inside and turned on the lights.

Maybe it was the tremendous fatigue weighing down on him, or maybe it was the fact of having slept in the open air, but in any case he'd got a chill.

So he went into the bathroom, took off his clothes, and got into the shower.

He immediately felt much better, and with this improvement in his condition, a powerful hunger came over him.

Slipping on a pair of underpants, he raced into the kitchen. His hunger led him straight, and unfailingly, to the oven. He opened it.

Oh, wonder of wonders!

Timballo di riso! God only knew how long it had been since he'd eaten any.

Not bothering even to set the table, he simply spread a large napkin over the oilcloth, set a bottle of wine and a glass down on it, grabbed a fork from the drawer, and attacked the *timballo* without removing it from the pan.

And he managed to make a miracle happen. That is, he didn't allow a single thought to enter his head. His brain had become a sort of blackboard on which appeared only expressions of praise for the flavor that began in his mouth and washed over his entire body all the way to the tips of his toes, from where it then resumed its journey back up to the top.

The rhythm of his eating began to slow down little by little as the contents of the pan diminished. The last two or three forkfuls were merely gatherings of the rice grains left in the pan.

When he'd finished eating he remained seated with his buttocks near the edge of the chair, intensely observing the design of the terra-cotta tiles of the kitchen floor.

Once the ecstasy had passed, he realized it was time to phone Livia.

He got up, went into the dining room, sat down, and dialed her number.

But then he immediately hung up, because he could still

feel the rice in his esophagus. He absolutely needed to take a walk.

So he put on a pair of jeans, a shirt, and a jacket and went down to the beach barefoot.

He touched the water with one foot. Freezing.

But he liked the sensation, and so he rolled the bottoms of his pant legs up to his calves and started walking in the water, letting it come up to his ankles.

Feeling something touch his feet, he bent down to look. There was a strange phosphorescence in the water, and he saw a great many tiny silvery fish swimming around his feet as in some kind of underwater slalom.

Then, as if some sort of signal had sounded in his head, he suddenly remembered the whole business with Osman. Fazio had confirmed to him that the doctor and the seam-stress had had a love affair.

And it must have been a serious matter if a man with as much self-control as Dr. Osman had let himself fall into such deep, disconsolate despair. It was completely different from the grief he'd seen in Trupia's face. And, come to think of it, Osman and Elena must have made a very handsome cou-ple, because their faces and manners were quite complemen-tary: He was as reserved as she was bright and cheerful, as closed as she was open.

And physically, too, they must have made a fine sight.

And so, if that's how it was, what obstacle had stood in the way of their relationship and broken it up?

Neither of them had a spouse, or any other kind of bond that might prevent them from being together.

Why had they left each other, or been forced to break up? Why hadn't they got married?

The mere thought of the word "married" called up a long, past history of his own, concerning himself and Livia.

He chased the idea from his head and started heading back to the house to call his longtime companion.

11

"Salvo! Finally! I couldn't wait to talk to you!"

"I'm sorry, Livia, but, you must realize, I—"

"Did you do it?"

"Did I do what?"

"Catch the killer! Did you?"

"Livia, don't be silly. I don't even know where to begin. Actually, you know what? I think you could help me out with this."

"How?"

"Tell me about Elena. When, for example, did you first make her acquaintance? What were the circumstances?"

"Well, I'm actually rather well prepared to answer that question. All I've been doing all day is thinking about Elena . . . The first time I saw her was about two years ago. I was walking past her storefront and saw some beautiful scarves in the display window. So I went inside and must have stayed there for at least two hours. I never told you about that?"

"No. Go on."

"I remember that we talked as if we'd already known each other for a long time. I, who normally talk very little about myself—I found myself telling her everything. I told her about you, about how we'd met, how long we'd been together . . ."

"And did she tell you anything about herself?"

"Not very much, really. Elena was the one leading the conversation and choosing the subject. I may have tried asking her about herself, but the more I think about it, my impression of her is that she was open and friendly, but only up to a point."

"Explain."

"I don't quite know how to put it . . . You know, when women are with women, they always end up talking about men, and yet she managed rather well not to tell me anything about her private life. She told me she'd married a man from Vigàta and that was why she moved down to your town. When I asked her if she was still married, I remember quite clearly that she said: 'No. He died.' But she'd said it in such a peremptory way that I didn't feel like asking her anything more about it. And, come to think of it, I would say that Elena made it clear she didn't want to go past a certain threshold. She was perfectly fine with our conversation as long as we were talking about me or her in a superficial way."

"And did you see her again after that?"

"Yes, a few more times. Always ending with the promise that we'd go and have an aperitif together sometime. We even exchanged telephone numbers, but it became clear to me that we would never meet anywhere outside her shop."

"So you don't know anything about Osman?"

"Osman? You mean the doctor for the migrants?"

"Yes. Apparently they were a couple for a while."

"What are you saying! They must have looked great together! But . . . but . . ."

"What's wrong?"

"Are you thinking he might be involved in this?"

"Livia, what are *you* saying! No, absolutely not. Osman was with me the night Elena was murdered."

"And have you got any suspects?"

"Yes, Livia. Though with no motive. Her most recent lover really has no alibi."

"So you're thinking it was a crime of passion?"

"I'm not thinking anything. I'm confused and so tired I can barely see. I haven't slept in my bed for two days . . ."

"What are you saying? In what bed have you been sleeping?"

At this point the conversation took a different turn.

Montalbano got angry. Livia got even angrier. They bade each other good night in a way that, in translation, meant "bad night," and hung up.

▬

It was a kind of funeral wake. Everyone was sitting in a row in the great room of the tailor's shop. There was Dr. Osman with one arm around Meriam; beside her was the old tailor, Nicola; beside him was the young tailor, with Enzo's arm around him; and the last in the row was Trupia.

Montalbano sat in the armchair looking at them all and slowly drinking a cup of mint tea.

They were clearly waiting for someone. Then Pasquano appeared in the doorway, holding Rinaldo in his arms. He approached the big worktable, set the cat down, and went to stand stiffly at attention next to the inspector's armchair.

"We can now begin!" Montalbano said in a loud voice.

Fazio came in with a ball of blue yarn, which he set

down in front of the cat. Everyone held their breath as though waiting for something extraordinary to happen, but the cat merely started playing with the ball of yarn, making it roll to the edge of the table without ever letting it fall off.

At a certain point the animal took one end of the yarn in its mouth and jumped down to the floor, trotted towards the doorway, and disappeared from sight. But it was clearly still playing in the hallway, because everyone could see that the ball of yarn on the table was turning and turning and getting smaller by the second. At a certain point all that was left of the ball was the other end of the yarn.

Montalbano stood up and started following the woolen strand. He went out into the corridor. The yarn disappeared through the door that led upstairs. He followed its path. The strand went up the stairs, which the inspector climbed one at a time. He reached the apartment. The strand continued down the entire length of the hallway and then turned, disappearing into Elena's bedroom. He went in. The yarn ended right in the middle of the floor. It looked like a sign traced in blue chalk.

Rinaldo had disappeared.

Montalbano woke up, wondering what that sign might mean. But he still needed to get more sleep and didn't feel like wasting any time with Jungian or Freudian interpretations.

When he showed up at the station, Catarella informed him that Dr. Cosma was already there and waiting in the waiting room.

"Is Fazio on the premises?"

"Yeah, Chief, totally onna premisses."

"Tell him to come to my office."

Montalbano went and shook Osman's hand.

"How are you feeling?"

"Terrible, but better."

"Do you feel up to . . . ?"

"Of course, let's do it."

Montalbano put his arm around him and led him into his office.

Fazio, who was already sitting down, stood up and also lent a hand to Osman.

"Please sit down," said the inspector.

The doctor took his place in the chair opposite the desk and Fazio sat down in the other.

"Let me make a preliminary statement," Montalbano began. "You, Dr. Osman, are here as someone informed of the facts of the case. There are no charges whatsoever against you, nor could any sort of accusation be made against you, since at the moment of the crime you were with me. In spite of this fact, you could avail yourself, if you wanted, of the help of a lawyer. Therefore, if you wish, we could suspend our discussion and postpone the meeting until such time as you had such assistance."

"I don't need any lawyer," said Osman. "And I'm ready to answer all of your questions."

"Thank you," said Montalbano. "I never had any doubt about that. I would, however, like Fazio to take down your declarations."

After Osman nodded his assent, Fazio opened his computer.

"Can you tell me, Doctor, what sort of relationship you had with the victim?"

"I first met Elena eight years ago. She came to me as a patient. I'd been recommended to her by Meriam, who had already been working at her shop for a while. What struck me most when she came into my office—and I still remember it as if it was yesterday—was her smile. We're all a little nervous when we first come into a new dentist's office. But not her. She was smiling and chatting, and sat down in the chair full of questions about all the buttons she saw around, touching them all, one after another. It was thanks to Elena herself—her spontaneity, how naturally she put me at my ease—that I, the long-faced, dour Muslim that I am, found the courage to invite her out to dinner. That's how it all began."

"How what began, Doctor?"

"A beautiful, passionate, genuine love story."

"How long did it last?"

"It's still ongoing, but in a different way."

"Please explain what you mean."

"Just as our doctor/patient relationship changed after our first encounter, we just as quickly became lovers after only a few days. And we were both surprised and happy with the intensity of our feelings. Our love was overwhelming and mature. The sort of affair that you can only have if you are free and open to life. And this was perhaps, and still is, the greatest lesson that Elena taught me. To be ready for life. To be able to accept what life has to offer."

"And how did that change later on?" asked Montalbano.

Osman looked at him with admiration.

"You mean how did it change from love to friendship?"

"Yes."

"It happened just as fast and naturally as the first change. One day, five years later, we were together in bed and were surprised to find that our bodies no longer felt that original urgency, but only a need for a tender embrace. And so we realized that we had to accept this new situation. I have often wondered what we would have done if we had had children."

"And why didn't you?"

"Elena never wanted children."

"And why did you never get married?"

"Elena was always adamantly against that, too. She'd been married once and didn't want to repeat the experience. And she didn't want us to live together, either."

"What do you know about her marriage?"

"I only know what Elena wanted to tell me about it, which is very little. She had this husband, they married very young, and they both lived in the north. They were in the same line of work, and they opened a tailoring shop together. At Rovigo, or Treviso, I forget. But then he took his own life. Elena never wanted to tell me the whole story. Even when she saw her sister-in-law, Elena was always very careful to steer the discussion away from that period of her life. And I respected her desire for silence. But now I would like to see clearly on this. I simply can't understand why anyone would want to kill her."

"Well, in order to gain some understanding of it," said Montalbano, "I need as much information as possible on Elena's life. I met her only twice. You practically lived with

Elena for five years. So what I'm asking you is to search your memory well, try to really concentrate to see if you can call up a forgotten recollection of any oddity, any change, however minor, in Elena's normal, daily behavior."

"Inspector, I haven't been able to sleep because of that very question. And during the night I've tried to bring together all my memories of those five years. Even the smallest details. And I must say that only twice did I find myself wondering why Elena didn't want to fill me in on something she was going through that I knew nothing about."

"Explain a little better."

"We would meet at either my place or hers. One evening we were having dinner at her place, and while Elena was busy in the kitchen and I was setting the table, the phone rang. 'Could you get that?' she said to me. When I picked up the receiver, a woman asked me if she had reached Elena's place, and when I said yes, she hung up on me. Elena asked who'd called, and when I told her what happened, she fell silent. The second time was the following day. When the telephone rang, Elena raced to answer it. And I heard her say: 'I can't talk right now. Don't call me anymore. *I'll* call you tomorrow morning.' Then she sat down at the table, but she was visibly shaken."

"And you didn't ask her anything?"

"Of course I did. But Elena replied that it was none of my business. I don't quite know how to put it, but she didn't mean to be rude; she was really trying to tell me that the matter had nothing to do with me."

"And you don't know where the phone calls were made from?"

"No, Inspector. But I do remember that Elena's mood changed after those two calls. She was irritable and nervous. Clearly something was bothering her, something unknown to me, which I had no way of ever finding out. Yet, despite how close we were to each other, I respected her wishes and never asked her about it again."

"What else can you tell me?"

"Nothing, for now. But I'm hoping I'll remember something that might help us."

Montalbano stood up.

"Thank you for your cooperation. We'll see you again very soon. But now, please, go and get some rest."

Osman looked at him and almost smiled. His eyes seemed to be saying: *I'd like to see you try to rest in my situation!*

As soon as Fazio returned from seeing him out, the outside line rang. And at that moment Mimì Augello appeared.

It was that enormous pain in the ass of a prosecutor, Tommaseo. Montalbano turned on the speakerphone.

"I am genuinely surprised at your manner of procedure, Inspector," said Tommaseo.

In a fraction of a second, the inspector realized that the prosecutor wasn't entirely wrong to be angry at him.

"What have I failed to do, sir?"

"Everything, Montalbano, everything. Does it seem right to you that it's only through your written reports that I should learn how far along you are in your investigation of the murder of that splendid, gorgeous woman who worked as a tailor?"

The inspector could easily imagine the twinkle of morbid

desire in the eyes of Tommaseo, who literally lost his head whenever he had a case of a beautiful murdered woman on his hands, since, apparently, the man had never managed to get his hands on a living woman in all his life. Montalbano decided to lay it on thick.

"On top of that, sir, you've only seen her in photographs. You should have seen her when she was alive!"

"Oh, yeah? Really?"

"But do tell me what I did wrong."

"You were wrong not to come in person to talk to me about the case. Because, you see, it took very little for me to put the investigation on the right track."

"And what would be the right track?"

"I've just released a notice of impending arrest for Diego Trupia, her lover."

"But, sir, if I may, that seems a little hasty to me, because there's still—"

"There's still what, Montalbano? Don't make me laugh. We weren't born yesterday, were we? The solution is obvious. Trupia has a quarrel with his girlfriend. Two or three days later he goes to see her, hoping to patch things up with passionate, pacifying sex. The woman refuses, of course, and Trupia, in an irresistible fit of lust, grabs her and pulls her roughly against his own body, and, as the woman continues to deny his request, the man, now blind with passion, grabs the scissors and shreds the body he so craves. And that's not all I can tell you. He spares her breasts because he didn't have the heart to disfigure a part of her body he loved, desired, yearned for with such—"

"Your Honor, please, if you'll allow me . . ."

"No, Montalbano. I'm not going to give in to your tortuous excogitations this time. The truth of the matter is much clearer than your far-fetched fantasies."

Montalbano decided to cut the conversation short.

"Then please tell me how I should proceed."

"Listen to me closely. You have twenty-four hours to put the screws to Trupia. As soon as he confesses, and I guarantee you he will, I will take the proper measures to request and validate his arrest with the investigating judge."

"As you wish, sir. Talk to you soon," the inspector said, hanging up.

"For once," said Augello, "I agree entirely with Tommaseo."

"Oh, do you?" Montalbano retorted. "Too bad you're not free at the moment, or I could have given you the assignment of interrogating Trupia."

"But I *am* free," Mimì said, smiling broadly, "and just this morning I got a call from the commissioner, who informed me that, as of today, our unit is relieved of providing support for Sileci. Except, of course, should unusual circumstances dictate otherwise."

"So much the better," said Montalbano. "All right, then, summon your erstwhile friend Trupia, make sure he has a lawyer present, and put the screws to him, as the prosecutor said."

"With pleasure!" said Mimì, getting up and leaving the room.

Fazio twisted up his mouth.

"What's bothering you?"

"Chief, if the defense lawyer finds out that Augello is Trupia's friend, don't you think he's going to use that to his advantage? It'll be very easy to contest the interrogation."

"Why, do you somehow think that hadn't occurred to me?"

"So you think Trupia had nothing to do with it?"

"Let's just say I'm ninety percent certain he didn't."

"But he has no alibi."

"That's exactly why. He came here of his own accord knowing perfectly well that he would be the prime suspect and had no line of defense."

"On the other hand, it might actually be a smart move."

"Yes, of course, and that covers the other ten percent. But I'm not gonna send a man to jail, not even for a day, if I'm not absolutely certain."

"And so? How are we going to get Trupia out of this?"

"Why should we get him out of anything? Let's wait for the results of Mimì's interrogation. Clearly he's going to do everything in his power to screw the guy. And if Trupia manages, in spite of everything, to give us even the slightest clue in his favor, that's what we'll have to work on."

There was a pause.

Fazio started staring intensely at his shoe tops. He always did that when he'd taken some initiative on his own and was afraid to tell Montalbano about it.

"Out with it," said the inspector. "Tell me everything."

"Chief. You have to believe me when I tell you that I ran into Nicola by accident today. Remember him? The old tailor who worked for Elena?"

"Of course I remember him."

"Well, this Nicola managed, between sobbing and wailing, to tell me a few things about everyday life at the shop, and how everyone had got along like newlyweds on a honeymoon until two months ago."

"Why, what happened?"

"What happened is that from one day to the next, Lillo Scotto, the younger tailor, who's just a kid, fell in love with Elena. Worse yet, he felt that she must certainly feel the same way. And that's when the trouble began."

"Meaning?"

"He just would never let up for a minute during work hours. He'd follow her all over the store and never leave her side. When Elena was upstairs in her apartment, he would find every excuse for going up and spending a few minutes with her. At first she laughed it all off, which only stirred Lillo up even more. Apparently on a couple of nights, after work, he'd even gone and knocked on her front door. At this point Elena couldn't take it anymore, so she talked it over with Nicola and Meriam and decided to sack him."

"When was he supposed to leave?"

"Ten days from now, at the end of the month."

"Thank you for that," said Montalbano. "Now you know exactly what you need to do."

"Yeah, Chief," said Fazio. "I'll get on it right away." And he left.

The inspector sat there alone for a spell, trying to think things over.

But he was unable to, because the door flew open and crashed against the wall with a tremendous boom and then bounced back and closed again with equal force.

"Uh, sorry, Chief, my 'and slipped," came Catarella's voice from behind the door.

"Okay, come in."

"I can't, Chief. 'Ss not passible. If I try an' make the same move as before, iss gonna make even more rackit."

Montalbano got up and opened the door.

Catarella's face was all bloodied and he looked like a Christmas tree. In his left hand he was holding a cat carrier with Rinaldo inside, and the animal looked ready to kill someone. Hanging from the same left arm were two small plastic bags, while a litter box was precariously balanced on his right arm, and the right hand held a child's bucket full of sand.

The inspector stepped aside to let him in.

Catarella came forward ever so cautiously, but as he was about to set the cat carrier down on the chair in front of the desk, the bucket slipped out of his hand and the sand spilled all over the floor.

Montalbano cursed the saints.

Looking like a battered dog, Catarella set all his ornaments down on the floor and reassured the inspector.

"Don' choo worry, Chief, I'll be right back," he said.

He disappeared.

Montalbano went and sat back down behind his desk as Catarella reappeared with a broom and a small shovel. It didn't take him long to get the sand all back into the pail. Then he came and stood stiff as a rail in front of the desk, holding the broom as though standing at ground arms.

"What did you do to your face?"

"Iss nuthin', Chief, bu' when they brough' me the cat, I

tried a take 'im outta the kitty cage, bu' he din't wanna come out an' so 'e scratched me."

"Cat, do me a favor. Go and wash your face, disinfect the scratches, and then come back. And please close the door, 'cause it looks like a zoo in here."

Catarella obeyed.

His curiosity aroused, Montalbano got up and went to see what was in the bags.

Catarella had spared no expense. One bag contained kibble for the cat; in the other, aside from a pair of small bowls for the cat's food and water, there was also a little cloth mouse, a clump of catnip, and a ball of yarn.

A ball of yarn!

Exactly like the one in his dream.

Montalbano crouched in front of the carrying case. He looked at Rinaldo, and Rinaldo looked at him. Montalbano realized he was in no danger.

12

He opened the little door, and a few seconds later Rinaldo stepped forward, came out, and climbed into the inspector's lap.

At that exact moment the door came crashing open again. Catarella appeared. Terrorized, the cat sank its claws into Montalbano's leg, and the inspector, cursing all the while, unstuck it roughly from his thigh and threw Rinaldo at Catarella, who stepped aside as the cat fled down the corridor.

It took the intervention of at least three policemen to catch the cat and put it back in the cage.

Catarella had an idea:

"Chief, seein' as how the cat ain't familial wit' dese offices, d'ya tink I cou' bring 'im home wit' me?"

"But this is not a stray cat, Cat. We'll have to give him back to his owners."

"Y'er right, Chief, but the owner was killed!"

"Okay, but maybe her sister-in-law . . ."

Catarella looked so crestfallen that the inspector changed his mind.

"Listen, tell you what: Take him home with you for a few days, and then we'll see."

"Tanks, Chief. Oh, an', sorry again, Chief, but d'ya mine if I make a few sep'rit trips to move all 'iss stuff? Utterwise iss possible I'm gonna make anutter mess."

"All right. Make as many trips as you like."

Montalbano waited for Catarella to clear out the office, then got up himself and went out to eat.

He'd probably been a bit excessive in slaking his long-neglected hunger, and therefore a stroll along the jetty became not only a necessity, but an urgent one.

When he got to the flat rock, it seemed to him the right time to make a phone call.

"Hello, Meriam, how are you doing?"

"Hello, Inspector. How do you expect me to be doing . . . ?"

"Do you think I could come and see Signora Messina this afternoon?"

"Actually, they just returned Elena's body to her a few hours ago. Teresa's in the morgue with her husband and I don't think she'll be moving from there. The funeral's tomorrow morning at eleven."

"All right, there's no hurry. Would you feel like meeting with me? There are a few things I need to ask you."

"Of course, but I can't right now. How about if we meet after six?"

"Could you come to the station?"

"Yes."

"All right, then. I'll be waiting for you."

As he was smoking a cigarette, he reflected that, up until that moment, he had been nothing more than a recipient of information.

He had been passively storing a great deal of data but had so far taken no initiative on his own.

He felt uneasy about this, as though he was unable to press the right buttons.

The real problem was that he was having trouble bringing the real Elena into focus, inside her proper frame. It was as though part of her remained in a sort of chiaroscuro that prevented him from seeing her actual contours.

The way everyone described her—an image that he himself had been able to confirm in person—as a person completely open to the world and to other people, might actually have been a kind of screen.

Better yet, that image might hide something that, depending on one's point of view, could seem either true or false.

Perhaps the right path to take was to follow his standard procedure. To try not to let himself be influenced by this great quantity of information and data, and especially not by people's judgments of Elena.

From this point forward, he would move only on the basis of confirmed, concrete facts. And so he decided to do something immediately that he should have done sooner.

He phoned the forensics lab.

The chief of the lab was Fernando Leanza, who'd taken over a few months earlier, and with whom Montalbano felt a mutual sympathy.

Leanza replied that he had a few interesting things to tell him, but he couldn't see him for another hour or so.

Since he had the time, there were two things Montalbano

could do: stay out there on the jetty, or get immediately in his car and go visit the Greek temples, which he hadn't seen for a very long time.

He got in his car and drove off.

Contrary to expectation, there were quite a few groups of tourists, dressed like tourists, milling about between the majestic ruins, faces half-hidden by either cameras or cell phones.

He was overjoyed to discover that, within the archaeological park, a plot of land had been fenced off for breeding Girgentana goats.

He stopped to look at them.

They were so beautiful!

They belonged to an endangered species, and perhaps because they were disappearing, Montalbano found them to be the most beautiful goats he had ever seen. They had coats of rich, long hair, light brown in color, and gentle, feminine muzzles, large, pink udders, and wonderful, incredibly long horns, upright and spiral.

Want to bet that Borromini drew inspiration from these goats for the bell tower of Sant'Ivo?

Then, all at once, with a disturbing sound, a large, broad-winged bird swooped across his field of vision. Montalbano stepped aside as a little girl beside him started crying and screaming loudly.

He had just enough time to see that it was a seagull snatching a cookie out of the hand of a young foreign tourist girl. Her father and mother tried to console her.

The inspector walked away thinking that not only had

seagulls forever lost their maritime dignity, they'd become back-road brigands.

Dejected, he decided it was time to go to the crime lab.

As for the sympathy Montalbano felt for Leanza, the new chief of Forensics, there was a personal reason at the bottom of it.

When Leanza was transferred from the Palermo forensics lab to Montelusa, the TeleVigàta journalist Pippo Ragonese, the one with the purse-lipped face that looked like a chicken's anus, had given the new arrival a welcome you really couldn't call benevolent.

For whatever reason, Ragonese had seen fit to present a whole sequence of suppositions for the reasons behind this transfer, all of them leading to a mountain of suspicions concerning the newcomer's private and public conduct.

Since, however, Montalbano was well familiar with the journalist's own public and private conduct, he had no doubt whatsoever that Leanza must, as a result, be an honest man and therefore worthy of his friendship.

And, indeed, the chief of Forensics, who'd now been in Montelusa for eight or nine months, had shown himself to be an intelligent, reasonable man who had absolutely nothing to hide.

And therefore, when he saw the inspector coming into his office, Leanza got up and greeted him with open arms.

"Hey there, Fernando," said Montalbano.

"Have a seat, Salvo. Can I get you anything?"

"At this hour I wouldn't mind a whisky, but obviously, here in the office . . ."

"Whoever said that?" Leanza replied, standing up. He

went over to the closet at the back of the room and returned with a bottle of whisky and two glasses, which he filled halfway, handing one to Montalbano. They both then raised their glasses at the same time and made a silent toast.

They sat there for a few minutes without saying anything, savoring the whisky and looking each other in the eye. Montalbano then took a deep breath, which Leanza took as a signal to begin the discussion.

"A nasty affair, eh?" he said.

"Very nasty. And I'm still unable to say that two plus two equals four."

"I don't think any of our findings will really help you much. I can tell you straightaway that the killer removed the victim's computer and cell phone from the apartment. Which in my opinion means, obviously, that they contained evidence of contacts between the victim and the killer. Therefore they definitely knew each other prior to the killing, as we saw from the fact that they had dinner together."

"What have we got in the way of fingerprints?"

"In the apartment, every kind of fingerprint you'd ever want, Salvo. One thing is certain, however: The killer used the tailoring scissors and, after killing her, was very careful to clean them off, since there are no fingerprints on either the handles or the blades."

"What did he use to clean them off?"

"That small piece of fabric lying on the table, which he left there."

"Go on," said the inspector.

"After killing her, he went upstairs into her apartment. He was clearly all covered with blood. And so he got undressed and took a shower in the bathroom off the victim's bedroom. Inside the shower stall we found traces of Signora Elena's blood but no fingerprints, and none on the taps, either. These, too, had been carefully cleaned. Which leads to a question."

"If the killer's clothes were all bloodstained, how was he able to go back out into the street? Is that the question you mean?"

"Yes, that's the one."

"Let's get one thing straight: Do you also think we're looking at a crime of passion?"

"Absolutely," said Leanza.

"Then, if our theory is correct, the killer did not bring a change of clothes. Therefore, one possibility is that he came by car, parked nearby, and, after killing Elena, took a shower, got dressed again as best he could, and slipped quickly back into his car. But there's still another possibility: If it was someone who'd come from out of town and was Elena's houseguest, he might have had a suitcase with him with other clothes in it. Incidentally, do you remember, Fernà, what the guest room was like?"

"Of course. The bed had been made up for that night. But it hadn't been used."

"Just like the guest bathroom, spick-and-span," Montalbano remarked.

"Whatever the case, we didn't find any extraneous fingerprints in either room."

"Apparently the killer had all the time in the world to erase all trace of himself. And what can you tell me about Rinaldo, Fernà?"

"Who's Rinaldo?" Leanza asked, alarmed.

"Oh, sorry; he's Elena's cat."

The chief of Forensics grinned.

"But tell me something, my friend: Was that bed by any chance made up for you?"

"Use your brain, Fernà. If I'd been going to spend the night there, there wouldn't have been any need to make up the guest bed. That's obvious, no?"

And since Leanza kept giving him that sly look, the inspector felt he needed to explain.

"Listen. I knew Elena, but I'd only seen her twice because she was making a suit for me . . ."

"But how much do they pay you at Vigàta Police, anyway, for all of you to have suddenly become so chic?"

"C'mon, Fernà, let's talk about something else. That suit was born under a bad star," said Montalbano, cutting him short. "Tell me about the cat instead."

"The cat's fur was soaked with the victim's blood. He may even have attacked the killer and scratched him. But we were unable to isolate any DNA under the animal's claws, because apparently he cleaned himself carefully afterwards, on the carpet next to the victim. And there you have it."

"Any idea why the killer spared her breasts?" the inspector asked.

"Well, it's certainly a sign of something, a conscious decision. But, sorry to say, I'm not in any position to interpret it."

They looked at each other.

Leanza threw up his hands.

Montalbano got up, thanked his friend, said good-bye, and headed back to Vigàta. Along the way he glanced at his watch. He was going to be right on time for his appointment with Meriam.

The first thing that struck him was the woman's obvious fatigue.

She seemed utterly exhausted. Tiny wrinkles that Montalbano had never noticed before had appeared on her face.

Being a smart girl, Meriam immediately understood the meaning of the inspector's look.

"This has been such a terrible blow for me. I still can't find any reason for it."

"I'm sorry," said Montalbano. "I'm sorry if I'm prolonging your suffering, but unfortunately I need some information from you."

"I want to help you in any way I can, Inspector. I'm entirely at your disposal," said Meriam, forcing a hint of a smile.

"I've been told about that young assistant at the shop, Lillo Scotto. Were you aware that Elena was intending to fire him?"

"Yes, of course I was. She talked about it with me and Nicola. Believe me, Inspector, Elena tried to avoid it, right up until the end, but the situation kept getting more and more intolerable by the day."

"Please explain."

"Lillo had been working at the shop for a couple of years. He's an excellent tailor, and had always been a good kid and a hard worker, always punctual, polite, and well-behaved. And he knew his place. But then . . ."

She stopped, as if to put her thoughts in order, and then continued:

"Then his behavior suddenly changed, and we didn't know why. But we realized immediately that he'd fallen hopelessly in love with Elena."

"But what could have happened to trigger that kind of passion? Had Elena perhaps taken on a somewhat more, let's say, affectionate attitude towards him?"

"No, Inspector, absolutely not. It wasn't triggered by anything specific, believe me. Lillo just lost his head over Elena. He stopped working, he wanted always to be the last one out of the shop, and he was forever finding excuses for sticking close to Elena. At first we just laughed at him, and Elena did, too. We figured it was just a hormonal thing, then some sort of illusion of love that Lillo harbored within himself and wanted to live out with Elena. But then this love, or infatuation, never diminished. On the contrary. Lillo only became more and more obsessed. Just imagine, when he would answer the phone and there was a man at the other end of the line asking for Elena, he would hang up in that person's face. Elena tried talking to him about it—at first gently, with affection, like a mother. Then she became more stern and imperious, but even that didn't work. Lillo wouldn't listen to reason. He wanted Elena and was convinced—though it's anybody's guess why—that sooner or later she would give in."

"But was there a specific episode that led to Elena's decision to sack him?"

"I can't think of any in particular, but just a few days ago I heard them arguing. I was in the fitting room. And after that Elena refused to go back on her decision. Lillo had to go."

"Let me ask you a very specific question," Montalbano

cut in. "Do you think he would be capable of committing a violent act? Do you think, for example, that if he was alone with her, an even firmer refusal than all the others from her could have caused him to lose all control?"

Meriam didn't have to give this any thought before answering.

"No, Inspector. But, given the kinds of things you read about in the papers, I couldn't really swear to it. Still, in all good conscience—and this is why I hadn't mentioned him to you—I don't think he would be capable of what you're thinking. Lillo always limited himself to courting her intensely; I am quite sure he never laid a hand on Elena."

Montalbano's question was a rhetorical one, since the killer had actually had dinner with the victim, and, given the way things were, Elena would never have invited Lillo Scotto into her apartment, in the evening, with her there alone.

He changed the subject:

"And what can you tell me about Diego Trupia? Did you know about her affair with him?"

"Yes, Inspector, of course. He would often drop in to say hello to her, and a few times we even went out together."

"I'm sorry, Meriam, but I know they had a serious relationship."

"I don't know how to put this, Inspector, but I've seen Elena when she's in love. And she was not in love with Trupia. She liked spending time with him, of course; she enjoyed his company, they sometimes went away together on vacation, but nothing more than that. Trupia was not the love of Elena's life."

"Was Osman?"

"He used to be. I'd never seen such a beautiful couple. And the friendship that came after their love affair was also a beautiful thing."

There was a knock at the door, and Mimì Augello appeared, hair sticking to his sweaty forehead.

"Sorry to interrupt, but I have to tell you something important."

Montalbano stood up and said to Meriam: "Excuse me. I'll be right back." And he went out into the hallway, closing the door behind him.

"I turned Trupia inside out like a sock," Augello said, assailing him with a dark stare. "That son of a bitch made me work, made me sweat like a pig, but he wouldn't confess."

"And so?"

"And so the only objective fact is that he has no alibi. He claims he stayed at home that whole evening and didn't even receive any calls. But he's the only person with a serious motive."

"And what would that be?" asked Montalbano.

"He admitted he'd quarreled with Elena. And probably what he's not saying is that their quarrel was maybe final."

"Did you say 'probably,' Mimì?"

"Yes."

"Mimì, 'probably' never sends a person to prison."

"Well, I hate to tell you this, but that's not Tommaseo's opinion. I've just been given orders to seize Trupia and bring him to the prosecutor in Montelusa. And I am certain, since Tommaseo's already told me, that the bastard will not be spending tonight in his own bed."

"Have a pleasant journey," said Montalbano.

And he turned, went back into his office, and sat down.

"Sorry about that," he said to Meriam. "Are you up to telling me a little more about Trupia?"

"I haven't got much more to add, Inspector."

"Then tell me something: Did Lillo Scotto know about Elena and Trupia?"

"Yes, and he even hung the phone up on him several times. Lillo lived inside a bubble of his own creation and seemed unable to get out of it."

"Do you know how he reacted to the news of Elena's death?"

"Yes, he called me on the phone but was unable to get a single word out. He was sobbing like a child and ended up passing the phone to his mother. I should call him back to find out how he's doing."

"One last thing. When Lillo Scotto found out he was going to be fired, did he lose any of his self-control?"

"Actually, Nicola and I were both present when Elena fired him. Lillo turned pale and dashed out of the room. I ran after him. Luckily there were no clients around. He went and shut himself up in the fitting room, where I found him lying on the floor, trembling all over, in the throes of an epileptic fit. That was his initial reaction. But the strange thing is that with Elena he kept on acting as if nothing had happened. He didn't try in any way to save his job and get Elena to change her mind . . ."

Montalbano sat there for a moment in silence, thinking about what Meriam had just said.

Something odd was happening: Whenever a possible culprit emerged who had some cause for conflict with Elena, immediately that same suspect was exonerated as someone incapable of committing violence.

He didn't think Trupia killed Elena, in the same way that Meriam didn't think Lillo did, either. Osman was out of the question.

And so?

Maybe they should be looking for someone outside Elena's daily world.

This last thought led to his next, rather specific question for Meriam.

"I've learned from Dr. Osman that when they were together, Elena would sometimes get phone calls that left her shaken and upset. When Osman, who was naturally curious, asked her about it, she hadn't wanted to answer. Nicola told me that on the day she was killed, Elena hadn't received any personal phone calls. Can you confirm that?"

"Now that you mention it . . . Of course, there was no way Nicola could have known . . . Before lunch, Elena asked me to accompany her to the bank. She had to make some withdrawals and didn't want to go alone. When she came back out of the branch office, her cell phone rang, and when she saw who was calling, she stepped away from me. Which she normally never did. She didn't want me to hear that phone call."

"But were you able to hear something anyway?"

"I just remember her saying: 'Okay, we'll talk later.' Or something similar. But I'm not sure. But maybe she did seem a little upset. Then, after the fitting, she sent us all home. But I don't think there was any connection between that phone call and her chasing us out."

"And what about before that? During all the years you spent working with her, did you ever see her upset after getting a phone call?"

Meriam closed her eyes and wrinkled her brow, searching her memory.

Then, weighing each word, she said:

"I don't know if I'm being influenced by what happened to Elena and by what you're asking me, but I remember a kind of situation that was repeated several times over the years but to which I'd never granted any importance until now."

She closed her eyes again, as if to concentrate better, then resumed speaking.

"It would happen every three or four months, almost on schedule, as if prearranged. Around eleven in the morning Elena would get a call and then hastily ask them to call back in the evening. There wouldn't be any exchange of greetings or friendly remarks. Anyway, after receiving these calls, Elena would seem distracted and nervous for a while. But I wouldn't say upset. Of that I can assure you."

"Therefore should I rule out that those were work-related calls?"

Meriam opened her eyes wide.

"I would rule that out completely."

"You've told me that over the past few months, it was Lillo Scotto who often answered the phone at work. Did Lillo ever call out to Elena and tell her who was on the phone?"

"Of course, Inspector, but those were work-related calls. Whereas the ones we're talking about—and I forgot to tell you this, sorry—were always on her cell phone."

Montalbano had an idea.

It was something, yet again, that he should have done long before.

13

He picked up the receiver and rang Fazio.

"Have you got the keys to Elena's store?"

"Yeah, Chief."

"Did you remember to remove the seals?"

"Yep."

"Then give the keys to Catarella. Oh, and another thing: Summon Lillo Scotto to my office for nine o'clock tomorrow morning."

"Okay," replied Fazio.

Montalbano set down the receiver and looked at Meriam without saying anything. The amazing thing was that there was no need to open his mouth, because Meriam did so first:

"Tell me what you're thinking."

"Would you feel up to coming with me to Elena's shop?"

The woman's face suddenly changed, assuming an expression bordering on fear, and she quickly replied:

"No, no, no . . ."

"I understand perfectly," Montalbano said, standing up. "I'll see you again soon."

He shook her hand by way of good-bye.

Meriam tried to justify herself.

"You must understand, Inspector. For me, going back there . . ."

"It's not a problem," said Montalbano, cutting her off.

Meriam squeezed his hand, headed for the door, opened it, went out, and closed it behind her.

The inspector sat there staring at the door.

Naturally, Meriam would have been of help to him, but he could also manage without her.

Somebody knocked lightly.

"Come in," he said.

The door opened and Meriam reappeared.

"I think I can come with you," she said.

Without saying a word, Montalbano put on his jacket. When passing Catarella's station, he asked him for the keys to Elena's shop.

"Am I coming in your car?" asked Meriam.

"No," said Montalbano. "It's better for each of us to take his own car, because I think I'm going to stay there a while."

There was one parking spot in Via Garibaldi, and Montalbano signaled to her to take it. He drove on a little farther and finally found another spot for himself.

Backtracking, he caught up with Meriam and together they walked the remaining ten or so steps to Elena's front door.

But then Montalbano froze, as still as a statue, to the point that Meriam, who was a step behind him, crashed into his back.

"What is it?" she asked.

"Look," the inspector said under his breath.

On the stair before the front door, sitting motionless on its haunches with forelegs perfectly straight like some Egyptian statue, was a white cat.

"Rinaldo!" Meriam said in astonishment.

The animal must have escaped from wherever Catarella had put him and had known the way home, following that mysterious trail of scents that cats leave.

When Montalbano drew near to him, Rinaldo didn't shy even one millimeter away. The inspector bent down, stroked his head, and moved him slightly to the side. Then he slipped the key in the lock and had no sooner pushed the door open a crack than the cat vanished fast into the gap. Entering, Montalbano and Meriam saw him already positioned outside the door of the apartment, and when this was opened, Rinaldo was again the first to go in, disappearing who-knew-where.

What most struck both Meriam and Montalbano was an unbearable smell of rot. As the woman dug through her purse for a handkerchief to put over her nose, the inspector ran into the kitchen and opened the window wide. Forensics had looked inside the garbage pail but hadn't emptied it.

"Let's go downstairs," said the inspector. "There's nothing to see here." As they were descending the stairs, Montalbano asked:

"Where did Elena keep her computer?"

"Let me show you," said the young woman.

She took three steps and pointed to a small table pushed up against the wall in the hallway with a telephone on it.

"She had one in the desk in her bedroom, and another, smaller one here, inside this drawer. She also had a strongbox in which she would put money for payments she needed to make, or for receipts from the business."

Montalbano made a mental note to have a look at it later.

When they entered the large workroom their noses were assailed by yet another odor: the sickly-sweet smell of blood.

Meriam made another expression of disgust, but luckily didn't realize what she was smelling. But then she blanched and staggered when she saw the dark stains beside the silhouette outlined on the floor in chalk.

Montalbano held her up, led her to one of the armchairs, and set her down in it. He sat down in the other.

He let a little time go by for Meriam to get hold of herself. Then he asked her:

"Feel like answering a question?"

"All right, go ahead."

"Look carefully around this room, especially the area around the table and the shelves. Do you see anything different from the way you left it?"

Meriam scanned the room carefully with her eyes and said:

"There was a large pair of scissors on the table, but nothing else."

"Are you sure that piece of cloth wasn't there?" Montalbano asked.

"I'd put everything away before leaving."

"Would you do me a favor? Could you go and look at that piece of cloth closely without touching it?"

"Why?"

"I want to know whether it's a scrap from the fabrics that came in the day before yesterday."

The woman stood up and went over to the table, on the side opposite to where the outline of the corpse was. Montalbano came up beside her.

Meriam looked at the piece of cloth for a few moments and then said:

"Could I take something off the shelf?"

"Go ahead."

Meriam turned, took the longest route to the stacks of fabric to avoid stepping on the chalk silhouette, and, leaning forward, stuck a hand into one of the shelves, pulled out a bolt, and came back to the table.

"Here, look. This is the one most like that scrap, but it's not the same. They're both blue but very different in tone."

Montalbano noticed that the first part of the bolt had been torn.

"Meriam, why is this fabric ripped?"

"Signora Elena did that. I told you she was very upset that afternoon and tore up some of the new rolls with her hands. But I can assure you, Inspector, this scrap wasn't from any of the new orders. I can even add that this piece of fabric is, well, already worn out. In fact, it looks old to me."

"Thank you," said Montalbano. "That'll be enough for today."

Meriam put the bolt back on the shelf, and as soon as she'd laid it down she burst out crying so desperately she could barely stand up.

Montalbano embraced her and, almost by force, led her out of the room. Holding her by the waist, he had her climb the stairs, guided her into the living room, and sat her down. Running into the kitchen, he poured a glass of water, ran back, and gave it to her. Meriam drank it as if she was dying of thirst.

"I'll be okay in a second," she said.

"I'm in no hurry," replied Montalbano, taking the glass.

When he returned from the kitchen, Meriam was on her feet.

"If you don't need me anymore . . ."

"I'll see you out," said Montalbano. "You've no idea what a big help you've been to me."

"Thank you, Inspector."

"One last thing, Meriam: Where will the funeral be held?"

"At the Chiesa Matrice, tomorrow morning at eleven."

Montalbano followed her with his eyes as she descended the stairs, and stood outside the door to the apartment until he heard the front door close downstairs.

Then, walking slowly, he made his way back into the big room and sat down in the usual armchair, eyes fixed on the piece of cloth.

Some questions started to come to mind. Where did that scrap come from, if it wasn't part of the new deliveries? And the follow-up: Why had it been pulled out and left on the table?

He stood up, went over to the large table, and opened the two large drawers located under the top. There he found all manner of scissors, needles, threads, shoulder pads, and measuring tapes, but no scraps of fabric.

Then he went back out into the corridor, stopping at the little table. He opened the drawer. He immediately noticed that the computer was gone, whereas to one side was the small strongbox, which had not been opened. Apparently the killer wasn't interested in money.

At that point he heard a sound coming from the apartment, pulling him out of his thoughts. It was a soft, muffled sound, but constant. Then it suddenly stopped, and he distinctly heard a plaintive meow.

It was surely Rinaldo. But what was he doing?

Montalbano sprang to his feet and went upstairs into the apartment.

The cat was outside the closed door to Elena's bedroom, scratching the wood and complaining.

He wanted to go inside.

Montalbano opened the door. Rinaldo scampered quickly across the room, jumped up onto the bed, and remained standing there, as though inviting the inspector to come in.

Montalbano took a few steps forward, until he was standing in the middle of the room.

The cat was now looking in another direction.

The inspector followed the animal's gaze and his eyes landed on the blue desk. The surface was completely empty.

He grabbed a chair, sat down, and opened the first drawer on the left. It was full of receipts, payments, notes, invoices, packing slips: all business-related stuff.

He closed the first drawer and opened the second: the same things, except that these were documents from the previous year, gathered together in so many folders.

He opened the third and last drawer on the left: more work-related documents. He went over to the right side. The first and uppermost drawer contained an assortment, this time, of personal documents: expired passports, ID cards, health-care cards, old checkbooks, bank withdrawal slips, and so on.

He closed it and opened the second. He rummaged a bit through the papers, these ones also personal. Postcards, letters, a few photos, and above all two large envelopes shut with rubber bands. He opened them and found a sort of detailed documentation of Elena and Osman's love affair. Feeling almost ashamed, Montalbano cast a quick, superficial glance at it all, as if he had no right to pry into the private life, not so much of the victim—since he would have only been doing his duty—but of Dr. Osman.

He opened the third and last drawer.

It was completely empty. No computer here, either.

He then pulled the drawer entirely out of the desk, slid the chair back a bit, and rested the drawer on his lap.

Elena had covered the bottom with a piece of wrapping paper. He lifted this. Underneath he found only a tiny triangle of thick paper. He picked this up and looked at it closely. It was clearly photographic paper. But he couldn't quite make out the image. Looking harder, he became convinced that what he was seeing was a child's shoe with its little foot inside. He put it back in its place, laid the paper back on top, slipped the drawer back into its slot, and sat there thinking.

He came to a conclusion, but one which had nothing to support it. Namely, that that same drawer had also contained personal papers and photos of Elena's, which, if he was right, had been taken away by the killer.

He was about to stand up when Rinaldo suddenly leapt into his lap, as if to tell him it was too early for him to leave that spot.

And so Montalbano picked up the cat and set him down on the desktop, then crouched back down and pulled the empty drawer entirely out again. He stood up, knelt down, and looked deep inside the hollow left behind by the drawer. Way down at the bottom there was something whitish.

He bent farther down, reached out with one arm, felt around, grabbed the piece of paper with two fingers, and pulled it out. The small scrap was rolled up from the opening and closing of the drawer. It looked like part of a letter. There were a few words written on it: *The fever is gone now. The pediatrician says that . . .*

It was clearly a woman's handwriting.

He stuck the piece of paper into his jacket pocket, then put everything back in place and sat down to think.

How could there not be any trace of Elena's prior life anywhere in that apartment? He had to keep searching.

He stood up and went over and opened the big armoire. It was stuffed full of clothes. Beneath them, however, were six large drawers. He opened them one by one. All he found in them was intimate apparel, stockings, socks, camisoles. Nothing else.

A strange sort of frenzy came over him. He grabbed a chair, pushed it up against the armoire, climbed onto it, and felt around on top of the armoire, but his fingers encountered only dust.

Stepping down from the chair, he went over and opened both nightstands. Nothing.

As he walked into the sitting room, he felt discouraged. There were too many magazines and books to sort through. Once again, he had come up empty-handed. He had found nothing.

He went back downstairs to the great room. He searched everywhere, in every imaginable place, and finally realized that he was wasting his time in there.

Climbing the stairs again, he walked down the hall, descended the other stairs, opened the front door, went out into the street, locked the door behind him, and headed for his car.

He was opening its door when his cell phone rang. It was Fazio, confirming the appointment with Lillo Scotto.

He bent down to get in and then froze.

Matre santa! He'd forgotten Rinaldo!

He called the station to talk with Catarella. But a voice he didn't recognize answered the phone.

"Montalbano here. Who are you?"

"Officer De Vico, sir."

"Where's Catarella?"

"I'm sorry, sir, but Catarella went back home this afternoon to check on the cat, and when he saw that it wasn't there, he practically lost his mind and is now looking for it all over town."

"Okay, thanks," said the inspector.

He rang Catarella on his cell phone.

"No, no, no, sir," Catarella said at once. "Ya shou'n't be callin' me, Chief, 'cuz I'm not woity to talk t'yiz."

"Cat . . ."

"Nah, nah, Chief, f'hivven's sake, don' talk to me! I did a wicket ting! I let Rinaldi get aways an' now I don' know where to find 'im. An' until I get 'at cat an' my honor back, I'm too disgraced to set foot inna p'leece station!"

"Cat! What is this, the puppet theater or something? I found Rinaldo myself."

At the other end the inspector heard a shout that sounded like a cross between a Tarzan yell and a horse's whinny.

"Y'er a reggler Moilin the Wizzid, Chief!"

Then, voice cracking with joy:

"Bu' didja rilly find 'im, Chief?"

"Yes."

"Y'er a magishin, Chief! Ya woik magickal mirakles! An' where'd ya find 'im?"

"He went back home."

"Bu' I looked fer 'im all over the place a' my house, e'en downna drain! An' inside the oven! An' even inside the warshin' machine—"

"Lemme speak for a minute, Cat. The cat went back to his own home, where Signora Elena lived."

"On Via Calibardo?"

"That's right."

"Man, 'a'ss so lucky! I'm juss rounna corner. I'll be over in a sec."

Montalbano turned around, went back to Elena's front door, sat down on the step, and set fire to a cigarette. He'd smoked half of it when he saw Catarella appear at a run, holding the cat carrier in one hand.

"'Ere I am, Chief," he said, stopping in front of the inspector and panting heavily.

Montalbano handed him the house keys and said:

"You go and get him yourself. I'm going home."

The first thing he did when he entered his house was take off his clothes and get into the shower.

Not that he was particularly dirty, but he felt sticky all over, as though the aura of Elena's life, which he had profaned by poking his hands into her memories and thoughts, had remained attached to his skin.

He got dressed again as best he could and, since it was a cozy evening, sat down on the veranda and started smoking, thinking back on every move he'd made in front of Meriam in the tailoring shop, and then after she'd left.

Well in the background inside his brain, there was a small detail he'd noticed and momentarily formed an opinion about, but which had later slipped his mind.

He saw himself moving about in the shop, as though watching a film.

But he still had that same feeling of discomfort.

He decided to watch the film one more time, and all at once the cause of his malaise appeared clear as day.

He glanced at his watch.

Surely Leanza was no longer in his office at that hour. He would have to call him on his cell phone, and it might even be too late, but his urgent need for an answer to the question spinning around in his head won out.

He dialed the number.

"Sorry to bother you, Fernà. Montalbano here."

"No problem. What is it?"

"Listen, do you remember seeing a piece of blue cloth on the large worktable in the tailor's shop?"

"Yes, the one the killer used to clean the scissors."

"Well, Elena's assistant has told me that it's actually a piece of old cloth. Did you notice that it had been torn?"

"Yeah, sure, I remember quite clearly."

"My question is this: Would it be possible for the forensics lab to determine whether that rent is recent or as old as the scrap itself?"

"Of course. At least, I think so. And there may be a logical explanation for it."

"For what?"

"For the rent. If it turns out to be recent, the killer could have made it while wiping off the scissors."

"Yes, of course, that's certainly likely," said Montalbano. "Thank you, and my apologies for the disturbance."

"What the hell does that mean?" asked Leanza. "How do we leave things? Shall I go and get the scrap of cloth myself or will you send it to me?"

"I'll bring it to you personally in person."

"Then I'll see you tomorrow. Good night."

While he was at it, he might as well call Livia.

As he was about to dial her number, the phone rang.

"Oh, Inspector, Inspector . . ." said a desperate voice. It was Meriam.

"What's wrong, Meriam? Has something happened?"

"I just now found out from Nicola that Lillo tried to kill himself. He's been taken to the hospital in Montelusa."

"So how did that happen?"

"This afternoon Nicola got a call from Lillo's mother, pleading with him to come to their house. Lillo was beside himself: yelling, bashing his head against the wall, drooling! He seemed to be having an epileptic fit. Do you remember that you asked Fazio to summon him to your office?"

"Of course."

"Well, ever since that moment, he's gotten worse, if that was possible. When Nicola arrived, Lillo's mother went out to the pharmacy to get some tranquilizers. But Nicola wasn't able to see Lillo because he'd locked himself in the bathroom and wouldn't open the door."

"And then what?"

"And then he tried to talk to Lillo through the door, but

when Lillo stopped answering, his mother returned and together they forced the door open and found him in the tub with his wrists slashed. But he was still conscious, and he managed to whisper to Nicola, 'Without Elena my life has no meaning.'"

Montalbano listened to Meriam's words with astonishment. This was one turn of events he hadn't even vaguely expected.

He didn't know what to say.

"Thank you, Meriam. If you find out anything else, call me, no matter the hour. Don't hesitate."

He didn't know what to think.

Lillo's act could, of course, be considered an admission of guilt, but it could equally be taken for the opposite.

The inspector had taken one step towards the French door when the phone rang again.

"Sorry to call, Chief, at such a late hour, but something nasty has happened."

"What is it, Fazio?"

"I've just been told that Lillo Scotto tried to kill himself this evening. He's been admitted to Montelusa Hospital."

"Already taken care of," said Montalbano.

"Huh?" said Fazio, confused.

"Nothing, sorry. I just meant to say I already knew."

"What do you say I hop over to the hospital and then give you a call and tell you how things stand?"

"Okay."

He hung up and made a move towards the veranda, when the phone, which apparently was determined to be a pain in the ass, started ringing again.

"Salvo! What's new?"

At the sound of this simple question, Montalbano felt overcome by a doglike rage and, more than speak, he barked:

"What's new??? I'll tell you straightaway: Elena's last lover is in the slammer because the public prosecutor, who's in cahoots with Mimì Augello, decided beyond a shadow of a doubt that he is the culprit. Lillo, the boy who would have liked to be her lover, has just tried to kill himself and is in the hospital. And I'm in deep shit up to my neck. Her computers have vanished, her cell phone can't be found, and there's no trace of anything. The only clues are: a piece of torn fabric, a piece of a photo with a small child's foot, and a piece of a letter with a sentence I can't make heads or tails of. Elena's body is in the morgue; the funeral is tomorrow at eleven o'clock sharp at the Chiesa Matrice. And what else? Ah, yes. Catarella lost the cat, but then I found it."

"Good night," said Livia, ending the conversation.

14

The tirade did him good, to the point that five minutes later, as he was sitting out on the veranda, he suddenly felt hungry.

He went into the kitchen for the usual inspection. Every once in a while Adelina would decide to make him a *sfincione* with meat. And there it was. It gave off an aroma so pleasing it could have been used as cologne. He heated it up in the oven and then took it outside. Not bothering to set the table, he merely put down a bottle of wine and glass. And there was no need for cutlery.

Adelina, as usual, had been generous. The *sfincione* was big enough for four, and in fact the inspector felt terribly disappointed that he could only manage to eat half.

So he went and took a large sheet of wax paper, wrapped the remainder of the *sfincione* carefully in it, and put it in the refrigerator.

He was heading for his bedroom when he heard his cell phone ring.

It was Meriam.

"I'm sorry to call so late, Inspector, but I wanted to let you know I went to the hospital and they told me Lillo Scotto is out of danger and they think they can release him as early as tomorrow afternoon."

"Thank you for that, Meriam," said Montalbano. "I hope you can get a little rest now."

"Thanks. You have a good night, too."

He left the cell phone beside the television, headed for his bedroom, lay down with satisfaction, closed his eyes, and was taking a deep breath when he was interrupted halfway with the ring of his cell phone.

Cursing the saints, he got out of bed and answered. It was Fazio.

"Just on my way back from Montelusa, Chief . . . Lillo Scotto's out of danger and—"

"Already knew that," said Montalbano, feeling almost ashamed. He was exacting too much revenge on poor Fazio.

"Did you know that they want to discharge him tomorrow afternoon?"

"Yeah, I knew that, too."

"Well, since you seem to know everything, I'll let you sleep in peace, though there actually was something I wanted to ask you. Good night."

"Wait!!!" the inspector yelled. "So you're going to get pissed off at me at this hour of the night?"

"Sorry, Chief, you're right. But when you keep saying you already know things, it starts to get on my nerves."

"Well, imagine how I feel!" replied Montalbano. "Now speak. What did you want to ask me?"

"If the kid recovers, can I summon him for the day after tomorrow morning?"

"Have him come in at nine," said Montalbano. "Thank you, and good night."

He lay down and fell asleep at once, only to wake up again moments later, sitting up in bed with his eyes wide open.

A thought had flashed through his head like a kind of luminous, lightning-fast snake that he was unable to grab, not even by the tail. Damn it all! What was it? Nothing. Total darkness.

He lay back down and closed his eyes, and only then did it come back to him that the elusive thought had something to do with Elena's phone calls and something he hadn't done relating to them. What had he forgotten to do?

"Damn my fucking old age!" he cursed.

But he could do nothing about it. And so he lost another hour before he could fall back asleep.

And he didn't open his eyes again until the morning light was already bright.

But he decided he could stay in bed for a bit, since he had nothing urgent to do at the station.

Then he changed his mind.

He got up, put the coffee on the burner, shaved, drank a mug of black espresso, and slipped into the shower.

Instead of getting dressed, however, he put on a bathing suit and headed off for a long walk along the water's edge. This lightened his spirits and cleaned out his lungs.

When he drove off for Vigàta, it was nine o'clock.

As he entered the station, he stopped in front of Catarella's closet and asked him:

"What's new with Rinaldo?"

Catarella grimaced, as if in displeasure.

"Chief, 'e jess don' like me. 'E's continually cryin' in continusity. 'E wants to run away alla time. Poor ting! 'E was useta bein' witta woman an' iss too bad I'm jess a man. When I c'n manatch t 'old 'im still an' pet 'is head 'tween 'is ears, isstead of purrin' 'e jess goes all hissy like 'e wants ta 'tack me. 'E won' even lemme give 'im no Vissikassi."

"You know what I say, Cat? I say that, since I'm going to have to see Meriam again sooner or later, I'll tell her to take the cat."

"But now I'm startin' a get a tatch to the cat, Chief."

"You can adopt another white cat off the street and do a good deed. Listen, do you still have the keys to Elena's shop?"

"Yessir, Chief."

"Gimme 'em."

Catarella pulled open a drawer and handed him the keys.

"Now please go," said Montalbano, "and get me a small plastic bag."

"Fer goin' shoppin'?"

"No, Cat, one of those little bags for evidence specimens."

Catarella bent back down, opened another drawer, and handed him a transparent bag still unsealed.

Montalbano put the bag in his pocket.

"I'll be back in half an hour," he said.

He got back in the car and drove off in the direction of Via Garibaldi. Luckily there was a parking space right outside Elena's front door.

He parked, unlocked the door, climbed the stairs, went quickly down the corridor and down again to the great room, set the little plastic bag on the table, picked up the scrap of blue cloth with two fingers, and slipped it into the bag.

He then retraced his steps and was on his way out, but when he put his hand on the front door handle to open it, he froze. There was something troubling him. It was that luminous snake of the night before again, the one that had made him sit up in bed. Once again he had that distinct feeling he was neglecting to do something he absolutely needed to do.

But what?

He stood there for several moments without moving a muscle, but nothing came to mind.

And so he opened the door, got back in his car, and returned to the station.

"Is Fazio here?" he asked Catarella.

"Yessir, Chief."

"Send him to me."

He went into his office, and Fazio appeared at once.

"Hello, Chief."

"Have a seat and let's talk a little. What do you make of Lillo Scotto's suicide attempt?"

"What can I say, Chief? I talked it over a little with Augello as well, but he totally rules out any chance it might be an admission of guilt. He's stuck on the idea that Trupia's the killer, and he won't budge."

"But what do you think?"

"I did gather some information on the kid. And there wasn't anyone, not one person, who considered Scotto capable of killing so much as an ant. In my opinion Lillo tried to commit suicide for no other reason than because he lost Signora Elena."

"Well, aren't we just brilliant!" Montalbano said bitterly. "We've got two potential killers in our grasp: one's in jail, the other's in the hospital, and yet, deep down, we're convinced that neither of them had anything to do with it."

"Maybe because we don't know the whole story yet," said Fazio.

"Explain what you mean."

"Chief, what I'm saying is that maybe we won't get any ideas until after we've questioned the kid. You became convinced that Trupia didn't do it after you talked to him. It's possible that after you interrogate Scotto, you'll think the opposite."

"Okay. We'll leave the question hanging and set it aside for the moment."

"Are you going to Signora Elena's funeral?" asked Fazio.

"Yes."

"You want me to come, too?"

"No."

Fazio realized that the inspector's monosyllabic replies of "yes" and "no" meant that their conversation had ended.

"I guess I'll get back to work," he said, getting up and going out.

Montalbano wondered how he was going to spend the hour remaining before it was time to go to the church.

He remembered his fictional colleague, that Inspector Schiavone, who'd been assigned to Aosta and whose first act in the morning, before going to the office, was to smoke a joint.

No, no, this was no time, so late in life, to start smoking weed!

He reached out melancholically with one arm, grabbed the sheet of paper sitting at the top of the pile, and gloomily started signing . . .

The Chiesa Matrice was packed. Elena's death had brought out half the town.

The coffin was lying on the floor in front of the main altar.

Meriam was sitting in the front pew on the left, with her arms around Teresa, who was dressed all in black. Behind the two women was Stefano, trying to keep the two ten-year-old children beside him quiet.

In the pew on the right sat a rather unusual couple: old Nicola, who was bent forward with his head in his hands, clearly weeping, and beside him, calm, erect, impassive, and more elegant than ever, Dr. Osman.

Among those present Montalbano recognized Enzo the restaurateur, the barman from the Castiglione, Augello, the greengrocer, and the tobacconist.

In short, everyone who lived on Via Garibaldi or nearby was there.

The inspector listened to the whole Mass in silence, and after the final benediction was given, Dr. Osman stood up and approached the coffin.

Three other pallbearers joined him and, together, they stooped down and raised the casket. The doctor rested it on his right shoulder as he lightly caressed the wood with his left hand.

Montalbano waited for everyone to leave, then slipped behind the last mourners. But at once he felt someone grab him by the arm. She was a woman of about fifty, shabby and disheveled and weeping.

"My son is innocent!" she said.

She must be Lillo Scotto's mother.

"You have to believe me, Inspector, he's innocent! I'm his mother and I can tell you! I can feel it deep down in my heart!" Still crying and sobbing, she continued: "My own flesh and blood would never be capable of doing a thing like that! My own flesh and blood would rather kill himself than kill somebody else."

"Please calm down, signora. You should go to the hospital. Lillo needs you there. Don't worry. You'll see: Very soon we'll clear everything up with your son."

He delicately removed the woman's hand, which was still clutching his arm, and headed out of the church.

The hearse was already pulling away, with three or four other cars following behind.

Montalbano walked towards his car, intending to head back to the station, but the moment he put his hands on the steering wheel, he instinctively pulled up at the back of the funeral procession.

When they reached the cemetery, he realized that the burial was going to take some time, and so he fired up a cigarette and started walking down the little lanes, always keeping the ceremony in the corner of his eye.

After his fourth cigarette, he decided the moment for condolences had come.

He embraced Osman, who'd come over to greet him, and got in line behind everyone else.

Meriam was still beside Teresa, and it was she who introduced Montalbano to Elena's sister-in-law. Without a word, the inspector shook the woman's hand firmly, and was about to let go when she said to him:

"Thank you, Inspector. I know you are doing a great deal for Elena."

"It's my duty. When you feel up to it, I will need to talk to you."

Teresa raised the little veil over her face. Montalbano was expecting to see two exhausted, sorrowful eyes red with tears, but the woman's gaze was instead that of a ferocious beast, two black, pinpoint pupils emitting flashes.

"Even now would be fine with me," she said. "I want to know who killed my Elena. Could you please wait for me for a minute?"

"Of course," said Montalbano, stepping away.

Teresa went and spoke to her husband; then she kissed the children and exchanged a few words with Meriam.

Coming back towards Montalbano, she said:

"We can go now."

"Where to?"

"Not far from here there's our family vault, with a bench in front of it. If you want . . . I'm sorry, but I need some fresh air, and that way we can stay a little while longer near Elena."

"All right," said the inspector.

After a short walk they sat down and said nothing for a few moments. Perhaps because they felt uncomfortable with the deep silence weighing down on them from all sides.

There was a rarefied air in the cemetery that softened even the sounds made by the cars passing along the road outside the enclosure wall. Montalbano noticed there were no birds in the sky above the cemetery.

There was only one other living being, some thirty yards away from them. An old woman in front of a small waterspout, changing the water for some flowers.

From where he was sitting, Montalbano could see before him an earthen grave with a large iron cross on top. On the tombstone were two round photographs of two lads in uniform. Montalbano managed to read the metallic letters on the photos: They were brothers, Antonio and Carmelo, who had died on a mission in Afghanistan.

The inspector thought that in all likelihood that tomb and that writing had been the work of the parents of the two fallen soldiers.

They represented an inversion of the natural order of things.

It should be the children burying the dead, not the mothers and fathers.

His thoughts were interrupted by the voice of Teresa, who apparently could no longer bear all that silence.

"Are you really so sure that Elena was killed by Diego Trupia?" the woman asked aggressively.

"And you're not?"

"No. At least, not too sure."

"Why not?"

"Because I know Trupia and I know the kind of relationship he had with Elena. They were lovers, yes, but they weren't very intimate. I'm not quite sure how to put it, but they were both aware that their ties would never be more than they were. They were on good physical terms, and things remained on that level. Do you have any evidence, any clues, that led you to arrest him?"

"The only clue is that he has no alibi for that evening," said the inspector, surprising himself with his sincerity.

"That doesn't seem like much. I don't have any alibi for that evening, either."

"Aside from the fact that you don't need one," Montalbano retorted, "I must tell you that my colleagues and I have somewhat differing opinions on the matter."

Teresa snatched this up like a mint.

"So do you have any idea who might have done it?"

"No, signora," said the inspector. "None at all, to be honest with you. And that is why I'm sitting here with you. I need to know as much as possible about Elena."

It was like opening a dike on a river in spate.

"You won't believe it, but I was sitting right here, on this very bench, when I spoke to Elena for the first time about my brother's death. And here I am today, on the same bench, talking to you about Elena's death. I first met her when she came to Vigàta with Franco's mortal remains, and this is where our friendship, a real friendship, was born. It wasn't just a family tie. Elena and I were true sisters. And I think it was on that day, on this bench, that Elena, alone as she was, decided to come and live in Vigàta."

"That was the first time you met her? Didn't you ever see her during the time she was married to your brother?"

"Well, Inspector, I was still very young at the time, and my parents wouldn't allow me to travel alone. I was never able to go up north and see them, and you have no idea how much I would have liked to, but my parents themselves hardly ever traveled very far. During his years with Elena, Franco came to see us only twice, both times alone. But we used to talk to him often over the telephone, and they would send me postcards, letters, photos . . . They were very busy trying to realize their dream, you know, and didn't have time for much else."

"What dream was that?"

"Franco and Elena wanted to become the biggest of all the Italian fashion designers. They met at a posh fashion school in Vicenza. Clothing had always been Franco's passion. I remember him spending evenings knitting, sewing, and darning with my grandmother when he was a boy. He even made dresses for my dolls. He always had a clear sense of things; he wanted to become a tailor. And when he graduated from high school with the highest marks, he asked my parents to pay his way to the Accademia in the Veneto. That was where he met Elena. They immediately saw their true selves in each other. And they got married shortly thereafter, but without telling anyone. We found out from a photo they sent us. What brought them together was surely her talent and his mastery. They were such a perfect couple in terms of work, that it was inevitable—as Elena later told me—that their relationship would also become intimate. They balanced each other out perfectly; he in technique, she in production; he

217

would get the ideas, and she would do the stylistic research. And the moment they graduated they found work. Elena in a prêt-à-porter company, while Franco began designing purses and handbags for a famous designer. But for them those were temporary jobs. Their dream was to strike out on their own. Elena told me they were living in a thirty-square-meter flat, doing everything possible to save the money they needed. And they would spend Sundays and holidays driving around visiting provincial towns, looking for the best place to set up their workshop. Elena, in the meanwhile, had become so good that she was appointed chief of a very important fashion line. And she was earning so much money that Franco was able to quit his job to devote more time to finding the right place and everything else they would need to set up their own company. In the end they decided on the town of Bellosguardo."

Bellosguardo! thought Montalbano, remembering a poem by Montale.

"And where is that?" he asked.

"In Udine province," replied Teresa, before continuing. "Clearly Elena couldn't move there right away. She had to serve out her contract and, most important, finish designing her personal line, and so, for the first few months, Franco settled there by himself."

"How long was it before Elena joined him?" Montalbano asked.

Teresa looked at him as though taken aback, and didn't answer right away.

Then she said very slowly:

"Why are you so keen to know about a story that's fourteen years old?"

"I don't understand your question," Montalbano replied, looking at her inquisitively.

"You're having me tell you a story that has nothing to do with Elena's murder. Tell me the truth: Do none of you know what direction to take with this?"

"No, signora, that's not true. I simply maintain that at the moment any information I can get on her could be extremely useful."

Teresa seemed unconvinced, but continued telling her story.

"Elena went and joined him after six months, if I remember correctly. Franco had already found the space for their workshop and had moved into a lovely cottage not far away."

"And what happened next?"

"What happened was that as clients began slowly to trickle in, and the workshop started doing well, their marriage began to show the first signs of stress. Elena told me that life in such a small town was a burden for her. She was unable to integrate with the local people and, given her personality, this made her suffer. On top of everything else, she'd also been made an excellent offer by the company she'd worked for earlier. Franco managed to persuade her to remain true to their dream, but Elena wasn't happy anymore. And then . . ."

The woman trailed off. Moments later, she said:

"I feel terribly uneasy about this."

"Why?" asked Montalbano.

"Because I'd promised myself never to tell anyone about any of this. Especially now that Elena and Franco are both dead. I feel as if I'm violating an intimacy that they are no longer able to protect."

"Signora, I understand you perfectly. But bear in mind that I am not a journalist but a policeman. The purpose of my questions is only, and exclusively, to help solve the case."

"What happened was that at a certain point Elena realized that Franco was treating her more like a business partner than his own wife. She also told me that he had changed ever since she'd moved to Bellosguardo. He was distant, engrossed in his work and not very involved in their marriage. She felt like she was losing him, and so she reacted in the most natural way for a woman to react: She told Franco she wanted a child. She said to me afterwards that the violence of his reaction almost frightened her. He claimed it would have been sheer folly to have a child at that moment, that it would greatly limit Elena's work possibilities, that it would be a burden, and that therefore there was no point in even talking about it. He attacked her, she told me in tears; I remember that perfectly. And so the rift between them began to grow by the day. And that, I think, was the beginning of their crisis."

"Forgive me," said the inspector, "for touching on an area obviously very painful to you. Did Elena ever tell you why, in her opinion, Franco committed suicide?"

"Yes. It was after a particularly violent quarrel brought on when Elena gave him an ultimatum: either they had a child or she would quit the workshop. Franco went out of the house that evening, slamming the door behind him, and was found the following morning, with his hands tied, dead by drowning in the town river."

"With his hands tied? How?" Montalbano asked in amazement.

"Franco was an excellent swimmer, and the police said he'd tied his own hands to prevent himself from giving in to the natural instinct for survival, and then threw himself into the river."

For a moment the woman seemed to have lost her breath. Two tears slid silently down her cheeks.

Montalbano felt like putting his arm around her, but restrained himself.

"But . . ." said Teresa, immediately stopping short.

"But?" said Montalbano, coaxing her.

"But I want to be utterly sincere with you. To this day, I have never been entirely convinced that Elena was telling me the whole truth."

"What reason would she have for not telling you?"

"I wouldn't know. Maybe Franco had somehow offended her womanhood. Or perhaps Elena wanted to spare me further details, thinking they would reopen old wounds. That's the feeling I've always had, that Elena was trying to protect me from something. I'd just lost my parents, and then Franco had to go in such an awful way. Maybe Elena was trying to avoid hurting me more."

"Some witnesses have told me," said the inspector, "that Elena would sometimes receive phone calls that left her very troubled and shaken. Did that ever happen in your presence?"

"No, never."

She smiled bitterly.

"But to tell you the truth, I'm starting to remember a rather 'bitter' phone call Franco received the last time he came to visit us."

15

"Why bitter?"

"He was simply furious, I remember. And he made some reference to an assistant at the workshop, a woman, who'd behaved badly, or something similar. But even though he cut the subject short, he remained in a terrible mood for the rest of his stay in Vigàta."

"As far as you know, did Elena remain in touch with anyone from Bellosguardo?"

"No. These past few days I've wondered several times whom I should inform of Elena's passing. And, strangely, I haven't been able to think of a single name from her past. My brother's suicide was so traumatic and devastating for her that she clearly wanted to bury that whole period."

She took a deep breath.

"Do you feel tired?"

"Frankly, yes."

"I can drive you home, if you like."

"Thank you," said Teresa, standing up.

They walked along the little lane leading to the exit. Then Teresa stopped, as though suddenly worried about something.

"But what about Rinaldo?" she asked. "What's become of Rinaldo?"

"He's presently in the care of one of our officers," replied the inspector. "I was thinking of asking Meriam to take him."

"No," Teresa said decisively. "I want him myself."

"That's not a problem. I'll have him brought to your house by the end of the day."

They were now out of the cemetery. The inspector walked towards his car, parked not far away, with Teresa following behind.

He opened the passenger's-side door and bent forward to retrieve from the seat the little transparent bag with the blue scrap in it. Then he stepped aside to let Teresa in, but the woman stopped dead in her tracks, her eyes affixed to the little bag.

"What is that?" she asked in a quavering voice.

At first Montalbano didn't know how to respond, since the truth of that scrap of fabric really would have been too brutal for Teresa. And so he took a roundabout path.

"It's a piece of fabric I found in Elena's shop and want examined by the crime lab."

"Let me see it," Teresa said gruffly. It was almost an order. Montalbano obeyed.

Teresa took the little plastic bag, raised it up to eye level, and studied it. Then she said:

"I know what this is."

The inspector stood there in silence, looking deep into her eyes. With her voice nearly cracking, Teresa continued:

"It's from the scarf that Franco used to tie his hands before throwing himself into the river. Elena kept it in a drawer with all the other things from her marriage."

"Which drawer?"

"Her desk drawer. In the bedroom. The third and bottom drawer on the right."

The one he'd found completely empty.

Teresa kept holding up the little bag, eyeing it attentively, and the inspector didn't feel up to taking it away from her. As she was studying it, the woman started shaking the bag to get a better look at the fabric.

"It looks to me like it's been torn," she said.

"Yes," said Montalbano.

"But the last time I saw it, it was whole. And it wasn't so dirty. What are these stains?"

Montalbano took the little bag out of her hand.

"That's what I'm taking it to the crime lab to find out."

And as he was congratulating himself for his excellent lie, he shut the car door for Teresa, who had finally managed to move, and then got in on the driver's side to head off to the woman's house.

Montalbano parked the car and went to open the passenger door. Teresa got out and stopped in front of him.

"You must make me a promise," she said.

"All right."

"I want to be the first to know the killer's name."

"You will be," said Montalbano. "And do not forget that I want to be the first to hear of anything you might remember in the meanwhile concerning Elena's past and present. Even if it's something that seems of no importance to you."

"I promise."

They shook hands. Montalbano waited for her to go through the front door, then got back in the car and, before starting it up, glanced at his watch.

It was two o'clock. He sped off in the direction of Enzo's trattoria.

Along the way he managed to blot the entire conversation with Teresa out of his mind.

He wanted to think only of eating while eating.

Upon entering the restaurant he almost collided with Beba, who was coming out with a large, steaming pot, followed by another woman with an identical pot.

There was no need for him to ask whether the dish of the day would again be "migrants' soup."

Beba greeted him hastily, and he replied with a nod and went and sat down at his usual table.

"No need to tell me anything," he said to Enzo as soon as the restaurateur approached. "Just bring me some of that soup."

Enzo thanked him with his eyes and went into the kitchen.

When the inspector left the restaurant, he felt heavy again, because, like the first time, he'd slurped down two helpings, along with a platter of fried baby octopus and shrimp.

The stroll along the jetty was rather labored, and when he went and sat on the flat rock, he was out of breath.

He waited for the sea air to blow a cool gust into his brain, and then started thinking again about everything Teresa had told him.

Two clear, indeed obvious, things jumped out from her words: that Elena spoke very little, if at all, about the period of her marriage, and when she was in one way or another forced to do so, she was careful to limit herself to singing only half the Mass. Even Teresa had noticed this in her sister-in-law's behavior.

What had happened in Elena's past that had to remain buried with her husband?

And might those telephone calls actually be an unpleasant echo of that past?

And if that was the case, who was the mysterious person at the other end of the line?

He realized that "line" might not actually be the correct word, since the phone calls to both Elena and Franco had all been made on cell phones.

Well, line or not, this was a lead to be further explored, because it just might prove to solve the case. Still, what had struck him even more was the story about Franco tying his own hands with the scarf to prevent himself from swimming instinctively once he jumped into the river.

How had the local police, or the carabinieri, been able to establish with such certainty that Franco had tied his own hands?

In other words: How had they managed to rule out the hypothesis of murder? This, too, was a fundamental point.

He took out his cell phone and called Catarella.

"Cat, there are two things I have to tell you. First, you must take Rinaldo to the house of Signora Elena's sister-in-law, in Via della Regione, 18 . . ."

"Ah, no, Chief! 'At'll break my heart! Jess iss mornin', isstead o' goin' all hissy hissy, 'e started purrin' for me . . ."

"I'm sorry, Cat. But I also want you immediately to find me the telephone number of the sexton of the cemetery and give it to me."

"Okay, Chief, le's see . . . Signor Sexton . . ."

"No, Cat. That's not his name. I don't know his name.

He's just the sexton of the cemetery—you know, the guardian."

"Sorry, Chief. Whatcha gonna do? 'Ang up or stay onna line?"

"I'll stay on and wait."

"Be right wit' yiz, Chief."

Catarella really wasted no time this time.

Two minutes later, the inspector was calling the sexton.

"This is Inspector Montalbano."

"What can I do for you, sir? I noticed I had the pleasure of seeing you here just this morning."

Only a sexton could use the word "pleasure" to describe seeing someone at the cemetery.

"I would like to ask a favor of you. I want you to go into the Guida family vault and tell me the date of Franco Guida's death."

"Of course, I can do that! Want me to call you back, Inspector, or will you call me?"

Montalbano gave him his cell phone number.

He sat there watching a fishing trawler slowly enter the port.

The cell phone rang.

"Inspector, Franco Guida died on February 19, 2002. Do you need anything else?"

"No, nothing else, thanks. Have a good day."

He wrote the date down on a piece of paper he had in his pocket.

Then he called Catarella back.

"I need you to do a search for me."

"Atcha soivice, Chief," Catarella said enthusiastically.

"Get me all the death notices for Franco Guida that you can find. To repeat: Franco Guida," said the inspector, pronouncing all the letters explicitly. "He died on February 19, 2002, and you should look in the newspapers of the Friuli region. I repeat: Friuli. But also look for anything you can find in our local papers as well."

"Awright, Chief, 'iss kind o' ting's rilly easy nowadays wit' the interneck."

The inspector headed back, one slow step at a time, to his car, but on the way he thought it best to make one more phone call.

"Ciao, Fernà. If I come to Montelusa right now, can you give me five minutes?"

"Sure, I'll be waiting for you. Is this about that piece of cloth?"

"Yes."

━━━━

"Gimme the cloth," Leanza said rudely, without saying hello, "so I can take it to Micheluzzi."

"Wait a second," Montalbano said, surprised. "What's wrong? Did I somehow offend you?"

"No, Salvo, you didn't. I'm just pissed off at my men."

"Why?"

"Because we attached no importance whatsoever to that scrap of cloth, whereas it was in fact very important, if now you're thrusting it in my face."

"No, Fernà, that's not right, because neither you nor me,

for that matter, knew at the time how valuable that scrap might be."

"All right," said Leanza. "Have a seat and wait for me. If you want I've got a little whisky to help you pass the time."

"No, thanks," replied Montalbano, "but do you think I could smoke a cigarette?"

"Tell you what," said Leanza. "I'll lock you in so no one can enter."

Montalbano had to smoke three cigarettes before Leanza reappeared.

"Micheluzzi says the tear is very recent. Whereas the fabric is more than ten years old. Now tell me why this scrap of cloth is so important."

"So, in your opinion, could the tear be attributed to scissors?"

"I've already got the answer to that: Micheluzzi says that if it had been made by scissors, the cut would have been clean. No, it was torn by hand. And another thing: They say that there are long folds across the entire piece, as if it had been folded and compressed for a long time, as if stored away. Make sense to you?"

"It makes sense to me," said Montalbano. "And thanks."

"What? And you're going to leave me hanging, just like that? Aren't you going to fill me in on anything?"

"You'll have to forgive me, Fernà, but I'm still pretty vague and confused about this whole story. If I tried to explain anything to you, it would probably end up being all bullshit."

They said good-bye, and Montalbano took the little plastic bag and headed back to the station.

"Did you take the cat to the lady?"

"Did it straightaways, Chief. But, man, it rilly broke my 'eart to do it. And when the lady saw the cat, she started cryin' an' 'enn she hugged it and kissed it all over. And so I decided 'at Rinaldo was in good 'ands, an' I felt a li'l better."

"Well, if you want to feel even better, there's a mama cat with two kittens right beside where I parked my car."

"Know what I'm gonna do?" said Catarella. "Since I got some cat food left over, I'm gonna go an' take it to 'em right now."

"Are you doing that newspaper research I asked you to do?"

"Assolutely, Chief! An' I even awriddy foun' two long arcticles. Bu' I'm still lookin', Chief, irrelentlissly. I ain't wastin' a single minnit."

"Thanks, Cat. Listen, is anyone here?"

"Yeah, Chief. Isspector Augello's onna premisses."

"Send him to me."

As soon as Mimì came in and quietly sat down, Montalbano could tell, from the dark expression he was wearing, that Mimì had some bad news.

"What's wrong?"

"What's wrong is that there's an enormous pain in the ass."

"Meaning?"

"Meaning that five minutes ago the commissioner called me to tell me to make myself and ten other men available to Sileci tonight."

"So that shit's starting all over again?" asked Montalbano.

"The commissioner said tonight is an exception. But, in essence, it's the same old story. The shears fly into the air and end up in the gardener's asshole. Apparently they're expecting about seven hundred desperadoes tonight . . . And that's only the first pain in the ass."

"And what's the second?"

"The second is that the investigating judge is not inclined to validate the arrest of that big turd Trupia."

"And why not?"

"Because the defense lawyer was very clever and managed to convince him that lack of an alibi is no indication of guilt and that there's no evidence against him. And then the judge said he would take twenty-four hours to decide. But I'm sure he's going to set him free."

"Tell me something, Mimì," Montalbano said with a grin. "If he'd been put on trial, would you have become a witness for the prosecution because he screwed a woman you wanted?"

"You are such an asshole, Salvo. I am deeply convinced he is the killer, and even if he's set free, I won't let him breathe freely for so much as one second. I will find no peace until I have proved his guilt."

Montalbano started applauding.

"What is wrong with you?" asked Mimì, taken aback.

"Brilliant! Splendid performance! I felt like I was watching an American movie. If you do it over again, with the same emphasis, I'll whistle the background music."

"Fuck off!" said Mimì, getting up and slamming the door on his way out.

A split second later, the same door opened again and Fazio appeared, and upon sitting down he noticed the little plastic bag with the blue fabric and sat there staring at it in silence, his face darkening.

"Have you suddenly lost your voice?"

"No, Chief. It's you who should do the talking."

"About what?"

"Well, for example, this piece of cloth, which the last time I saw it was on the worktable in Signora Elena's shop."

"Okay, I'll tell you everything. Do you remember that it was bloodstained because the killer had wiped the scissors with it, and that it was also torn?"

"Yes."

"Well, leaving out the finer details, I can tell you that I became curious to know whether that tear was recent, and so I went to the forensics lab, and they told me that the rip is quite new, but the fabric is rather old."

"And what does that mean?"

"It means what Signora Teresa explained to me."

"Please explain it to me, too."

"Okay, listen up. Franco, Elena's husband, took his own life by throwing himself into a river. To thwart his natural instinct for survival, he tied his own hands so he couldn't swim. With this same scarf."

Fazio's coppish instincts got the better of him.

"But how could they be so sure it wasn't somebody else who tied his hands? Such as, for example, the very same person who wanted to kill him and make it look like a suicide?"

"That's what I'm waiting for Catarella to tell me."

"For Catarella to tell you?"

"Yes. I asked him to collect all the obituaries from the papers concerning that suicide. But there's something that's had me thinking a lot. Which is this: The scarf had been kept along with papers and other stuff in the bottom drawer of Elena's desk. But when I opened that drawer, it was completely empty. Which, in plain words, means the killer took away everything that was in that drawer. The troubling question that all this raises is the following: Why did Elena pull that scarf out and take it into the big workroom? The only answer I've been able to come up with so far is that she wanted to show it to the killer."

"And why would she want to do that?"

"Dunno. In fact, at the moment, only God knows." After a brief pause, the inspector continued: "Any news about the kid?"

"I summoned him for nine o'clock tomorrow morning."

"Good. Listen, it's getting pretty late, so we can go home now."

The phone rang.

"Ah, Chief, 'ere'd a happen a be a Mister Measles onna line wantin' a talk t'yiz poissonally in poisson."

"Tell me, Cat, is he contagious?"

"Oh, my Gah, Chief! I don' know. Ya tink 'e might be contatious? E'en over the phone?! *Matre santa*, Chief! When I was a kid I got the mamps, but never the mizzles!"

"Do this, Cat: Put him through to me and then go and disinfect your ear with a little alcohol."

"Tanks, Chief. Ya rilly know so much!"

"This is Montalbano here. And you are Mr. . . . ."

"Aurelio Mizzillis," said a deep, gravelly, pedantic old man's voice.

"What can I do for you, sir?"

"Fifteen minutes ago I got back from Palermo."

Silence.

"Glad to hear it," said Montalbano.

Then, blocking the mouthpiece, he whispered to Fazio:

"I think we can have a little fun with this guy. You listen in, too."

He turned on the speakerphone. But since the man at the other end was still silent, the inspector prodded him.

"And do you intend to stay for a while in Vigàta?"

"I live here. In Via Giosuè Cusumano, number 22, where my family's been living for generations."

"My compliments," said Montalbano, winking at Fazio. "Got anything else of interest to tell me, Mr. Mizzillis?"

"Yes, sir, I do. In fact, I'm calling you because I need someone to help my wife deliver her burden."

"Why, is she pregnant?"

"No, Inspector, she's seventy years old, and I'm not kidding. And we have four grandchildren from our two sons, whose names are Antonio and Filippo."

"My warmest congratulations. And now I must say good-bye, because . . ."

"Please wait just a minute. You absolutely must help relieve Concettina of her burden."

"And Concettina would be your wife?"

"Yes, sir, and she absolutely must free herself of this burden, which she's been carrying in her heart and was unable to unload because I was away in Palermo."

"And what is this burden?"

"The burden is the fact that my wife suffers from insomnia at night, and so she spends her time watching."

"Watching TV?" Montalbano suggested.

"No, Inspector. Television only makes her eyelids flutter."

"So what does she watch?"

"She watches the building in front of ours."

One practically had to pull the words out of Mr. Mizzillis with pliers.

"And what does she see in the building in front?"

"Well, for example, she saw Diego Trupia."

Montalbano's and Fazio's expressions changed. The smiles they had on their faces vanished.

"And what was he doing?"

"Nothing, Inspector. He was sitting down watching television."

"Yes, but when was this?"

"Well done, Inspector. It's clear you're a great cop, as the concierge of my building said to me. And that's the weight my Concettina's been wanting to get off her chest: On the night that poor Signora Elena was killed, Diego Trupia watched TV until two o'clock in the morning. Then he turned off his set and went into his bedroom, but as soon as she saw him start to get undressed, my wife, who is an honest, chaste woman, turned her eyes to the window two floors above him, where she watched Signor Anzalone play cards with his friends until daybreak."

And so, just like that, Trupia suddenly had an alibi, and was now off the hook!

"Listen, Mr. Mizzillis," said the inspector, "would your wife be willing to come to the police station and make a declaration of what you have just told us?"

"Of course. Now that I'm back from Palermo, I can bring her to you."

"Then I would like to ask you a favor: Could you come right now?"

"All right, Inspector. We'll be there in half an hour."

"Thank you so much, and please, when you get here, ask for Inspector Augello, who will be waiting to take your deposition. Thank you again. You've been very helpful," said Montalbano, before hanging up.

Then he rang Augello's office.

"Listen, Mimì, I've just now got a phone call from a guy named Mizzillis, whose wife has some important information concerning Trupia. I'm hoping it's something that'll help you corner him. They'll be here in half an hour."

"Thanks, Salvo. You're a real friend," said Mimì.

Montalbano stood up, circled around his desk three times, humming and hopping first on one foot, then on the other, before Fazio's astonished eyes, which seemed to be saying: *What a great big son of a bitch my boss is!*

"I'm gonna go home now," said the inspector.

"Okay," said Fazio. "But I don't want to miss this."

"That way you can tell me about it tomorrow."

16

While heading home to Marinella, he suddenly felt terribly thirsty. He tried to produce a little saliva in his mouth, but it was like searching for water in a desert. He actually had trouble swallowing, and so the first thing he did when he went into his house was race into the kitchen.

He opened the tap, filled a glass, downed it in one gulp, and then turned off the water. Or, more correctly, he closed the knob, but the water kept coming out. Apparently the gasket was stripped. So he opened the tap again and then reclosed it forcefully. The result was the opposite of the desired one. The flow of water increased. *Matre santa!* In half an hour's time the kitchen was likely to be flooded. He went to close the main valve, then hurried back inside to look for the plumber's phone number.

He was sure he'd written it down in his little red address book.

But where had he put the book?

He started looking for it in the area around the telephone, then suddenly froze.

The luminous snake that had been flashing in his brain every so often had returned, with the difference that this time the thought was no longer vague and confused, but in fact clear and precise.

What a lamebrained dickh—well, let's just say feeble-minded old codger—he was! He'd completely forgotten to look for Elena's address book!

Not wanting to lose so much as one second of time, he put his jacket back on, checked to see whether he had the keys to Elena's shop in the pocket, as well as his cell phone, and then, leaving all the lights on, drove off to Via Garibaldi.

Given the hour and lack of traffic, he parked without difficulty, got out of the car, opened the front door, and climbed the stairs. He recalled that there were two phones there: one on a nightstand in the bedroom and the other on the small table in the corridor.

He started with the bedroom. There was no address book. He opened the drawer of the nightstand and found a pair of women's glasses, a book, a box of sleeping pills, and a handkerchief. He closed it and looked in the other nightstand. Nothing.

He went back downstairs into the corridor and pulled out the little table. Not a trace of any address book. Just to be thorough, he opened the drawers of the big table in the workroom and rummaged through the scraps of fabric, but nothing doing.

And so he sat down in the armchair to think.

And his cogitations led him to a negative conclusion. Probably, as had become the custom with most people, Elena no longer wrote her telephone numbers down in an address book but merely registered them on her cell phone.

For a moment he lost heart. Then he realized there was still one more chance, and he went back upstairs and sat down at the blue desk.

He opened the first drawer on the left, pulled it all the way out, took it in both hands, and set it down before him. He began taking the papers out by the handful, and with the second load, something red slid out from the mass of papers and fell to the floor: It was a little daybook exactly like his. From three years earlier. He picked it up, opened it just a crack, and saw that it was densely filled with names and numbers. Closing it, he put it in his jacket pocket, put everything back in place, and headed home.

He had unburdened himself, as Mizzillis might have said, of one worry.

So pleased was he that he caught himself singing a little Beatles tune in broken English: *Lov, lov mi du.*

When he got home, he went to set Elena's address book down near the phone, and since colors attract like to like, his little red book appeared on the shelf right in front of him.

He wasted no time calling the plumber, and they planned for him to come the following morning around eleven, when Adelina would be there. The man also told him how to resolve the problem temporarily.

He went into the kitchen, took a cork, and, using a knife, forcefully worked it into the mouth of the tap until it was snug. Then he took a rag and looped it under the cork, securing it with a tight knot. After reopening the main valve, he saw that the expedient held up.

The unexpected rediscovery of his own address book triggered a wolflike hunger in him, and so, while he was at it, he went and had a look at what was in the refrigerator.

And here he made a second discovery: rice *sartù* with fish, one of Adelina's glorious inventions. He put it in the oven to warm, then went to see if the conditions were right for eating on the veranda. They were, and so he went about setting the table. When he figured the *sartù* was warm enough, he took it outside, sat down, heaved a long sigh of satisfaction, and started eating.

Once he'd finished and cleared the table, he sat down in the armchair with Elena's daybook in his lap. Then he decided it was best for him to call Livia first, so he wouldn't be interrupted later.

"Hi, Livia. Sorry, but I've only got a minute. A ship with seven hundred migrants is coming into port, a lot of them children and injured . . . I'll be out all night."

"Poor Salvo, I'm so sorry! What a tragedy!"

"I know, but it's my job. Good night, Livia."

"Good night, my love."

He opened to the page with the letter A, and began looking at the names. Adamo, Salvatore, and number. Almirante, Rosalinda, who had three numbers: two land lines and one cell phone. There was also her home address.

When he got to the letter N, he became convinced the book contained only Sicilian numbers and addresses: The exchanges were all from Montelusa, Catellonisetta, Palermo, Trapani, and so on.

At the letter S, he was beginning to lose hope. There were only three names: Savatteri, Ernesto; Sirch, Nevia; and Siracusa, Valerio.

As he was about to turn the page, he flipped back to it. Nevia Sirch.

That was not a Sicilian name.

There were two numbers, for a cell phone and a land line, as well as the address.

Via Orta, 3, Bellosguardo.

Then he remembered that Teresa had spoken to him about that very same town, which was in Udine province.

So it wasn't true that Elena had burned all the bridges to her past.

He had a powerful urge he was unable to resist.

He got up, went over to the telephone, and dialed the number.

"Hello?"

It was a woman's voice, in a cadence so northern it was frightening.

"Hello, who is this?" the woman repeated.

Montalbano, to his surprise, didn't know what to say and hung up.

Then he had an idea and redialed the number.

"Hello? Who is this?"

"Then I guess they gave me the wrong number! This isn't the home of Signor Siracusa, is it?"

"No, I'm sorry, it's not. This is the Sirch home."

"Sorry to bother you," said Montalbano, ending the conversation. But he'd found out what he wanted to know. Nevia Sirch had not changed her phone number and was still in Bellosguardo.

He reviewed in his mind the various commissariats and police bureaucracies in that region, but couldn't think of any friends or acquaintances there.

It was too late to come up with any more ideas concerning this Nevia. It was probably best to wait and talk it over with Fazio in the morning.

He decided to go to bed, grabbing the first book that came to hand, and went into the bathroom. Afterwards, lying down, he opened the book and realized he'd brought with him the book of postal codes. Rather than get up again, he started reading it, amusing himself with the strange names certain Italian towns and villages had. Then he came to the towns with bridges: Ponte a Bozzone, Pontecuti, Ponte Este . . . and, little by little, his eyelids drooped and he fell asleep.

How long had he been asleep when the ringing of the telephone woke him up? He'd left the light on. He looked at the clock. It was two-thirty. Something huge must have happened at the docks. Cursing, he went to answer the phone, and from Augello's tone of distress he realized that his prediction was not incorrect.

"You'll have to forgive me, Salvo, but you need to go to the station."

"Why?"

"Because, as the migrants were disembarking, two women started shouting, and one pulled out a knife and severely wounded the other. All hell broke loose, Salvo, and I can't really tell you about it now because the friends of the first woman then started brawling with the friends of the other one."

"And what's the situation now?"

"The injured woman has been taken to the hospital in Montelusa, and the others are all on the bus, ready to leave."

"So what the hell has any of this to do with me?"

"It has to do with you because the knife assailant is at the station. So, if you want to leave her all night in the holding cell, that's your business. And seeing that you were so ready and able to worry about Trupia, I thought it was best that I worry a little about you."

So Mimì had decided to even the score.

Montalbano hung up without saying a word.

He would go to the station, but this brought to mind a serious problem. After the kind of day they'd had, he just didn't have the heart to wake up either Meriam or Dr. Osman.

And so? How was he going to talk to this woman? He wasn't. The only thing to do was to go back to sleep and to get to the station no later than seven-thirty the next morning, since Lillo Scotto would be coming in at nine.

Before closing his eyes, he remembered Mimì's words: *Two women started shouting, and one pulled out a knife and severely wounded the other.*

He didn't even feel like asking himself why these words had come back to him. There must be a reason, but he was too sleepy and in no condition to devote any thought to the matter.

The first thing Catarella did was hand him four sheets of paper.

"Chief, 'a'ss evveryting I foun' inna news inna newspapers, onna basis o' wha' ya tol' me."

"Very well done," said Montalbano, putting the pages in his jacket pocket. "Who's on the premises?"

"Fazio's on 'em."

"Send him to me."

He sat down and took the pages out of his pocket. Three of the newspapers were from the north. Only one, the *Giornale dell'Isola*, was Sicilian, and it devoted some ten lines to Franco's suicide. He took the time to read them. They were utterly generic and contained no new information.

At this point Fazio walked in.

"Why are you in so early today?"

"Chief, Inspector Augello called me last night after talking to you and told me about the stabbing, and after that I wasn't able to fall asleep."

"Okay," said Montalbano. "I'm going to call Osman now, because I'll need him if I'm going to question this woman."

"Already taken care of," said Fazio.

Montalbano could barely keep from flying across the desk and grabbing his assistant by the throat. Instead, he faked a coughing fit, to calm himself down.

"What does that mean, 'already taken care of'?" he asked.

"It means that this morning I looked through the peephole at this woman, and she was sitting there crying desperately. So I opened the door and comforted her, and since she spoke Italian, I questioned her. She said that the other woman had tried to steal a piece of bread from her three-year-old son. First on the barge, a second time on the motorboat, and a third time when they were disembarking onto the dock. At that point she lost her head and grabbed her knife."

Montalbano sat there for a moment in silence. Then he asked:

"Do you have any news of the woman who was sent to the hospital?"

"Yeah, Chief. She's out of danger."

"All right, then, let's do this: In half an hour, at the most, you call the prosecutor, explain the situation to him, and throw everything into his lap. I have other things to worry about. When Lillo Scotto gets here, I want you back in my office to make a written record of the interrogation."

"Okay, Chief," said Fazio, going out.

A short while later Montalbano stood up, crossed the hall, and went and had a look at the woman through the peephole, as Fazio had done.

She was a poor woman of about thirty, tiny and wearing a long skirt, a kerchief round her head, and a sort of shapeless sweater full of holes that must at one time have been green in color.

Closing the spy hole, he went back into his office and rang Dr. Pasquano.

"Good morning, Doctor."

Pasquano recognized his voice at once.

"Good morning, my ass! What the hell's going through your head to think of calling at this hour?"

"What happened? Did you lose at poker last night?"

"None of your fucking business. What do you want to know?"

"I would like to know whether a woman armed with a pair of scissors is capable of killing another woman."

"If the woman is as big a ballbuster as you are, then why not? Rage and hatred multiply anyone's strength, which is something you surely knew when you were young but have now forgotten, since old age is erasing your memory. And on that note, good-bye."

This changed the situation entirely. It was possible he now had to change the gender of the word and consider the murderer a murderess.

He resumed reading the papers. Two articles were from the *Gazzettino*, but published five days apart.

The first one reported the news of the mysterious death of Franco Guida, a promising young figure in the Italian fashion world, whose body had been found in the river near Bellosguardo with the hands bound by a scarf. This immediately led people to presume foul play, but the police came to a different conclusion, which was that the young man had tied his own hands together to prevent himself from trying to swim, as Teresa had said.

The second article basically reported the findings of the autopsy, which were that before throwing himself into the river, Franco had numbed himself with enough sedatives to kill him all by themselves. The police therefore concluded that this result confirmed the fact that he'd bound his own hands—in other words, that Franco had done everything possible to make sure he would die.

The third newspaper more or less hewed to the conclusion of the *Gazzettino*, adding one notable detail. The article's author had managed to speak with the widow, who admitted that on the evening of his death, Franco had left the house after quarreling fiercely with her. But the woman did not wish, under any circumstances, to reveal the reason for their quarrel.

There was a knock at the door. Fazio came in.

"All taken care of. The paddy wagon's on the way to transfer the woman to Montelusa prison."

"To the prison? Lately our esteemed national prisons don't confine anyone but these poor wretches anymore!"

"Yeah, Chief, but we're talking about attempted murder."

"Of course, Fazio, but attempted murder spurred by hunger and despair. Do you ever wonder where the people are who send these wretches to their deaths on these ships? They're all in the European Union, dictating guidelines on immigration while chowing down on our local fillet of sole!"

Fazio fell silent.

The telephone rang.

"'At'd be the Scottatis onna premisses, mutter an' son."

"Please show them in."

An odd procession entered in single file. The first to appear in the door was Lillo, who could barely stand on his own two feet; followed by his mother, who was holding him up by the shoulders from behind, practically pushing him; with Catarella bringing up the rear, also propping up the lady, who was clearly teetering, his hands on her hips.

Fazio shot to his feet and, to prevent the little train from derailing, grabbed Lillo and sat him down in the chair opposite Montalbano's desk.

Catarella led Lillo's mother to the other chair.

Catarella then left, closing the door behind him.

Montalbano was struck by the fact that Lillo's face didn't look as boyish as he'd remembered it.

The young man's wrists were bandaged, and he looked like a ghost.

He spoke first.

"I didn't kill Signora Elena," he said.

"He didn't do it! He didn't do it!" the mother cut in loudly. "I can swear it on my mother's grave. He was in his room all evening on that awful night!"

"Please calm down. So far nobody has leveled any accusations against your son. Did you receive any phone calls or visits that evening from anyone outside the family?"

"We sure did!" the woman said at once. "For the last week or more, once he got off work, Lillo would just shut himself up in his room, and didn't even want to eat or sleep or watch TV with the rest of us. And so round about eleven o'clock on the terrible night that Signora Elena was killed, he got so agitated, so nervous, so strange—and it was like he could feel wha' was happening at Elena's—that I called Dr. Camilleri and told him to give him something to make him feel a little better."

"And did the doctor come?"

"Sure he came. He's a good man! An' he stayed with my boy for at least forty-five minutes, talkin' to him an' tryin' to get him to take a pill so he could rest."

And this erased any doubt that might remain as to Lillo's innocence.

Since the youngster hadn't opened his mouth the whole time his mother was talking, the inspector turned to him.

"How long had you been working at Elena's shop?"

"In a week it would have been two years," the mother replied.

Montalbano moved his chair a little bit to get a better angle on the son.

"Tell me, Lillo, did you immediately feel comfortable with the other people working there?"

"He was all excited when he come home from work the first day, Inspector. They were all very fond of my son, you see . . ."

At this point Montalbano looked up and his eyes met Fazio's.

They immediately understood each other.

"Signora," said Fazio. "You're going to have to wait outside. Please come with me."

"Why?" the woman protested. "Why? I'm the boy's mother, for heaven's sake! And I want to hear everything you want to know about my poor Lilluzzo."

"Please, signora. Lillo is a legal adult," the inspector said firmly. "Please go and wait outside."

The woman stood up, went over and kissed Lillo once on the forehead, twice on the cheeks, again on the forehead, and then on the lips, until Fazio grabbed her by the arm and took her out.

"I had your mother leave because I need to ask you some strictly personal questions. Did you immediately fall in love with Signora Elena?"

Lillo blushed. He then brought his hands to his face and stayed that way for a few moments before replying.

"No, not immediately."

"When, then?"

"One day when Signora Elena was in her apartment she called me upstairs to lend her a hand in the bathroom, 'cause she cut her finger badly on a rusty tool. The blood was coming out so fast that I instinctively grabbed her hand and started sucking the blood. I was about to spit it into the sink when I thought maybe that was the wrong thing to do, and so I swallowed it. Then I opened the medicine chest and disinfected it for her and put some gauze and then a Band-Aid over it. But the whole time I was doing that I noticed she was watching me, an' she never stopped watching me. An' so I did my whole routine really, really slowly, 'cause I was starting to like feeling her eyes on me. Then, when I was done, Elena gave me a hug and held me tight and said, 'Thank you, Lillo, thank you so much.' But she said it in my ear, in a voice I'd never heard before that got me all worked up. I don't really know what happened to me. Maybe it was her blood, which I could still taste in my mouth. But from that moment on I lost my head. I couldn't stay away from her, an' all I could think about was her. It's like I wasn't myself anymore. I was like a puppet in the puppet theater, after he drinks the love potion. I was under a spell . . ."

Lillo trailed off and started weeping.

Fazio, the good Samaritan, ran to get him a glass of water.

"One last question," said Montalbano, "and then you're free to go. I've learned that a few days before her death, Signora Elena scolded you harshly and decided to terminate your employment with her. Can you tell me exactly what happened?"

"As I said, Inspector, I was completely out of my head, an' so I suddenly got insanely jealous an' would try to answer the phone whenever it rang so I could see if she had a lover or boyfriend. That day I was alone in the big room because Nicola had gone to deliver a garment to a client. Meriam was in the fitting room, and Elena was upstairs in her apartment. All of a sudden I heard a cell phone ring, and I realized Elena had left hers on the table," said Lillo, pausing for a moment. "Could I have another glass of water?" he asked.

Fazio got up and brought him another glass.

"As you can imagine," the youth resumed, "I didn't want to miss this chance. So I grabbed the cell phone and saw a name, but I couldn't tell if it was a first or last name . . ."

"Stop right there!" said Montalbano. "Think this over carefully and try to remember this name . . ."

"I'm sorry, Inspector, but I just draw a complete blank. But I can tell you it was a woman's voice, and—"

"Was her accent from around here or was she from another part of the country?"

"She was definitely from far away, Inspector. She had a strange way of talking."

"Lillo, did her name sound anything like the word 'navy'?"

"I dunno, Inspector. I just remember her asking me why Elena didn't answer instead of me, and I was telling her why, but then Elena came storming into the room, jumped on me, and yanked the phone out of my hand. Man, I never seen her so mad! She looked at the phone and then said: 'I'll call you back.' Then she grabbed me by my jacket and started shaking me like she wanted to shake something out of me, and she asked me in the strangest voice: 'What did she say to you? What did she say to you? Did she say she was coming here? Did she say when? Speak, speak, you fool!' I tried to tell her she didn't really say anything to me, but Elena wasn't listening anymore. She just turned her back and went upstairs with her cell phone, and I just sat there in a daze."

"And what happened next?"

"When she came back downstairs about ten minutes later, Inspector, she told me, in front of Nicola and Meriam, that she didn't want me coming back to the store after the end of the month."

"Okay, thanks, Lillo," said Montalbano. "You've been very helpful to me."

17

From the hallway came the loud voice of Lillo's mother.

"Wha'd they ask you, my boy? Tell me everything, dear, you must tell your mother everything."

It occurred to Montalbano that to be orphaned of a Southern Italian mother might not necessarily be a bad thing.

Fazio returned at once, closed the door behind him, sat down, and stared at the inspector.

"What is it? Do you not recognize me or something? Shall I introduce myself? Hello, I'm Inspector Montalbano."

"You may feel like joking, but I don't."

"What's got into you?"

"What's got into me is the fact that you still haven't told me what you're thinking. Why did you ask Lillo that question about the navy?"

"Fazio, it's not as if we've had a lot of free time. At any rate, here I am. I'll tell you the conclusions I've come to and how I got there."

It took him about half an hour to tell him the whole story, and when he'd finished he asked:

"So, does that make sense to you?"

"It makes enough sense, Chief, but there are a few things still on shaky ground. For example, there's no guarantee this

Nevia is the killer, just because hers is the only out-of-towner's name in an address book from three years ago."

"You're right," said the inspector. "But there are also some other things that don't add up. Elena's sister-in-law said that she'd broken off all contact with her prior married life. Apparently she was lying, since at least until three years ago, she still had a relationship with someone from that world."

"And there's another thing," said Fazio. "If this murderess, as you call her, got so covered in blood that she needed to take a shower, how was she able to leave the house in all her bloodstained clothes? Being from out of town she would have had to take some kind of public transportation, and she would have been noticed."

"Unless she came here in her car."

"But then she wouldn't have been able to get out of the car until she was back home in Friuli. She couldn't very well have gone into some roadside restaurant to pee or gotten out to refill the gas tank . . ."

Fazio's point was a good one, and at that moment Montalbano had an idea. He started looking for something on his desktop. He found a small piece of paper and started pressing buttons on the telephone.

"Meriam, I'm sorry, but I need you again."

"What is it, Inspector?"

"Could you meet me in half an hour outside Elena's front door in Via Garibaldi?"

"Certainly."

"What are looking for?" asked Fazio.

"I'll tell you when I get back."

He pulled up outside Elena's front door, parked the car, got out, and looked around. Meriam wasn't there yet. He fired up a cigarette and had barely the time to take three drags before Meriam drove up.

"I'll go and park."

"I'll wait for you upstairs," said the inspector.

He left the front door ajar, climbed the stairs, and headed into Elena's bedroom.

He stopped in the middle of the room, in front of the white armoire.

"Where are you?" Meriam called.

"In here. In Elena's bedroom."

"Hello, Inspector. Have you discovered something?"

"Maybe. But only you can help me. Could you tell me if there are any dresses missing from Elena's armoire?"

Meriam looked at him inquisitively.

"Do you live alone, Inspector?"

"Yes, why do you ask?"

"Because otherwise you would know that no woman can really tell you exactly what is supposed to be in her wardrobe. So you can imagine how well I'd be able to tell if a dress was missing from Elena's. She must have owned hundreds."

"Here's another way to look at it," said the inspector. "On the day Elena was killed, when I came here in the afternoon, she was wearing a green dress, but it was a special sort of green . . ."

"Ultramarine," said Meriam.

"But when she was found dead, she was wearing a different dress, which you would have no way of knowing. Do you think you could find that green dress?"

"Of course. Elena was very orderly."

She opened the armoire, and Montalbano noticed that Elena arranged her dresses according to color. And there were many green ones, in different shades of green.

Meriam started going through them one by one. A short while later, she said:

"It's missing. Not here. Maybe it's in the laundry." As she was saying this she went into the bathroom to have a look inside the hamper. "No, I can't find it."

"Maybe she took it to have it laundered."

"I can check," said Meriam, taking her cell phone out of her pocket.

A minute later they had the laundry's answer: no dress.

"So where could it have gone to?" Meriam asked herself.

Montalbano preferred not to answer.

"Listen, there's another favor I need to ask of you. Please come with me," he said as they were about to go downstairs into the tailoring shop. "Remember when I last saw you, I asked you about a piece of fabric that was on the table?"

"Yes, the piece of old fabric."

"I asked you to go and have a closer look at it, and you did. Could you do the same again?"

Meriam, a bit confused, did as she was asked.

"Then I walked over to you," said the inspector as he approached her. "And then, all of a sudden, you made a move to get a new roll of fabric. Could you do that for me again?"

"Of course," said the young woman.

She walked past him, turned her back to him, and reached out to the shelves.

"Okay, thanks, that's good enough," said Montalbano.

They went back up and down the stairs, and when they were in the doorway, the inspector said:

"Thank you so much. You've been extremely valuable to me, as always. By the way, do you have any news of Dr. Osman?"

"Yes, he's taking some time off to rest. He said he was going to Tunisia, to an archaeological dig that an old friend of his is working on."

After she left, Montalbano closed and locked the door this time, retraced his steps up the stairs and back down to the big room, and sat down in the usual armchair.

He started thinking about the movements he and Meriam had made, and as he was reviewing them, it was as if he was seeing them again.

He saw himself come into the big room followed by Meriam, then Meriam went behind the table to look at the fabric.

He saw himself approach Meriam, who then walked in front of him and reached out towards the shelves.

Cut.

The two images disappeared.

Then he and Meriam reappeared and went through the exact same motions.

Cut.

From the top again.

This time the first person entering the big room was Elena, who was speaking, but there was no sound.

She was talking to a woman of almost the same height as her, who was standing behind her.

Then Elena stopped and pointed at the table, and the second woman went and positioned herself in the exact same spot where Meriam had been standing moments before. Elena approached her and spoke again; the woman replied, Elena retorted, the woman spoke again, this time with a sneer; Elena raised her voice, but this time she did not do the same as Meriam; she didn't pass in front of the woman but turned her back to her and reached out with one arm towards the shelf.

Cut.

He closed his eyes and concentrated deeply. He could feel himself sweating intensely from the effort. Then he felt ready and, keeping his eyes closed to avoid all distraction, he replayed the scene again from the top.

Elena came in.

She spoke to the woman following behind her.

"... *to show you* ..."

Montalbano managed to grasp only these three words.

The other woman went over to the table and bent down to look at the cloth.

She said something that might have been: *"I remember."*

Elena spoke for a long time. But this time there was no voice. Nor could he hear the words of the other woman, who again had a sneer on her face.

Still speaking, Elena then turned her back and reached out towards the shelf.

Darkness.

Montalbano saw only a pair of scissors in the air being thrust violently downwards.

More darkness.

Elena's bloodied body now conformed perfectly to the chalk outline on the floor.

The images vanished.

He opened his eyes.

Yes, that must be what had happened.

He stood up, turned off the light in the great room, climbed the stairs, walked down the corridor, turned off the light in the corridor, went outside, and locked the front door.

"Find what you were looking for?"

"Yes," said Montalbano. "Here's the solution to the puzzle: The murderess—because I no longer have any doubt that it was a woman—after taking a shower, put on the dress that Elena had worn earlier that day and had probably left on the bed."

"So what do you think you'll do now?" asked Fazio.

"If my hypothesis is correct," said the inspector, "this woman came down here from the north. She may have driven in her car, or she may have taken the train, or she may have flown. That's what you need to find out."

"Chief, if she came by car or train, we're screwed," said Fazio. "Our only hope is that she flew down here and then rented a car."

"Then we'll start with the plane hypothesis," said Montalbano. "I'm giving you ten minutes to inform yourself."

Fazio shot off like a ball on a tether.

He returned seven minutes later with a smile so big, it was as if he'd seen a choir of angels pass.

"You were right on target, Chief. Nevia Sirch took a plane from Trieste to Trapani on the day Elena was murdered. Her flight landed in the afternoon, and she'd already reserved a car from the car rental, which she returned the following morning, two hours before boarding the flight back to Trieste."

They'd done it.

"Now I need another favor from you."

"At your service."

"Find out more about those flights: departure times, arrival times . . ."

"Why, do you want to go up there?"

"It'll be a pain in the ass, but that's the only place I'll ever find the answer to all of this."

Fazio stood up and left the room.

Montalbano looked at his watch.

Matre santa! It was already half past two. He grabbed the telephone.

"Enzo! Be sure to leave me a piece of bread."

"Actually we're just now sitting down at the table. We'll wait for you."

Montalbano was off like a rocket.

While he was eating a sumptuous seafood salad, the inspector noted that the dish was not featured on the menu. For his second course he ate a sort of potpourri of all the leftover fish parts fried up in a skillet, the kind of thing that has you licking your fingers down to the bone. In short, and in conclusion, Enzo's family treated themselves even better than they did their customers. This was something to bear in mind. It might be better, henceforth, to arrive late at the trattoria more often.

He came out feeling heavier, to the point that it took him twice as long as usual to reach the flat rock under the lighthouse.

He put a flame to the usual cigarette.

"How's it going?" he asked the crab staring at him from under the rock.

The crab seemed not to appreciate the question. Not only did it not reply, it disappeared underwater.

Montalbano felt as if he'd drunk an extra glass of wine.

Knowing he was just a few steps away from solving the case made his blood flow faster than usual through his veins. He observed that if the murderess hadn't made the biggest mistake of her life—that is, forgetting on the table the scrap of scarf she'd used to clean the scissors—the investigation would still be lost at sea.

That scarf was the key to everything.

But if it had also been the motive for the murder, this meant that the unknown woman—or rather, the woman named Nevia Sirch—had had something to do with the death of Franco Guida.

This second hypothesis had yet to be verified.

He therefore had no choice but to take the route he'd already told Fazio he would take: to go to Friuli and talk to Nevia.

He didn't feel one bit pleased about this choice; but it was his duty to make it.

He decided to smoke a second cigarette. It was a nice day, and he filled his lungs with sea air thinking—and already feeling melancholy about it—that where he was going there wasn't so much as a hint of sea air.

He started telling himself that if he ran into even the slightest wisp of fog he would be lost. The two or three times in his life that he'd found himself inside a fog bank he'd actually gone into a panic, feeling as if he was the only survivor left on the face of the earth.

A short while later, he sighed long and deep, stood up, and headed back to the office.

"I've got all the schedules, Chief," said Fazio. "As I said, there's a morning flight, at ten, from Trapani to Trieste, and then the same plane flies back to Trapani in the afternoon."

"Do you know how long it takes to drive from Trieste to Bellosguardo?"

"About two hours, Chief, if there's no fog."

The mere mention of the word "fog" elicited a long sigh from Montalbano.

"So I'm going to have to rent a car at the Trieste airport?" he asked dejectedly.

"Of course," said Fazio.

Montalbano imagined the scene: him inside a car that stank of car deodorant, lost, with no chance of finding his way, in a secluded mountain pass, maybe even the same one where they'd found Ötzi, the iceman.

"With a driver," said the inspector.

"What?"

"The car. I want a driver for it. I'll pay for it out of my own pocket, if I have to."

"I'll arrange everything," said Fazio. "I'll call some of our colleagues in Trapani. When do you want to leave?"

"Tomorrow. I'll go to the commissioner's right now and explain everything. See you back here in about two hours."

"Please be brief," Bonetti-Alderighi said brusquely. "I haven't got much time."

"I'll be telegraphic," said Montalbano. "Found likely killer Elena Biasini. Stop. Request authoriz—"

"Knock it off, Montalbano," the commissioner snapped, as though bitten by a viper. "This is no time for jokes."

"But I wasn't joking, sir. I really didn't want to waste any of your time . . ."

"Stop being a wise guy and tell me everything in full detail."

And so the inspector began telling the whole story.

The commissioner sat there without interrupting him even once. When Montalbano had finished, Bonetti said:

"Now go and report all that to the prosecutor."

"No," said Montalbano, "I don't think it's time for that yet."

"What do you intend to do, then?"

"I would like authorization to go and talk personally with the suspect in the province of Udine. In the fog."

"Eh?" said the commissioner, not understanding. "What's this about fog?"

"Er, nothing, sir. I was speaking metaphorically."

The commissioner thought about this for a moment, to the point that Montalbano felt he had to prod him a little.

"Is there some problem with that?"

"My good man, the whole thing is starting to look like a violation of territorial jurisdiction. If I don't have in hand a written and confirmed request based on some minimum of evidence, I can't ask for a reimbursement of your expenses for travel, accommodation, car rental . . ."

"Tell you what," said the inspector. "I'll pay for everything myself, and that'll be that."

"I cannot allow you to do that," the commissioner said firmly.

"Then I request two days' leave," the inspector replied with equal firmness.

"I'll grant you your two days, Montalbano. But you should proceed very carefully. If you need to make an arrest, you'll have to call the local authorities into action to do it for you."

"All right," said the inspector.

—

"I've done everything," said Fazio. "The people in Trapani already have your reservations. If you give me the authorization from the prosecutor's office, I'll pass that on to them right away."

"No, Fazio. There's no authorization. I'm going for my own amusement. I just suddenly felt like having a coffee in the central piazza of Bellosguardo."

"So should I buy you the ticket?"

"Right you are, Fazio. Just one way. 'Cause I might find a good trattoria there and decide to move to Bellosguardo."

"Okay. Gallo'll come and pick you up tomorrow morning at seven-thirty."

Fazio was about to go out, but Montalbano stopped him.

"Everything arranged with the driver?"

"Yes. They even asked whether I wanted a man or a woman."

"And what did you tell them?"

"A woman, Chief."

"Well done."

On top of everything else, Triestine women were famous for being beautiful, so that if and when he got lost in the fog with her, it would be a pleasant experience.

Fazio wouldn't let him leave the station until he'd signed some urgent documents.

When he got home it was eight p.m.

He decided to call Livia and tell her he had to leave Vigàta for two days to go to Palermo, for a meeting of law enforcement functionaries.

"So you would rule out any chance of coming to see me?"

"Livia, it breaks my heart, but I don't see how I could manage . . ."

"All right, then, have a pleasant journey and a good night," Livia said snarkily, hanging up.

The feast he'd eaten late on his lunch break didn't prevent him from having a peek at what Adelina had made for him.

Luckily he found a rather light dish. For once, his house-keeper had turned her back to the sea and gone into the countryside: a *pitaggio* of fava beans, peas, and artichokes.

To judge from the aroma, Adelina had outdone herself!

Later, when bringing the first bite to his lips, he awarded Adelina a gold medal for the dish.

When he'd finished eating, he went down to the beach and started walking along the water's edge.

For an hour he tried to plan his first meeting with the murderess. Was it better to accuse her right off the bat, or to let her stew in her own juices before moving on to direct questioning?

He decided in the end that he would make his moves depending on how the woman reacted once she learned that he was Inspector Montalbano of the Vigàta Police.

At this point he stopped in his tracks, assailed by a very real concern: What if, upon arriving in Bellosguardo—assuming of course that he managed to get there—the woman wasn't there? Maybe she'd taken a few days' vacation, and it was anybody's guess where she'd gone . . . Or maybe she worked somewhere outside of town . . .

The best thing would be to ask around for information. And to find out, first of all, if there was a police or carabinieri station there.

He went back home and sat down in front of the telephone, and the first thing that came to hand was Elena's little red address book.

Without realizing what he was doing, he dialed the number for Nevia Sirch.

"Hello, who is this?"

He immediately recognized the same voice as the last time.

"Am I speaking with Signora Nevia Sirch?"

"Yes, but who is this?"

"This is Inspector Montalbano. I'm calling from Vigàta."

He stopped, waiting for her reaction.

"Vigàta? I have a very dear friend in Vigàta," said the woman, showing no surprise whatsoever.

"That's precisely why I'm calling. I wanted to talk about her."

"Why? Has something happened?"

"Unfortunately I have some very bad news."

"Oh, my God!" said the woman.

"Elena Biasini has been murdered."

It was as though the person at the other end of the line had vanished into nothingness. No matter how hard he tried to prick up his ears, Montalbano couldn't hear any breathing. He became convinced they'd been cut off.

"Hello!" he said. "Are you still there?"

"Yes," the woman replied, practically whispering. Then she immediately said: "Excuse me for just a second."

Montalbano started counting. He'd reached twenty-five when she returned, and she asked only one question.

"Who did it?"

"We don't know yet. That's why I'm calling. The killer seems not to have had any plausible motive."

"But how . . . how . . . how was she killed?"

"Stabbed to death with a pair of scissors."

The woman started crying. Audibly, this time.

"You must try to be brave," he said.

"I'm sorry, Inspector, but it's such a terrible blow. I can barely stand up. Please wait a second while I get a chair."

She returned a few moments later.

"And what do you want from me?"

"I've been hearing what all the people who were close to Elena have to say, and so I—"

"I'm sorry, but who gave you my phone number?"

"I found it in an old address book of Elena's . . ."

"Ah . . ." said the woman, adding nothing more.

"I wanted to know if we could meet tomorrow in Bellosguardo, in the afternoon. At three. Would that work for you?"

"I'll be waiting for you at Via Orta, number 3. But now you'll have to excuse me, I'm unable to speak anymore," said the woman, hanging up.

Her behavior seemed perfectly normal. To the point that Montalbano began to wonder whether he'd got it all wrong.

18

Before going to bed, he prepared a small suitcase, packing just a shirt, a pair of underpants, and a pair of socks, since he was expecting to be away for only a day. He set his alarm clock for half past six.

He slept soundly and deeply, and when he woke he felt in perfect shape. Opening the window, he noticed something strange: The air was rather milky and sort of damp. He went and made his customary pot of coffee, drank it down, took a shower, shaved, put on the first pair of trousers that came to hand, and instead of donning a sports coat he grabbed a heavier zip-jacket. Then he took his toothbrush, comb, and everything else he needed and put them in a plastic bag, which he packed into the suitcase together with a spy novel that would help him sleep, since, as always happened when he watched spy movies on television, he never understood what was going on.

Gallo arrived exactly on time and then, as soon as Montalbano was in the car, took off again in his usual fashion, as though he were on the track at Indianapolis. But the inspector had no time to protest before they'd gone from the State of Indiana and into a kind of Dantesque limbo. Taken by surprise, he didn't understand why they could no longer see a thing beyond the windshield.

"Goddammit!" said Gallo.

"What is happening?"

"We're in the middle of a fog bank," Gallo replied, slowing down. "This is the first time I've ever seen that around here."

He'd asked for it!

Montalbano remembered a line of verse that went: *A joyous start is the best of guides . . .* And he immediately wanted to tell Gallo to turn back. If the fog had come all the way to his front door to find him, he could only imagine what would be waiting to welcome him up north.

They slowed down to a crawl. Even a horse-drawn carriage would have gone faster.

At one point Gallo nearly came to a stop.

"You have to do me a favor, Chief," he said.

"What?"

"You need to get out of the car and walk in front of me, because I can't read the road signs, which means that I might end up taking us to Palermo instead of Trapani."

Cursing the saints wildly in his head, Montalbano got out, walked over to the front of the car, and the slow procession began.

Then, as if by magic spell, the fog suddenly vanished, the sun appeared in triumph, and Gallo was finally able to find the track at Indianapolis again.

When they got to Trapani airport the loudspeaker was already announcing the boarding of his flight.

Once the plane was in the air, the passengers were told not to undo their seat belts because of turbulence. The usual stewardess started making the usual strange gestures, pointing first to the right, then to the left, while a metallic voice gave instructions on what people should do in case of an emergency, which was merely a nice way to say *in case of certain death*. In a kind of superstitious desire to ward off disaster, Montalbano memorized the plasticized sheet with little drawings that showed how to don the life jacket should the plane fall into the sea, as if all you had to do was whistle and help would soon be on the way; how to administer oxygen to oneself when the last thing you think of doing, when you can no longer breathe, is to put on a mask; and how one should remove high-heeled shoes and throw oneself onto the escape chute and into the sea where the sharks were surely waiting with mouths open wide.

And he got so scared that when he heard the announcement that the plane had begun its descent into Trieste, he seized his armrests forcefully and closed his eyes, expecting the worst.

But in fact it was a smooth landing.

He went to the car rental desk and, after signing about twenty papers, was given the keys to the car.

"There seems to have been a misunderstanding. I asked for a car with a driver."

"Ah, yes, sorry about that," said the woman, reaching under the counter and pulling out a strange metal gizmo. "Here's your GPS."

"GP what? I was told I could have a woman driver!"

"That's not a problem. I can program it for a woman's voice. Where do you have to drive to?"

"To Bellosguardo. In Udine province," the inspector said dejectedly.

The woman started fussing with the little machine.

"Okay, it's all set. All you have to do is follow Esther's instructions, and she will take you to your destination."

Confused and unconvinced, he went into the parking lot, looked for post number J44, and got into the car, which stank of car deodorant.

He took the GPS and set it up on the dashboard.

"Go straight until you reach the roundabout," said the gizmo.

He had to admit it, the woman's voice was pleasant. And that wasn't all. She was also extremely precise in her instructions, to the point that more than once Montalbano found himself saying:

"Thank you, Esther."

Of fog he saw nary a wisp. To make up for it, everything was a lush green, with high mountains in the distance, glistening with snow.

Suddenly Esther told him to turn right, and, as if by magic, the name *Bellosguardo* appeared on the road sign.

She really was very good, this Esther.

When he parked in the main and perhaps only square in town, he felt as if he'd entered a poem by Palazzeschi:

> *Three little houses with pointed roofs,*
> *a small green lawn*
> *and a slender torrent*

He glanced at his watch. It was time to eat. Even if Palaz-zeschi made no mention of it, there had to be a trattoria somewhere nearby. And indeed he needed merely to take a look around to read: *Al Leon d'Oro*—At the Golden Lion. The name was reassuring. He went in. It was a homey restaurant, with few tables, all of them vacant. As soon as he sat down a waiter appeared.

"Today we have *jota e frico*," he said.

"Eh?" said Montalbano, feeling lost.

"*Jota e frico*," the man repeated.

Since he had no choice, the inspector told the waiter to bring him both.

With great satisfaction he scarfed down a concoction of onions, butter, potatoes, and sauerkraut in the silence of the restaurant, where he remained the sole customer.

He paid the bill, which was very little, then asked the waiter if Via Orta was anywhere nearby.

"It's a ten-minute walk. Go out and take a right, keep walking straight, and it's the second street on the left," the young man replied.

The inspector went out and, before going where he had to go, stopped at a bar and asked for a triple espresso to put some order among all the ingredients wreaking havoc in his stomach.

He found Via Orta easily. Number 3 corresponded to an old four-story building.

The front door was locked, and so he went up to the intercom and buzzed the button next to the name Sirch. There was no reply. He tried again. Nothing.

He decided to smoke a cigarette and wait. Then he heard a clatter of high heels and saw a woman of about forty appear, walking briskly. He was hoping she would stop at number 3, but she kept on going. He went back to the intercom and was raising his hand to buzz when the front door opened.

He found himself face-to-face with a well-dressed man of about fifty, who asked him:

"Are you looking for someone?"

"Yes, I'm looking for Signora Sirch. I had an appointment with her."

The man seemed momentarily confused.

"I don't think you'll find her at home today. I saw her leave this morning with a lot of luggage. Signora de Amicis, who lives on the third floor, may know how to get in touch with her."

Montalbano felt himself sinking into a bottomless well, but wanted to grab on to any thread of hope that might exist. Without thanking the man, he raced up the three flights of stairs. Reaching the top floor, he rang the doorbell on the left.

"Who is it?"

He tried speaking, but his mouth was so parched that only a bizarre voice came out.

"Who is it?" repeated the woman's voice behind the door.

"Inspector Montalbano, police."

"Ah, yes!" said the woman, opening the door. She looked about sixty and wore her hair in a bun.

"I had an appointment," said Montalbano, "with Signora—"

"I know all about it," said the woman, interrupting him.

"But do you know where she went?"

"No, she didn't tell me."

"A gentleman I met downstairs told me you would know how to reach her."

"No, no. I'm sorry, but she didn't tell me anything."

The thread of hope snapped, and Montalbano began sinking again.

"But she did leave a letter for me to give you," the woman continued.

The inspector's fall stopped in midair. He suddenly realized that the phone call he'd made the previous evening was a fuckup of tremendous proportions.

"Ah, here's the letter," said the lady, handing him a closed envelope.

Montalbano took it. The envelope was heavy. He put it in his jacket pocket.

"Thank you," he muttered. "Have a good day."

And he started going down the stairs on two legs that could barely sustain his weight, so that he had to lean on the bannister the whole way.

Swimming around in his head was just one word, directed at himself.

Dumbfuck. Dumbfuck. Dumbfuck.

He went back to the bar in the piazza, fell heavily into a chair, and ordered a double whisky, neat.

Dumbfuck. Dumbfuck. Dumbfuck.

He took the letter out of his pocket, set it down on the table, and stared at it.

No. He couldn't bring himself to open it without another strong boost.

"Bring me another," he said to the waiter.

He sipped it slowly. Never taking his eyes off the envelope.

When he'd finished his drink, he reached out, grabbed the letter, tore open the envelope, and pulled out the contents. There were five pages covered with dense handwriting, bearing no date and no opening greeting. He started reading.

If you have managed to track me down, due to some mistake on my part, it means that you have already somehow figured out more or less what transpired.

I thought I had got rid of any trace of my relationship with Elena, but apparently not. I know that you wanted to meet me not because you wanted more information from me, but to put my back to the wall. At first I even thought I would wait for you to come, but then I told myself that by meeting with you I would be losing the freedom that is mine by rights. Your phone call had an extraordinary effect on me. That is, in an instant it allowed me to recover a lucidity I had lost for years, living under a pall of hatred and the desire for revenge. It is this same lucidity that now enables me to recount my story to you, which I am telling for the first and only time.

I met Franco in Udine one afternoon in July. It was 5:22 p.m. He came into the real estate agency where I worked, and I immediately knew that he would be the man of my life.

Franco quickly explained to me what he was looking for, and the whole thing was rather complicated. He wanted first of all to find a town in our province where he could eventually move to, and also a large space in which to set up a tailoring shop. One next to the other, if possible. The idea was to settle not in a tourist town but somewhere not far from one, and to arrange it so that the atelier's name could get around and become known through some intelligent advertising and well-coordinated word of mouth. And so we began our search, and I decided always to accompany him on his visits. We spent whole days driving around looking at towns in the Udine area. It took two months before we finally settled on Bellosguardo. And during those two months we fell in love, even though Franco always maintained, to the very end, that he did not love me, and that it was I who had seduced him. But I had noticed the way he looked at my legs, the way he smiled so affectionately at me. And I could tell he was shy and needed a little encouragement.

I knew he had a wife who worked far away, and that one day she would rejoin him, but at the time I didn't really care.

As soon as he moved into the apartment in Bellosguardo and started renovating and outfitting the tailoring shop, I would go and visit him almost every day. He would sometimes say he didn't want to see me, and he would pretend not to desire me. But he was shy, and I knew that, deep down, he loved me, too.

My constant absence from my job led to my firing. I decided to move to Bellosguardo to be close to Franco, and

when I told him he didn't raise any objection. I was
pregnant. Franco begged me to have an abortion, but I
refused. After Elena, his wife, arrived, I went through days
and days of real torment, since we were spending less and
less time together and our encounters took on an air of
secrecy, which I simply couldn't bear. And so our
relationship grew more and more bitter. I demanded he tell
his wife everything and come and live with me, but I
quickly realized that Franco was incapable of making so
radical a decision. But then chance met us halfway. I'd
gone to the general hospital in Udine for a maternity
checkup, and when I walked into the waiting room I heard
them call for Elena Guida. She was a beautiful woman,
very elegant and cheerful. I later learned that she was there
for treatments to try to increase her chances of getting
pregnant. I waited for her at the exit and introduced myself
as the real estate agent who'd helped Franco, and I invited
her out for coffee. As we were sitting at a table in the café
and Elena was stirring the sugar in her cup, I told her I
was expecting a baby boy, and that Franco was the father.
She looked at me as if she couldn't quite believe what I'd
said, and finally she stood up in a huff and left. I felt a
certain satisfaction at the thought that from that moment
on, their life as a couple would become impossible. When
the baby was born, I named him after his father. But
Franco didn't even come to see me. So I wrote him a letter,
of which I also sent a copy to Elena, in which I asked him
to acknowledge paternity of the child. His only answer was
to burst into my house in a rage. He no longer seemed
himself. He insulted me, accused me of setting him up, and

told me I should get any idea of him ever recognizing the boy as his own out of my head. He actually claimed he wasn't the father. After that I didn't see him again for a very long time. And in the meanwhile, Franchino wasn't growing, was always crying, and was never sleeping. He clearly wasn't well. So I took him to see the doctor, who told me he had a terrible congenital disease and that he would need some very expensive care. At that time I was in dire economic straits and didn't know what to do. So I finally decided to ask Franco for money, again in writing. A few days later Elena showed up at my place. She wouldn't even look me in the eye. She came inside and ran straight to the infant's crib. And she took him into her arms without asking. She noticed that he was small, too small, and instinctively held him to her breast, raising her sweater and putting his mouth up to her nipple. Cradled like that in her arms, and resting against her breasts, little Franco fell asleep immediately. And he slept for hours, for as long as we needed to come to an agreement concerning his support. Elena told me she herself would see to making sure that Franchino never wanted for anything, but that I must never, for any reason, tell her husband.

On February 17 I took my son to the hospital, and they kept him there. Around midnight on the night of the 18th, after I'd already gone to bed, someone knocked at the door, and I got up to see who it was. It was Franco, very upset, and I think he'd been drinking. He must have had a heated argument with Elena, and he wanted me to return the money she'd given me without his knowing. I started feeling an intense, unbearable hatred of him growing inside *me. But I tried to calm him down, and offered him another glass of wine, into which I put all the sleeping pills I had in the house. But that wasn't enough, because Franco kept shouting at me that I'd ruined his life by telling Elena about our affair. And he said it was my fault that he was unable to get her pregnant. Since his emotional state seemed to be getting worse and worse, I got dressed and suggested that we go for a walk. Once we were outside we started walking towards the river. It was a nasty night, and luckily there was nobody about who might see us. Franco was staggering and yelling that when we got to the river he was going to throw me in. When we reached the riverbank, he collapsed. Since it had been raining for a long time, the river was quite swollen. That was the moment when all the sleeping pills I'd dissolved in his wine took effect. Franco fell asleep. I removed the scarf he was wearing from his neck and tied his hands with it, so that if upon contact with the cold water he happened to wake up, he wouldn't be able to swim. Franco was an excellent swimmer. The riverbank was all muddy and slippery, and I gave him an extra push with my foot, to make sure he fell in. Then I turned my back and went home. The next day, in the afternoon, I was questioned by the carabinieri. I told them almost everything, but mentioned nothing about our walk to the river. I said that Franco had left my place in anger, threatening to kill himself and slamming the door behind him. Elena then moved for good to Vigàta, selling their house and workshop a few months after Franco's death, but before she left she promised me she would continue to help us. My baby didn't live to see his first birthday.*

But I never told Elena, and she never found out. I was
entitled to that money.

I kept on sending her photos of little Franco, but they
were actually of a nephew of mine of almost the same age.
Elena asked me many times if she could see him, but I
always told her that the boy wasn't yet ready to know the
truth. We carried on this way for years, then a month ago I
got a very long letter from Elena, in which she offered me,
in exchange for granting her custody of Franchino, a sort of
lifelong annuity in my name. It would have been nice to
accept, but how could I? Franchino was gone. And so, to
stall, I told her that it might be better to work things out in
person, and I could come to Vigàta for this. Obviously at
Elena's expense, and in fact she accepted my offer and I
still don't really know what I was thinking when I made it.
And so on the appointed day I flew to Trapani, rented a
car, and got to Elena's shortly before dinnertime. I found
her different from the way I remembered her. She seemed
worried and spoke very little, and our dinner took place in
almost total silence. She didn't even ask me about
Franchino. When we'd finished eating she asked if I would
come with her downstairs into the shop. And so I followed
her down there. We went over to the big worktable, on
which there was only a piece of cloth and a pair of scissors.
She asked me to have a good look at the scrap of fabric; I
immediately recognized it as Franco's scarf and said so.

Upon hearing my words, Elena began inveighing against
me. She said Franco would never have been able to tie his
own hands with that fabric, which was too fragile and
delicate and would have torn easily when pulled. As she

*was saying this, she picked it up and tugged it, and the
fabric immediately gave way.*

*I tried to object that the scarf may have become fragile
over time and because it had been underwater.*

*"No," Elena said to me, getting more and more angry.
"I got more of the same fabric yesterday morning. I'll show
it to you. You're a murderer." And she turned towards the
shelf to get it. But the sound of the word "murderer" had
sent me back in time. For a moment I was back on the
riverbank, tying Franco's hands, and when I returned more
or less to the present, I grabbed the big scissors that were on
the table and started stabbing her wildly. I spared her
breasts because that was where Franchino had found a
moment of peace. When my rage subsided I was all covered
in blood, and so I got undressed, took a shower, put on a
dress that I found on the bed, stuffed all my dirty clothes in
a shopping bag, and began my journey home.*

*I won't be getting any more money from Elena, but I
finally feel free again.*

And there you have it.

At the bottom of the last page was her signature, written
bright and clear: *Nevia Sirch.*

Although the woman had played him for a fool, Montalbano couldn't help but feel a certain satisfaction.

The inner workings of his brain had functioned well,
just a little too slowly.

The letter had served to fill him in on a few details, but
otherwise the general thrust of his investigation had been
correct.

He put the letter back into the envelope and summoned the waiter. He paid for the whisky and inquired whether there was a police or carabinieri station in town.

There were the carabinieri.

He asked for directions to their compound and headed off. After identifying himself, he was received by a marshal who gave him a funny look, no doubt owing to the unprecedented phenomenon of a police inspector asking anything at all of the carabinieri.

Montalbano told him the whole story, and when he'd finished he handed him the letter.

He waited for the marshal to finish reading and then asked:

"What do you intend to do?"

"It's too late," replied the officer. "Too late to set up any roadblocks, I mean. But I'm going to get busy immediately trying to find her. Could you leave me your cell phone number?"

"Why?" asked Montalbano.

"Aren't you interested to know how the case develops?"

Could he really tell the marshal that he didn't care anymore at all about the whole affair? No, he couldn't. He gave him the number.

And what now?

Should he look immediately for a hotel right there in town or get back in the car and drive back to Trieste with Esther? But he rather liked Bellosguardo, and so he decided to spend the night there.

They gave him a beautiful room at the hotel that was also called the Leon d'Oro.

And now he began to feel the fatigue of the day. He settled into a nice velvet armchair and turned the television on to help pass the time.

Less than an hour later he got a call from the marshal, who informed him that Nevia Sirch had been pulled over by the police in a routine check, and even though she didn't have any insurance on her car, they'd let her go. And she'd gone.

Montalbano's thought was that at least he wasn't the only fuckup in town.

"At this point," the marshal added, "she's probably gone off to Slovenia."

"And why would she do that?"

"She has relatives there. Sooner or later we'll find her, you'll see."

Montalbano thanked him, and two minutes later the telephone rang again.

It was Livia.

"Salvo! I want you here! You promised. And I've thought of a solution that will save you some time."

"Time for what, Livia?"

"You see? As usual, you've forgotten. Tomorrow's my friends' renewal of the vows."

Maria, beddra matre! Montalbano cried out in his head, but not into the phone.

"Giovanna and Stefano," Livia continued, unstoppable as a swollen river, "are expecting you, and you will come. I've looked at all the schedules, and there's a flight from Trapani to Trieste tomorrow morning. After you land you can rent a car at the airport and we'll meet up directly in Udine."

"In Udine?" asked Montalbano, interrupting her. "Why in Udine?"

"You see? You forgot that, too, of course. The renewal is taking place in Udine. I'll be arriving there tomorrow at three in the afternoon on the train from Genoa."

Udine?

"Udine?" Montalbano asked again, completely confused.

"Yes, Salvo, we'll meet at the station tomorrow afternoon at three."

The inspector finally decided to have his revenge.

"I'm already there."

"Come on, don't be silly," said Livia.

"Let me correct myself," said Montalbano. "You can consider me already there."

Livia sent him a kiss that was so loud that it made his ear ring, and then she hung up.

Montalbano got more comfortable in the armchair. He felt at peace with himself and the world. Now the only problem facing him was finding a place where he could buy a nice suit ready-to-wear.

Author's Note

As usual, the characters and situations featured in this novel have no connection with any real events or persons.

I would like to thank Valentina Alferj, who helped me to write this book, not only physically but also by intervening creatively in its drafting. In other words, now that I am blind, I would not have been able to write this story (nor those that I hope will follow) without her.

Notes

36 Cosma and Damiano always appear together . . . there was something saintly about Dr. Osman: Saints Cosmas and Damian (died ca. AD 287) were Arab Christian martyrs, reputedly twin brothers, who practiced medicine charitably, won many converts to the new faith, and perished in the anti-Christian persecutions of the emperor Diocletian. There are many churches in Italy dedicated to the two saints, called Cosma and Damiano in Italian, though none to one brother without the other.

37 Arab sheiks come to visit the Valley of the Temples: The fictional town of Montelusa is modeled on the real-life Sicilian city of Agrigento (Girgenti in Sicilian), which features, on its outskirts, an astonishingly well-preserved group of ancient Greek temples from the period when Sicily formed part of Magna Graecia. These, too, are called collectively "the Valley of the Temples," though this is something of a misnomer, as the complex is actually somewhat elevated.

52 the Day of the Dead: In Italian, *il giorno dei morti*, corresponding more or less with All Souls' Day in the English-speaking world, November 2.

67 Marianna Ucrìa . . . Catarella's becoming interested in literature!: Italian author Dacia Maraini (born 1936) wrote a book entitled *La lunga vita di Marianna Ucrìa*, published in 1990.

85 The shears fly into the air . . . : A Sicilian saying (*sàvuta 'u trunzu e va 'n culu all'ortolano*), which means essentially that it's the little people who always bear the brunt of misfortune.

95 *Chi l'ha visto?*: A national television program about missing persons and unsolved mysteries. The title means "Who has seen him?"

118 *ciambella*: A sweet, doughnut-shaped Italian cake, varying in ingredients according to region and tradition, and usually much bigger than an American doughnut.

145 *tressette*: An Italian card game played with the traditional Italian forty-card deck.

145 **pasta with *bottarga***: *Bottarga* is cured salted fish roe, often used as a condiment for pasta or a supplement for other sauces and dishes.

157 *Timballo di riso*: A Sicilian rice-casserole dish with a variety of possible other ingredients ranging from vegetables to fish to meat.

206 *sfincione*: Also spelled *sfinciuni*, this is a Sicilian sort of thick-crust pizza that can be served with a variety of toppings including, as in this case, meat.

241 **rice *sartù* with fish**: *Sartù* is a Neapolitan rice timbale usually featuring many ingredients, including vegetables, eggs, meat, or, as in this case, fish.

267 *pitaggio*: A Sicilian vegetable soup (from French, *potage*).

284 **the unprecedented phenomenon of a police inspector asking anything at all of the carabinieri:** In Italy, the police forces of the Commissariati di Pubblica Sicurezza, such as Montalbano's, constitute a bureaucracy separate from the carabinieri, who form a national police force under military command, and the two institutions are often in competition with each other and see one another as rivals. The phenomenon has given rise to many popular jokes, usually at the expense of the carabinieri.

Notes by Stephen Sartarelli

ANDREA
CAMILLERI

"Camilleri is as crafty and charming a writer
as his protagonist is an investigator."
—*The Washington Post Book World*

For a complete list of titles,
please visit www.prh.com/andreacamilleri

 PENGUIN BOOKS